W9-CRD-734

Double Daggers

a novel of history by

Jamie Clifford

ISBN 0-89754-217-7 // $16.95

Fiction:

Copyright © 2006 James R. Clifford all rights reserved. Contact publisher for reprint rights.

This book is a work of fiction. While names of characters are sometimes historical, the events described did not happen. Any resemblance to real people, living or dead is coincidental.

Cover painting used by permission Scala/Art Resources, NY.
Art by Vincenzo Camuccini (1771-1844)

Photo of Brutus Ides of March Denarius courtesy of Stack's Rare Coins, NY.

Cover design by Johnson Design

Dan River Press
Thomaston, Maine 04861

For Alex and Regan

Acknowledgements

Special thanks to Gene Kizer whose enthusiasm and professional expertise were instrumental in helping make ***Double Daggers*** the best book possible.

And to Julie, thanks for everything.

The Beginning

Woe to the hand that shed this costly blood!
Over thy wounds now do I prophesy—
A curse shall light upon the limbs of men; . . .
                    -Shakespere, Julius Caesar

The folly of man, with his endless, insatiable pursuit of money and power has existed since the dawn of time. That fine, almost indefinable line between good and evil has become so blurred over the ages that even God must find it difficult to tell the two apart in his most precious and complex of creations.

Life continuously and predictably repeats itself, and the lessons of the past are so simple, yet inexplicably, they remain beyond man's grasp. Since he first walked the planet and gazed into the heavens with yearning and wonderment, his true nature has remained the same. What makes a man laugh, cry, desire, love and hate, has never changed, nor will it ever.

Chapter 1

March 44 BC

He stood hidden in the shadows, watching in horrid fascination as the clandestine figures cloaked in long white tunics rained a thousand blows down upon the condemned man. Then, as fast as they had sprung upon him, the faceless killers drifted away from the dying man.

The man in the shadows watched as, one by one, the assassins dropped their murder instruments. He stared down at the collection of knives and daggers covered in blood. Slowly, he looked up. The assassins' eyes were now upon him. They were waiting. He was the final assassin, the only one who could deliver the death knell that would end the life of the greatest man the world had ever known. A man he loved but hated. A man he worshipped, but also despised. A man he owed everything to.

The conspirators parted and he slowly made his way between them tightly gripping the razor-sharp dagger.

The tyrant's once white tunic had turned a gruesome crimson color and his breath came in short ragged gasps. He stood directly over the dying man who whispered up to him.

"What? What did you say?" he commanded.

"Fili mi," the tyrant gasped.

The final assassin took a step back as the words sent a wave of revulsion through him. Did he call me . . . my son? Did the others hear his words?

He gripped the dagger even tighter. It was too late. The confession didn't matter because the man's fate had been set long ago. He raised the dagger high into the air. The tyrant lifted his head and a pained smile spread across his face.

The assassin couldn't bear the torment any longer and thrust the dagger deep into the tyrants heart. A spray of hot blood splattered across his face.

He stared back down at the dead man's face and what he saw made him gasp in horror. The face he now saw on the body of the tyrant was his own. What had he done? An immense wave of doom filled him. He dropped the dagger and fell down to his knees. Then, he screamed.

Marcus Brutus felt as if he was suffocating. His lungs burned for oxygen and just when he thought he was going to die—

He jerked up in bed, struggling for air. His heart pounded and he couldn't catch his breath. His body was drenched in a cold sweat.

"Brutus! Brutus! Are you all right?" his wife, Porcia asked. She moved closer and gently began rubbing his back. "You were screaming in your sleep. Are you all right?"

Brutus couldn't stop shaking and he hated himself for it. He didn't want his wife to see him in such a weak, troubled state. "I'm fine. It was just a bad dream."

"Another?"

He inhaled deeply, still trying to catch his breath. He turned towards her and replied wearily, "It's still early. Go back to sleep."

Porcia ran a hand through his soaking wet hair. "You are doing the right thing for Rome. This will soon be over."

He stared into her eyes, haunted by self-doubt and fear. "Am I, Porcia? Tell me. Am I?"

She hugged him. "Yes. Your name will be honored forever. Romans will sing your praise a thousand years from now. You will be a hero. A legend."

He kissed her on the forehead. "Go back to sleep."

She squeezed his arm and rolled over leaving him to contemplate his nightmares and what the future held. Brutus knew he wouldn't be able to go back to sleep, not now. He got out of bed still trying to calm his breathing. He needed some fresh air. He stripped off his damp nightshirt, pulled on a wool tunic and slipped on his sandals.

Brutus walked down a long hall then stepped out into the atrium. The sun had yet to rise and a chill hung in the clear air. He stared off into the early morning sky. The few remaining stars shined dimly on the horizon.

He stared at them, not moving for the longest time then he finally spoke, "O' gods! Tell me! What! What have I done?"

Chapter 2

The general restlessly paced the floor of his study with tight fists clenched behind his back. Gaius Julius Caesar had only been back in Rome for six months and already he had grown tired of the decadent city.

Almost every night he left his villa to walk alone through the streets of Rome. Caesar found it depressing that his nightly excursions were his only respite from the lies, pettiness and aggravations of dealing with an endless stream of senators and incompetent bureaucrats. His solitary walks also made him question if all the blood he had spilled to gain control of Rome was really worth it.

The city seemed as if it could collapse upon itself at any moment. More than a million people lived among the seven hills and Rome had grown into a crowded, dirty metropolis and it was suffocating him. Rome still possessed much of her beauty, but Caesar no longer saw the splendor of the enormous columned buildings, the stately domes of the temples, the public parks lining the city or the magnificent baths and gardens.

Instead, no matter how hard he tried, all he saw was crumbling seven story apartment buildings, streets clogged with refuse, animals running amuck and a never-ending array of harassing merchants trying to peddle their goods any way they could. Rome, no city on earth could match its splendor and beauty, nor its rampant poverty and ungodly mass of humanity.

He walked over to the window of his study and stared at the small garden in the corner of the atrium. Pale, golden streaks of the last of the day's sunlight shined onto the grounds. The simple, natural beauty of the scene brought a smile to his lips.

A loud rap from outside his study door interrupted his thoughts, causing the smile to leave his face.

"Enter!" Caesar yelled, swearing under his breath that it better not be some administrator asking for a personal favor.

The door opened and standing there with his trademark 'devil may care' grins was his most trusted and loyal advisor. "Marc Antony!" Caesar called out, happy to see his good friend.

Antony stepped into the room. He was a large, stout man with a thick jaw, dark curly hair and a full, masculine face.

"Caesar," he said in a husky, deep voice. "I hope you have been well?"

"I am now." He walked over to Antony and clasped his shoulder. "I wasn't expecting you back till after the Ides. To what do I owe the pleasure?"

"Oh, I grew bored with country life. There's no one to drink with except a bunch of goats. And besides, my wife's driving me crazy."

Caesar laughed. "Your wife is beautiful and I have always heard you preferred the company of goats. So, why the early return?"

Antony hesitated as if measuring his words. "I returned back to Rome because I'm concerned. I have caught wind that a plot may be brewing. It appears some in the Senate are up to something."

Caesar waved his arm. "And when isn't that the case? Those sneaky whoremongers are always up to no good."

"I think this time is different. I have received word—" Antony's voice trailed off.

"Go on."

"I fear Brutus might be behind it."

Caesar could hear the acrimony in Antony's voice. It was no secret that Antony despised the man. Caesar turned his back to Antony and walked over to the window. He stared into the now dark atrium. During the civil wars that had plagued Rome over the previous twenty years, Brutus had consistently acted against him; and despite that, Caesar had repeatedly promoted him in both position and power.

But Brutus' treachery reached a new level when he actually sided with Pompey during the battle for Rome. After Caesar defeated Pompey, Antony had pleaded with him to execute Brutus. It was one of the few times they had ever seriously quarreled. In the end, Caesar rejected Antony's call and once again pardoned Brutus.

Caesar continued to stare out the window. He knew if he gave Antony the order, Brutus would be dead by sunrise. Antony was right, Brutus was a threat and he should have executed him long ago, but he just couldn't bring himself to do it—he had his reasons.

Caesar turned back from the window and walked over to the wine table. He poured two glasses of red wine.

"Here," he handed Antony the glass. "I'll heed your warning about Brutus and the Senate." He raised his glass. "To our health," he toasted.

Antony raised his glass then took a large drink. Caesar knew his actions regarding Brutus must drive Antony mad, although, he also realized Antony had his suspicions as to why he treated the man the way he did. It was no secret that he and Brutus' mother, Servilia, had carried on a love affair for quite some time when they were both younger. But wisely, Antony knew when to hold his tongue, and had never brought the subject up, even during their arguments over Brutus' fate.

Caesar poured more wine into Antony's glass. "Come here." Caesar motioned towards his desk. "I have something to show you." He unrolled a bundle of maps with a large smile on his face.

"And what is this?" Antony asked with a bemused grin.

Caesar knew, like himself, Antony was a soldier at heart and the battlefield was the only place either man would find true happiness.

He pointed down to the war plans. "It's time to gather the legions again my friend. We have a new battle to fight. The Parthians are causing trouble along the eastern border. I want to have the army ready to leave by the end of the month."

"Parthia," Antony said with a wide smile. "It is about time we destroyed those savages."

Caesar looked his loyal friend directly in the eyes. "When we return from our great victory, no one will be able to stand in my way. No one will be able to deny me what is rightfully mine. Not the Senate. Not Brutus." Caesar hesitated and then pronounced, "When we return, my friend, I will take the title— King of Rome!"

Chapter 3

Brutus sat alone in his villa, brooding. He turned the silver coin over and over. His discontent had reached a boiling point.

"The audacity and conceit of Caesar knows no bounds!" he cursed loudly.

To think that the Roman Republic has flourished for over five hundred years, yet this single man, this usurper, threatened to destroy the greatest state, the greatest civilization the world had ever known. Brutus had long suspected that Caesar's ultimate design was to completely eliminate the Senate so that he could proclaim himself King of Rome.

And if anyone needed any further proof, this coin was it. Brutus stared at it with contempt. Never before had a living person been portrayed on a Roman coin—even the thought of it was considered a sacrilege because no individual was greater than the Republic. There had been thousands of great men in Rome's history, and not one of them ever dared to be as bold and contemptuous as this man.

Heroic men like his own ancestor, Lucius Junius Brutus, who five hundred years earlier overthrew Tarquinius Superbus, the last Roman king, destroying a foreign monarchy that had ruled Rome for centuries. And after dismantling the monarchy, Lucius didn't seek to rule Rome as its leader; instead, he established a Republic so men were not subject to the whims and cruelty of a single king.

And now, with this new threat brewing, Brutus understood it was his destiny to defend the Republic and his ancestor's honor from yet another tyrant.

Brutus stood and walked over to the small serving table. He poured himself another glass of wine and caught his reflection in the mirror. Despite the internal strife that had caused him so much distress over the last months, he still carried a youthful appearance that defied his forty-one years. He ran a hand through his thick, closely cropped black hair. He was a tall, fit man who possessed strong, handsome features and a pair of dark black eyes. Porcia liked to tease him that he was the most handsome man in all of Rome, and that he should smile more to reflect it.

But he was a serious man who believed smiles and laughter were best left to women and children. He walked back to his desk with the wine bottle in hand

and sat down. He picked the coin back up. Caesar's portrait stared back at him.

Brutus shook his head. "Caesar!" he spat.

He studied the coin closely. He was obsessed with the portrait and his burning hatred of the man continued to grow stronger. Brutus remembered that just two months earlier, the Senate had been forced to name Caesar dictator for life; and now this, a coin with Caesar's portrait on it.

By minting a coin with his portrait on it Caesar had done what no one Roman had ever dared—he placed himself above the Republic. The man had no respect for the Republic, or for its glorious and mighty history.

Brutus smirked. On the coin, Caesar wore a wreath upon his head, further showing the man's vanity. It was no secret that Caesar was embarrassed by his receding hairline and took great pains to cover it.

Brutus read the inscription behind Caesar's wreathed portrait—CAESAR DICT—obviously flaunting his success in forcing the Senate to name him dictator for life. Brutus turned the coin over. The goddess Juno Sospita was depicted in a galloping chariot with a spear in one hand and shield in the other.

Brutus threw the coin across the room in disgust. He poured another glass of the strong red wine. He had been drinking too much, but the wine seemed to be the only thing that could calm his nerves.

He was waiting for his brother-in-law, Cassius, to arrive and then the final plans could be made. The point of no return was soon to be crossed, and after tonight, events would unfold rapidly.

As he held his wineglass Brutus noticed his hands were trembling and he knew he would not have a moment of peace until Caesar was dead. He alone carried the personal burden that the very survival of the Republic rested upon his shoulders.

He had just finished another glass of wine when a slave led Cassius into the room. He gave Cassius a cold stare. "Where have you been?"

Cassius glanced at the slave then back over to him with a look of caution.

Brutus understood his point. No one could be trusted, especially the slaves. "Go fetch us another bottle of wine," he barked to the servant.

"Well, should I guess as to your delay?" Brutus asked again, after the slave had left.

"Marc Antony has arrived in Rome."

Brutus felt a chill run down his spine. "What! I thought he wasn't supposed to be back for weeks."

Cassius shrugged his shoulders. "Nevertheless, he's here."

Brutus pondered the news for a moment. "It doesn't change anything," he finally said.

"But he has allies in the Senate, Brutus. If Antony even suspects a conspiracy—all will be lost."

"Antony's arrival makes our mission more dangerous, but the plans can't be stopped."

"There is more," Cassius replied.

Brutus noticed the neck of his brother-in-law beginning to turn red. The man had a penchant for flushing when he was nervous.

"What?"

Cassius shifted his feet and began to speak but paused when the slave returned with a new bottle of wine. Cassius poured a glass and continued only after the slave had left the room.

"Caesar is going to announce a war campaign against the Parthians. He's planning to leave before the month is out."

Brutus' mind was already dazed from too much alcohol and he could only stare at Cassius in stunned silence. Everything had been planned so carefully, and despite the alcohol, Brutus did grasp this fact—a victory over the Parthians would seal the fate of the Republic. Upon his return, Caesar would be able to declare himself King, and there would be nothing he, or the Senate, could do to stop it.

"That settles it, Cassius. We must act immediately. We have to act before he leaves. It's the only chance the Republic has to survive."

"But we don't have enough time," Cassius protested. "The date was set for the Parilia."

Brutus slammed his fist down on the table. He had chosen the Aprilis date because it was a religious holiday celebrating the founding of Rome by Romulus and Remus—a significant date in the history of the Republic.

"I don't care what we had planned! We can't let Caesar leave Rome alive or all will be lost. Don't you understand that?"

The redness in Cassius' neck was now crawling up towards his cheeks. "We don't have enough time," Cassius protested again. "What about the others? I don't know if . . ."

Brutus raised his hand. "I'll talk to the others. They will listen and agree with me. Sometimes, I suspect your loyalty to the Republic and the cause. If you want out, let me know." He knew that Cassius had no choice at this point but to continue on—his fate had already been cast.

Cassius lifted his glass. "To the Republic."

"To the Republic," Brutus toasted.

"But what about Antony?" Cassius asked.

Brutus waved a hand in dismissal. "Antony is nothing more than Caesar's puppet. The people will hail us. And without Caesar around to protect him, there is little he can do."

Cassius shifted nervously. "That may be true but we should still kill him. You never know what trouble he might be able to stir up."

Brutus shook his head. "Cassius, do you not grasp the situation we are in? We cannot appear to the citizens of Rome that we are nothing more than common murderers. After Caesar is eliminated, Antony will lose much of his power and we will appear as we should—defenders of the Republic."

Cassius still looked uncertain, almost scared. "So we just leave him to his devices? I think you underestimate him. If we are to carry this plan out we need more thought as to what happens after Caesar's death."

Brutus was quickly growing impatient with his brother-in-law and was not in the mood to argue any more. "I said I will take care of Antony if he becomes a problem."

"And what of . . ." Cassius paused slightly before continuing. "What of your mother?"

"My mother!" Brutus shouted. Cassius' comment inflamed Brutus' growing agitation. The mere mention of Caesar and his mother was a subject that he didn't care to discuss with anyone. He was fully aware of the gossip regarding the two of them and it made him sick. "What does she have to do with this?"

"It's just . . . that I know of her feelings towards Caesar. That's all," Cassius stammered.

Brutus couldn't believe he was bringing this up. He began to feel lightheaded and took a large sip of the wine knowing that the alcohol was not the answer to what ailed him.

He glared at Cassius. "My mother, like all Romans, will understand that I am acting as a defender of the Republic. There is no doubt that she will see her son as a hero."

Cassius shrugged. "Where do you propose we strike Caesar now?"

"Knowing that egomaniac Caesar, he will not leave on his military campaign before speaking in front of the Senate. It will give him a chance to boast and wallow in his self-grandeur. We will strike him there. He will never expect it on the grounds of the Forum."

"I still think we haven't planned for the aftermath carefully enough. There could be chaos. There could be—"

"The matter is settled," Brutus cut him off. "Go, talk to Cimber, Decimus and Ligarius. I will handle the others."

Cassius set his wine glass down. "It is done."

Brutus watched with growing uncertainty as his brother-in-law left. Cassius' hesitancy at such a late date was a warning. He was having second thoughts, which meant the other conspirators might be faltering as well. Brutus began to wonder how much longer he could hold his shaky coalition of senators together, and more importantly, could he still trust them?

As he thought about it, maybe Antony's return was a blessing in disguise. By forcing the issue and acting now, it would give his unreliable conspirators less time to back down, or, even worse, betray him.

Chapter 4

Brutus walked along the streets of Rome in great anguish. Tomorrow was the Ides of March, 44 BC, and what he had set in motion could not be stopped.

It was early evening and the city was still bustling with activity, but Brutus barely noticed. His mind raced with doubts and fears but his misgivings weren't strong enough to quench his hatred of Caesar.

He went over the plot in his mind. He would use Caesar's own success against him. His recruited assassins were ready. Brutus had to laugh. A few, like Cassius and Cimber, hated Caesar for personal reasons but most, like that fool Decimus, really thought they were protecting the Republic.

He felt a surge of excitement because it wasn't Caesar who would attain the title of king, it was him—Marcus Junius Brutus— who would lay claim to the title. What his co-conspirators were too blind to grasp was that he wanted Rome, and his lust for power knew no bounds. He would do anything to get it.

Brutus came to a shabby part of the city, run down by years of neglect. He passed an alleyway when he heard a raspy voice call out, "Bruuu-Tus."

He took a step back and peered into the dark alley. He saw an old woman sitting by a rickety table. Brutus stepped into the alley and asked, "How do you know my name?"

She smiled a toothless grin. "Doesn't every Roman know the name of our great Senator?"

Brutus walked closer. Her table had two candles on it illuminating her wrinkled face. The old hag must have been at least ninety-years-old.

"Isn't it late to be out, old woman?"

"Hah," she cackled. "It's not too late for me. But is it too late for you, Brutus?"

The light from the candles revealed thick cataracts on her eyes and Brutus wondered if she was actually blind. He watched in silence as the old woman reached into a small leather satchel. She pulled out a handful of small cubes carved out of animal bone.

Brutus recognized her instruments. They were used by gamblers and fortune-tellers. "Knucklebones, huh? I don't suppose you want to place a wager with me?"

She rolled them onto the table, and after a moment said, "Tomorrow is the

Ides of March."

"You need bones to tell you that?"

"Do you want to know?" she asked.

"Know what?" he asked sarcastically, wondering what kind of game she was trying to play with his mind.

"Come. Sit down and find out."

"From a blind soothsayer?"

"For two denarii, I will tell you."

Brutus was not superstitious. Fortune tellers, palm-readers and soothsayers lined every street in the city and he considered them nothing more than petty thieves. But there was something about the old woman that made him want to stay.

He reached into his tunic and pulled out two silver denarii. He threw the coins on her table and watched as she quickly snatched them up. Maybe she wasn't blind after all, he thought.

"Sit, Brutus," she said, pointing a crooked old finger at the other chair.

He obeyed her and sat. The soothsayer picked up the bones, shook them close to her ear, then rolled them onto the table.

Brutus stared at them. The cubes were painted in different colors, and covered with strange, bizarre looking symbols.

The old woman studied her implements a long time before looking back at him. Finally, she said, "Beware of the Ides of March."

His heart began pounding. "What is that supposed to mean?" he asked defensively.

"The words speak for themselves."

"Who? Who should beware of the Ides?"

She looked at him with a quizzical expression. "You paid me, Brutus. Who else would I be cautioning?"

He stared at the old woman. The candles flickered and almost went out before the flames grew again. The alley was pitch black except for the candlelight, and their shadows danced eerily on the walls behind them. It was quiet and Brutus felt as if they were the only two people on earth. A rush of trepidation filled him.

"What else do you know?" he asked, almost in a whisper.

She wrapped her blanket more tightly around her. "That I am cold."

"That's all I get for two denarii, woman? A veiled caution about tomorrow?"

"No. Not a caution."

"What, then!" he raised his voice, "Wasn't that what you just said! Beware the Ides of March!"

The old woman looked directly at Brutus but didn't answer. She held his stare and picked up two of the black knucklebones then rolled them on the table.

She didn't even look down to see what the knucklebone revealed. "Some who accuse others are themselves guiltier than those they accuse."

"What is that supposed to mean?"

"The Ides last only one day, Brutus, but some sins are punished forever. Sometimes a man dies more than once. Take heed of this fact."

Brutus sensed danger and looked around to see if anyone was hiding in the alley. He stood up and said, "You are nothing but a cunning old woman."

Once again, she smiled a toothless grin at him. "You will remember at some point that I warned you, but it will be too late."

Brutus walked quickly out of the alley and back into the street. He took a few steps but couldn't get the warning out of his head. He had to know more.

He turned and ran back into the alley, but there was no trace of her. The old woman had vanished.

Chapter 5

Caesar stared out at the dismal afternoon. The Ides had started out sunny and bright, but now, the day had turned dark and dreary. He turned and looked at Calpurnia as she sat warming herself in front of the fire.

He couldn't help himself and smiled. Calpurnia was his third wife and a gentler, more caring creature did not exist. She had the thickest blackest hair he had ever seen, and despite her advanced years, she maintained a fresh milky complexion that made her appear years younger.

She caught him staring at her. "I beg you Caesar, don't go," she cried softly.

He went over to her and placed a hand on her shoulder. "Quit worrying, my love. I have faced enemies a thousand times worse than the Roman Senate. I will be back home before you even have a chance to miss me."

"But what about my dreams? I think something terrible will happen."

"Calpurnia, you are the most superstitious person I know. We go through this every time I leave for battle, or when there is any type of political unrest. You are just worried about the Parthian campaign. That's all."

"No. This time it is different," she protested.

Caesar chuckled. "You say those same words every time." He sat down next to her and held her tightly in his arms. "To be loved by one as sweet and lovely as you is indeed a blessing from the gods. How can I fear any man with a woman as good as you behind me?"

She looked up into his eyes, tears still falling, and said, "I dreamed of the Ides and I saw you, torn, ripped, bleeding. I love you so much. I don't want to see tragedy befall you."

"My love, the day is slipping by and there are matters that cannot wait. It was I who called the Senate together. Would you want people to think that Caesar is afraid to leave his own house?"

"Will you at least take the German bodyguards?"

"I am just as likely to get a knife in the back from one of those barbarians, than from any senator. We all must die one day. It will be my time when the gods have fated it. I could have a thousand guards posted around me, but if the Fates have chosen me . . . then it still wouldn't matter."

He stroked her cheek. "I promise. We will always be together—no matter what. That is our destiny."

She laid her head on his shoulder as servants began moving about, doing their evening chores. Caesar looked up as a trusted friend, Decimus Albinus, entered the room.

He hurried over to them. "Caesar, the Senate waits. We must get moving. They are liable to declare you King today. Would you deny yourself the crown which you deserve more than any Roman who has ever lived?"

Calpurnia looked at Decimus with pleading eyes but he continued, "Come, Caesar. It is time to go."

"He is right. I must go."

Calpurnia smiled weakly, obviously resigned to the fact that he had to leave. They both stood. She hugged him tightly and kissed him on the cheek.

Caesar squeezed her hand. "Good-bye, my wife."

"Good-bye, Caesar."

The litter dropped Caesar and Decimus off on a bustling street in front of the Forum—a vast area within Rome containing an array of temples, buildings, statues, gardens, public baths, open markets, theaters and shops.

Caesar strode purposely through the grounds acknowledging with a slight wave of his hand the cries of "hail Caesar," shouted out from his people. Decimus followed closely behind.

Caesar reached Pompey Theater when he heard a voice call out to him, "Caesar, please wait."

He turned to see the Senator approach. He relaxed. It was Cimber, a man he considered one of his few allies in the Senate.

"Cimber, what can I do for you?"

Cimber walked straight up to him and placed a hand upon his shoulder. "Caesar, sorry to disturb you but there is a matter I wish to discuss."

"Of course. What is it?"

"It is about my brother."

Caesar glanced over the man's shoulder and saw a group of senators rapidly approaching. What do these men want? He was in no mood to hear their petty grievances. He felt Cimber's grasp tighten on his shoulder, then suddenly, his toga was yanked above his head hindering movement of his arms.

"What is the meaning of this?" Caesar shouted.

He heard a muffled cry, followed by an explosion of pain that ripped across his upper chest deep into his collarbone. He screamed as a rain of blows descended upon him from all sides.

Caesar tried to fight back but even with the horror of what was happening, he knew it was futile as the senators came after him in a wave of fury. Caesar stumbled back against the attack and his toga fell back down from the top of his head.

Through blood and sweat-filled eyes, he now saw his attackers face to face: Sevilius Casca, Cassius, Decimius, Trebonius, Cinna and many more stabbing him with knives and daggers—Caesar saw blood thirst in their eyes.

He cried out in agony as another rain of daggers fell upon him. One, two, ten, twenty times. The excruciating misery shot through every nerve, every fiber of his body.

Caesar's worst fears were coming true—he would not succumb on the battlefield at the hands of a worthy adversary. No. He was to be assassinated by a group of cowards. The spineless jackals couldn't even kill him properly. Instead of delivering the fatal blow and letting him escape to his rightful place among the stars, they only weakly slashed at him prolonging his agony.

He tried to stand tall against the assassins. He didn't want to give them the satisfaction of cowering against their heinous attack, but finally, he could no longer endure the pain and loss of blood. His legs gave out and he slumped down to the ground. He could feel the life draining from his body, and from his days on the battlefield, he knew that the fading pain could only mean one thing—death was near. His vision began to blur but he could still see the outlines of men surrounding him, speaking to one another in hushed whispers.

Caeser raised his head. The struggle had pushed him back towards an alcove by the theater and he had fallen at the base of a statue. He looked up with blood filled eyes. Despite the realization that he was dying, what he saw made him laugh out loud. Maybe the gods did have a sense of humor after all. He was going to meet his end under a giant marble statue of Pompey the Great—the man he defeated to win Rome.

He felt a hand on his shoulder, then a voice, "Caesar."

"Brutus, is that you?" he asked.

"Yes, Caesar. It is I."

"Don't worry," Caesar said in a weak voice. "There is nothing you can do for me now."

Brutus knelt down beside him. "I haven't come to help you."

Caesar struggled to wipe blood from his eyes and watched as Brutus pulled a long dagger out of his toga. Caesar coughed violently and blood ran out of his mouth nearly choking him.

"Et tu, Brute, fili mi?" Caesar said, tears filling his eyes.

"What. What did you say?" Brutus asked, taking a step back.

"My son—" was all Caesar could manage, but the horrific sadness in his voice was unmistakable.

Brutus hesitated for a moment before revulsion followed by an uncontrollable anger filled him. He rushed forward and plunged the razor sharp dagger into Caesar's heart—sending him to his place among the stars.

Chapter 6

Brutus watched as Caesar's body convulsed violently from the blow. He pulled the bloody dagger out of Caesar's chest and stepped back. He dropped the murder instrument and stared at a large pool of dark red blood outlining Caesar's body.

"The tyrant is dead! The tyrant is dead!" he heard Cassius shout from behind him.

Brutus didn't respond. All he could think about was Caesar's dying words, "And you too, Brutus, my son." The same words he had dreamed about. He felt Cassius' hand on his shoulder. He turned. Sheer pandemonium had broken out around the theater. He eyed his group of assassins who milled about in a hesitant, uncertain fashion.

Brutus watched Cassius run out into the street shouting to a group of frightened bystanders, "Don't be alarmed. Caesar is dead. We are free again!"

The declaration didn't stir anyone into celebration and served only to scare the people even more. The crowd stared back at Cassius with a look of confusion before drifting off as if they sensed a hidden danger.

Cassius ran back to him. "Brutus, you should go to the Rostra and speak to the people. Proclaim that their freedom has been preserved, their liberty protected."

Brutus thought for a moment. He was assured of a crowd at the Rostra. The area served as the orator's platform where Romans came to speak and be heard, and there was always a large crowd during the daytime.

"Yes, let us go," Brutus said, still shaken over Caesar's dying words.

They left Caesar's body where it had fallen at the base of the statue of Pompey, and walked down the wide avenue towards the Rostra. News of Caesar's death had spread quickly, and much to Brutus' consternation, the reaction was not what he had expected. Everywhere he turned, people appeared to be in great distress, filled with anxiety and fear.

Upon reaching the Rostra, Brutus tried to reassure a small crowd of their noble intentions, but with every passing minute, chaos seemed to have taken hold of the streets.

Cassius looked dumfounded. "Brutus, forget the speech. It is too much of a shock for the people at the moment. Let's go to the mint instead."

Cassius led him away from the Rostra and out of the Forum. As they made their way to the mint, Brutus knew it was important to their cause to get the mintmaster to halt production of all Caesar's coins, but more importantly, he had to give the mintmaster the designs for a new coin. He had spent months thinking about the design which would tell the world of how he saved the Republic from Caesar's insidious plot.

The Senators entered the enormous mint building and Brutus hesitated before realizing the deafening roar reverberating throughout the building was the sound of coins being pounded on top of stone tables.

He had been in the mint only once, a few years ago, and the enormity of the operation still astounded him. It was obvious by the flow of work that the news of Caesar's death had not yet made it to the mint.

"There he is." Brutus pointed out the mintmaster to Cassius.

When Mettivus saw the two Senators smeared with patches of blood, warning bells began sounding in his head. Something had happened. He had a sixth sense when it came to changes in Rome's political landscape, and he could tell something monumental had occurred.

With an instinct finely crafted from witnessing many leaders come and go over the years, Mettivus knew he would have to play the survival game again. He lived by only one rule—never take sides, and never give allegiance to any politician because, as his father often had lectured him, "politicians crave only two things—wealth and power. If you align yourself with one party, or make an enemy with another, you are sealing your fate because, as sure as the seasons change, so does the power."

The two Senators approached him. Mettivus bowed and greeted the men, "Senators, good day."

"Mettivus, can we speak somewhere more quiet?" asked Cassius, his eyes nervously darting around the building.

"Of course," he said. "Please follow me."

They followed the mintmaster back through the building and into his office. Mettivus shut the door eliminating enough of the noise that Brutus could finally hear himself think again.

He didn't waste any time to announce the news, "Mettivus, Caesar is dead."

Mettivus held back a gasp. He felt as if he had been punched in the stomach. He had expected something big, but the news of Caesar's death floored him. Despite his personal rule of neutrality, he carried an immense respect and loyalty towards Caesar; but he knew his role and his instinct for self-preservation quickly took over.

Mettivus looked at Brutus and grew even more nervous. The Senator appeared on the verge of a breakdown. His hands shook and beads of sweat mixed with blood glistened on his forehead.

"The Republic has been saved, Mettivus," Brutus continued. "The people are free. The first order of business is to immediately halt all production of Caesar's coin issues. Is that clear, mintmaster?"

Mettivus nodded solemnly and answered, "Of course."

Brutus unrolled the scroll on top of Mettivus' design table. "I have designed a new coin and I want you to start work on it at once."

Mettivus looked at the design and disgust filled him, but he forced himself to maintain his composure.

Brutus pointed at the coin design. "This coin will forever commemorate the fall of a tyrant and the liberation of the Roman Republic. Romans, thousands of years from now, will sing praise to our heroics when they hold this coin in their hand."

Mettivus picked up the design and it answered his questions as to what happened to Caesar. The obverse showed a portrait of Brutus, apparently the chief conspirator, with the inscription BRVT IMP.

Mettivus was confused—Brutus said his actions were necessary to save the Republic, yet now he was proclaiming himself Imperator?

The reverse of the coin displayed the liberty cap, the symbol of the freedom that is granted to all Romans citizens. On each side of the liberty cap were the daggers, which told Mettivus that Caesar had been stabbed to death. Below the liberty cap was the inscription, EID MAR, today's date. The date that Julius Caesar, the most beloved man in Rome, conqueror of the world, had been murdered at the hands of his own countrymen.

"How soon can you have the coins ready?" Cassius asked.

Mettivus took a deep breath. "We have unstamped flans that have cooled to the appropriate temperatures. I can have the dies completed by tomorrow. Then we can begin minting."

"Excellent," Brutus said. The thought of his portrait on a Roman silver coin excited him in a way he didn't think possible. He would be only the second living person to have his portrait on a Roman coin. In his excitement Brutus had almost forgotten the most important part, "And Mettivus, I would like you to do me a personal favor."

"Of course."

"I want you to personally mint the first coin for me. Inscribe it with the numeral I following the EID MAR. When it is finished I want you to deliver it to me."

"It shall be done," Mettivus said.

The Senators left the mintmaster's office and Mettivus sat down at his die table to begin work on the new Brutus Eids of March coin. Caesar's demise was a shock, but Mettivus had seen it before and was likely to see it many more times. Anyway, it was out of his hands. He had a job to do.

Mettivus worked late into the night perfecting the die for the new coin and it was almost dawn when he finally set his tools down. He studied the final set of dies with an artist's eye—it was one of his best designs ever, but it didn't fill him with any sense of accomplishment.

He stood up from the table and stretched his overworked body. He was stiff and sore from working at the table for so many hours. He walked out into the mint and didn't like the silence that greeted him from the empty building. It was time for him to go home. Tomorrow, he would start minting the Brutus coin.

After only an hour or two of restless sleep, Mettivus returned to complete the process of minting the first series of Brutus coins. The mint was already bustling with activity when he arrived.

He went over to a large table containing the first batch of coins. He carefully studied them to make sure the flans had cooled to the correct temperature. When he was satisfied, he nodded to the frail-looking diemaster.

The man's face was so wrinkled Mettivus could no longer tell that he had once been a dark-skinned Syrian who had been captured and sold into slavery as a young boy. But, despite the man's seventy-one years of age, he was Rome's best. The diemaster had worked in the mint for over forty-five years serving Mettivus, his father, and his father's father.

Mettivus watched as the diemaster stamped the coin with expert precision. The diemaster grabbed a large magnifying glass with an arthritic hand, and inspected the coin for a full fifteen minutes before handing it over to Mettivus with a nod of approval. Mettivus barely glanced at the coin. If the diemaster had approved it, the coin was perfect. Mettivus took the coin back to his office and was surprised to see his son waiting for him.

"Lucius," Mettivus said. He knew the young boy realized something monumental had happened. He was old enough to grasp Caesar's death, but too young to understand its ramifications.

Lucius pointed to the coin. "What are you going to do with that, father?"

It is for Brutus," he replied with no emotion. "The Senator requested that I inscribe the first coin minted with the numeral I."

"What for?"

"I guess as a souvenir," Mettivus said, while sitting down at his table. He took out his cutting instruments and looked at Lucius, hoping that his son would never have to see the violence that he had witnessed during his life.

"Watch." Mettivus took the instrument and carefully inscribed the numeral I after the Eid Mar. He pointed at the inscription. "This coin is forever marked with I. It will be the only one of its kind, ever."

Lucius stared intently at the coin then pronounced, "It is a mark of evil."

The boy's words and tone surprised Mettivus. Seldom had he seen his son upset. He forced a smile and patted Lucius on the head. "Be a good boy and go play with your friends. I have more work to do."

His son left and Mettivus returned to the Brutus coin. He sat at his worktable with a growing sense of unease. The double daggers, and what they meant, mesmerized him. Mettivus was above the gossipmongers who filled the city but still he wondered—had Brutus murdered his own father.

Mettivus yawned deeply while rubbing his sore eyes. He had barely slept in two nights. He felt himself drifting off as sleep began to overtake his weary body.

Mettivus found himself standing in an open, treeless plain. He sensed that he was not alone. He slowly turned and saw Brutus standing about thirty yards away, near the bank of a stream. Mettivus approached cautiously. Brutus wore a military outfit and looked fatigued, disheveled. His breathing was labored and he looked ill-at-ease.

He approached to within ten paces. Brutus didn't even notice him. Mettivus watched as Brutus looked down at something in his hand. Mettivus was close enough to see that it was the Eids of March coin, the very coin he had specially minted with the inscription I underneath the daggers. He watched as Brutus suddenly squeezed the coin in his fist and let out a wail. Great fear and anxiety was etched across Brutus' face.

Mettivus stood in silence as Brutus reached into his tunic and pulled out a long dagger, a dagger that looked exactly like the one on the Eids of March coin. Mettivus began to speak but stopped as Brutus cried out, "Forgive me father! I have betrayed you!"

Brutus then raised his arm and in one swift motion, thrust the dagger deep into his chest. Mettivus ran over to the stricken man but there was nothing he could do. Caesar's assassin was dead.

Brutus still clutched the coin and Mettivus reached down and pried it from his fingers. He could feel the coin burning the inside of his palm. A strange notion overcame him. It felt as if the coin had a life of its own—a cursed existence born from an unspeakable act.

Mettivus felt as if he was partly responsible. He had created a coin commemorating the most heinous of all crimes—patricide. Brutus had committed a double murder by assassinating his own father, and the Father of his Country.

Mettivus was overcome by a sudden realization that he couldn't destroy the coin, even if he wanted to. But, he could hide it, hopefully, forever. He walked over to the bank and threw the coin into the middle of the stream.

Mettivus' head jerked back and he snapped open his eyes. He felt panicky. His mind was in a fog as he stared around the room. It took a moment for him to realize that he must have fallen asleep at his worktable and had been dreaming. Beads of sweat ran down the side of his face and he could feel his legs trembling.

He opened his fist. Inside of it was the double dagger coin. As he stared at the daggers, the dream flooded back into his consciousness. "Cursed," he said, quickly dropping the coin onto the worktable.

He stood up. His only desire now was to get rid of the coin as fast as possible. He grabbed a satchel and threw the coin into it. He rushed out of the mint, straight to Brutus' villa and delivered the coin to the assassin.

After all, Brutus deserved it.

Chapter 7

After the mintmaster left, Brutus sat alone on his terrace. An unsettling combination of power and fear surged through him as he stared at his portrait on the Eids of March coin. It had turned out far better than he ever expected.

The coin was a welcome victory in what had been a taxing couple of days. Caesar's assassination had gone exactly as planned but the public's apprehension in the aftermath was causing Brutus much distress. He had expected it might take a few days for the shock of the assassination to wear off, before Rome hailed him as a champion of freedom, a savior of liberty; but, there had been no shouts of glory for his noble deed.

Instead, an uneasy pallor had fallen over Rome, and to make matters worse, most of his co-conspirators had deserted him by retreating to the safety of domains outside of Rome.

Since Caesar's death, he had hardly slept, and when he did, he was tortured by dreams of Caesar's last words: "Even you, Brutus, my son."

Even in death, Caesar still haunted his mind. "Damn him!" Brutus cursed while squeezing the coin in his palm. Caesar deserved his fate. He stared out at the sky as the sun slowly set in the horizon. A group of high puffy clouds filtered streaks of fading sunlight producing a strange array of bright and dark colors across the iridescent sky. However, the natural beauty of the scene did nothing to ease the doubt and dread that had begun to consume him.

He watched the sun fall below the horizon. He knew it was too late for misgivings, but he also realized he hadn't considered the potential aftereffects as carefully as he should have. Events were spinning out of control and there seemed to be nothing he could do about it.

"Brutus!" he heard his mother call out.

He winced as Servilia appeared from the foyer with a pained look on her face. Brutus' blood began to boil. What was she doing back in Rome? He had sent her to his country estate to keep her out of the way.

She rushed over to him. "Brutus! What have you done! Do you not know what you have done!"

He stared at her in disbelief. Surely, his own mother would be grateful for what he had done to save Rome. "What are you talking about?"

"Caesar!" she spat. "Why Brutus? Why?"

"Mother, don't you see, someone had to save the Republic for all of our sake. I'm sorry if this has caused you distress."

"For everyone's sake!" she screamed, cutting him off. "What are you talking about? You are a fool!"

Brutus' melancholy turned to anger. "Why do you say these things!" he shouted.

Servilia began to weep uncontrollably but Brutus remained seated, not willing to give comfort after her outburst. She quickly gathered herself and looked him straight in the eyes. "I loved Caesar."

Her words stung him. He looked away but she continued, "You stood against him every step of the way. Even after you betrayed him, he looked favorably on you. Caesar kept you from being executed more times than I can count, and this is how you repay him, by stabbing him in the heart? You are nothing but a cold-blooded murderer!"

He looked back at her in fury. "How dare you come into my house and talk to me in such a fashion!"

"Brutus, stop! You can't fool me. I know your true character and it makes me sick to think that you are my own flesh and blood. You're pathetic, hiding behind the lie of trying to save the Republic. At least be a man about it and tell Rome you killed Caesar because you want to be emperor. Because that is the only reason you killed him. And you know it. You don't give a damn about the Republic. The only thing you care about—is Brutus!"

Her words angered him to such a point that it took all his willpower not to strike her. He sat there unable to move as she continued her tirade.

"For all these years you sauntered about with the grand notion that you were descended from Lucius Brutus. Oh, and how you loved to tell anyone who would listen that your ancestor was solely responsible for throwing the last king out of Rome. It makes me want to laugh because Lucius would be ashamed to even be in the same room with you. That much I know!"

"Mother . . ."

She cut him off. "All of Caesar's generals wanted to execute you after your treachery during the Pompey war. I know that Caesar personally spared your life and made sure your wealth and political standing were not harmed. Why do you think he did that?"

"Because he knew I was worth more to Rome alive than dead," Brutus answered.

Servilia rolled her eyes then broke out in a demeaning, cruel laugh. "Your worth to Rome is nothing. Do you think Rome would collapse if you were not around to save it? Everything you are, everything you possess, even your life itself, you owe to Caesar."

"Why do you keep saying that?" Brutus shouted, slamming his fist down on the table so hard that it caused the bottle of wine to fall off the table and shatter on the tile floor.

He looked down at the broken bottle and began to feel nauseous. The dark red wine spread slowly across the floor and Brutus shuttered—it looked exactly like the blood that had pooled around Caesar's body. He looked at his mother. Her face displayed pure contempt.

"Brutus," she said, almost in a whisper, "I'll tell you why I say these things. So you can no longer deny the truth—Caesar was your father."

With those damning words, Servilia turned and left. Brutus stared down at the coin. He ran a finger over the double daggers and closed his eyes. He saw Caesar lying in a pool of blood and, once again, he heard his father's last words, "Even you, Brutus, my son."

His nightmares had come true.

Chapter 8

Caeser's Funeral

He could not get the soothsayer's warning out of his mind— "some sins are punished forever." Brutus bit his lower lip, drawing blood. A blast of trumpets interrupted his thoughts and he watched the funeral procession make its entrance onto the giant stage. An elaborate bier draped in purple cloth held Caesar's body.

Brutus sat nervously behind the stage on the Rostra. This was perhaps his last chance to sway Rome to his side. It was an unseasonably warm day for March. Brutus placed a hand over his eye and looked up into the clear blue sky. A solitary eagle circled high in the sky and he couldn't help but wonder—

No! he thought. He wouldn't allow himself to think about it. What was done—was done.

He wiped a bead of sweat from his brow still finding it hard to believe that three days had passed since the Ides. Three excruciating days of turmoil, confusion and self-doubt; but now, he had his chance to win over the citizens of Rome. He stared out at the massive throng of people. It seemed as if every person in the city had come to witness Caesar's funeral.

A short blast from a trumpet cued him. Brutus was the first speaker. He rose and walked slowly to the front of the stage with a grave expression. The crowd was quiet, but Brutus sensed an underlying restlessness.

He began the most important speech of his life:

"Fellow Romans, I stand here with overwhelming sorrow in my heart—for I loved Caesar. Yes, it is true when I say I loved, even admired him. But believe me when I say—I love Rome even more.

"Caesar was a great man, but Caesar was only a single man whose ambitions and pursuits placed the very survival of Rome into question. Five hundred years ago, tyrants ruled this city and my ancestor, Marcus Lucius Brutus, expelled them creating the greatest civilization the world has ever known.

"Why should any of us bow to the desires or greed of a single individual— a single king? It is the Republic to which we owe our lives, our freedom, our prosperity too. Why would any one of us want to jeopardize that?"

A smattering of applause rang out from the crowd giving him much needed encouragement.

"Before you judge me my fellow countrymen, I wish to ask you a simple question. Is it better to live as free men under a Republic, or as slaves under a king?"

The crowd ended its uneasy pallor and shouts rang out, "As free men!"

Brutus took a deep breath and continued, "Believe me, for my honor. I love Rome. I love the Republic. It had to be done. There was no other way. Trust the Republic, and your trust and faith will be rewarded with the greatest gift a person could have—their freedom. Who among you would say they don't love Rome, or don't wish to live as free men?"

"No one!" the crowd now shouted in unison.

Brutus held out his arms dramatically, motioning for silence. "Never forget that our decisions now, affect Rome for years, centuries to follow. It would have been easy to grant Caesar the title he craved. To give him the king's crown he so desired. But I ask you, what of your children? And their children's children? What if they were enslaved under a vengeful tyrant? Would anyone here wish that upon their descendants?"

"Never!" erupted the crowd followed by chants of, "The Republic! The Republic! The Republic!"

Brutus held up his arms and motioned for silence. "I leave you with this, fellow countrymen. Just as I slew Caesar for the sake of Rome, I have a dagger for myself, if my country ever decides it wishes me dead!"

Brutus raised his fist toward the sky as he soaked in the applause and shouts of, "long live Brutus! Brutus for Emperor!"

He remained at the stage a few moments then bowed solemnly and moved back with the crowd still cheering.

Despite his appearance of great sadness, inside Brutus was ecstatic. He had done it! Judging by the crowd's reaction he had succeeded in convincing Rome that his actions were necessary to save the Republic.

He glanced over at Cassius who smiled, confirming his intuition of the success of his speech. He returned to his spot in the back of the Rostra and watched as Caesar's good friend and top general, Marc Antony, approached the podium. Brutus crossed his arms across his chest, confident there was nothing Antony could say now to win Rome back over to his side.

The crowd grew silent again and Antony began:

"Friends, I come to bid Caesar farewell. But first, I have an announcement. In Caesar's will, he bequests to each and every free Roman, the sum of three hundred sestertii."

Brutus felt a chill run down his spine as the crowd roared with delight over the inheritance gift. Antony raised his arms to silence the crowd and continued,

"Let us rejoice, my fellow countrymen, at the honors, titles, the battles and glory bestowed on Caesar by the Senate and his people."

Antony began reading from a piece of paper. "Julius Caesar, the man who defeated Rome's enemies: Gaul, Illyricum, Alesia, Iberia, Britiannia—" Antony continued reading the names of every great battle Caeser had won, every people Caesar had defeated.

Brutus grew wary as the crowd shouted, "praise Caesar!" after each victory was read. He looked over at Cassius whose face had lost its earlier look of confidence. He couldn't help but wonder if he had made a horrible misjudgment in allowing Antony to speak.

Brutus flinched when Antony suddenly yelled out to the crowd, "Romans!" He turned to Brutus and pointed. "Brutus says that Caesar was an ambitious man, and Brutus is a man of honor. But of all the enemies Caesar conquered, where did the riches go?"

Antony paused then answered, "It went directly into Rome's Treasury for her citizens. Does this seem ambitious?"

"No!" The crowd shouted.

Brutus felt sweat trickling down his back. Antony was inciting the crowd against him and there was nothing he could do about it. Brutus again looked over at Cassius whose face had grown more pale and grim.

The clamor died down and Antony spoke, "The noble Brutus told you that Caesar was an ambitious man. And yet who amongst you doesn't remember when our beloved general wept when the poor cried. And to his legions, his soldiers, he was a soldier just as you. Caesar fought next to you. He traveled with you. And he would have died next to you if it had been his time."

A large group of Roman soldiers standing around the giant stage began pounding their lances against their body armor creating a thunderous noise. Antony motioned for them to be still.

"Brutus says Caesar was an ambitious man, but three times Caesar was offered kingship and three times he refused the honor. I ask you friends, was this ambition?"

Cries of, "No! No! No!" caused Brutus to cringe. In a matter of moments, Rome had turned completely against him and now, his life was in jeopardy. He cautiously made his way over to Cassius.

Cassius covered his mouth with his hand and whispered to Brutus, "We're going to be cut to shreds."

"We have to get out of here," Brutus replied back.

They listened as Antony yelled out in a louder, more defiant voice, "Caesar was the greatest general Rome or the world has ever known! He conquered our enemies so we could live free! Free from fear and oppression. Yes, Caesar was an ambitious man. But I, Marc Antony, am here to tell you that Caesar was ambitious only for the glory of Rome and her people!"

The crowd erupted in a fevered pitch.

"Follow me," Brutus said to Cassius. They walked quickly to the back of the hall. Brutus turned and watched as Antony grabbed a lance from a soldier and jumped up onto the stage next to Caesar's body.

Antony held out the lance. "My heart is here with Caesar," he cried out, thrusting the lance down and picking up the bloody toga Caesar had worn. He lifted it high into the air, out towards the surging crowd. "Look Romans! Here is where Brutus stabbed Caesar. His so-called friend, a man he claimed to love! Is this how you repay friendship and love?"

Antony flung Caesar's bloody toga into the frenzied crowd. "Fellow citizens of Rome, I ask you, why was our great and noble Caesar stolen from us when we needed him the most?"

The soldiers in front of the podium started chanting, "Traitors! Murderers! Assassins! Kill Brutus!"

Brutus watched in horror as a large group rushed towards the stage holding Caesar's funeral couch. Brutus turned and ran for his life, but not before hearing Antony's last words to the crowd, "Brutus won't escape. Some crimes are punished for all of eternity!"

Chapter 9

Philippi Greece 42 BC
Two years since assassination of Julius Caesar

Brutus stared into the campfire, mesmerized by the dancing flames. He sighed deeply. He still found it hard to believe that two years had passed since Caesar's death and the chaos that had erupted afterwards.

He sat alone, outside a country villa in front of a large vineyard. The air was still and silent, and for maybe the first time since he left Rome, a mild feeling of contentment filled him. He gazed out at the empty countryside wondering how long it had been since he had a moment of peace. He randomly poked the glowing coals with a stick, thinking about the hardships and humiliations he had suffered since leaving Rome. Two years. It seemed like an eternity.

After Antony's eulogy, Brutus knew his cause was lost and he had fled to a sympathizer's house where he had hidden for two weeks as mobs searched the city killing anyone even remotely associated with Caesar's assassination.

Brutus only managed to escape by sneaking out of Rome under the cover of night, hidden in the bottom of an olive cart. He had made his way to eastern Italy where he found refuge and aid among old Republic supporters from the Pompeian Wars.

With their urging, Brutus had sent envoys to other parts of Italy requesting support to wage war against Antony in hopes of regaining control of Rome one day.

The response had been favorable and after a year of organizing, Brutus left Italy and traveled to Athens and Macedonia. He was well received by the Greek king who also contributed generously to his cause. So now, against all odds, he had raised a formidable army numbering almost a hundred thousand men.

Brutus yawned deeply but fought the urge to sleep. The nightmares came almost every night now. Horrific visions of the soothsayer's dire prediction, Caesar, blood and images of his own death tormented him.

He felt his eyelids closing. "Damn it!" he cursed, fighting his body's desire to sleep.

He threw another piece of wood on the fire and watched as burning embers drifted up into the dark sky. It was frigid for October and a cold mist permeated the air. He pulled the wool tunic over his shoulders and rubbed his hands over the fire.

An intense pain of sadness swept over him. How he wished his beautiful Porcia could be here to warm and comfort him, but it would never be. He had lost everything. He remembered the night the message had come telling him that his wife had grown so distraught over his forced exile that she had committed suicide by stuffing burning coals down her throat. The news of her death had caused him to break down and weep for days. How he wished he could take everything back.

Brutus took out a small leather satchel and removed the coin. He held it in front of him. "All over a coin," he spoke softly.

The double daggers reflected the yellow flames from the fire and he agonized about what he had done. The old soothsayer was right—he knew he had committed the greatest sin known to man and because of it, he was eternally doomed.

His mother had also been right. He had been blinded by power and the desire to achieve it at any cost. The simple truth was that he had murdered Caesar because he wanted Rome for himself, and he didn't care who stood in his way, even if it was his own father.

At this point in his life, he didn't seek redemption. It was much too late for that, but he swore that if he defeated Antony, he would return to Rome, not as an emperor or king, but as a senator. He vowed to spend the rest of his life defending the Republic against tyrants like Caesar, and more importantly, defending Rome from men like himself whose ambitions knew no bounds. But first, he would have to defeat Antony.

The final battle was rapidly approaching. Scouts had informed him that Antony's army was on the move and had begun to build a defensive position on the open plains of Philippi.

Winter was near, and Brutus wanted to engage the battle as soon as possible. He couldn't bear the thought of another cold winter away from Rome.

He shivered and stared at the numeral I next to the coin's EID MAR date. How would he be remembered when a Roman held his coin a thousand years from now? He had been told that Antony was melting them down by the thousands, and he wondered if any of his coins would even exist a millennium from now.

A hundred times he had considered throwing the cursed thing into a fire or down some deep gorge, but he forced himself to keep it as a reminder of his weaknesses and sins.

Again, he felt the inevitable force of sleep gripping his body and mind. He fought his body's overwhelming desire to sleep, but he knew that it would come eventually, followed by the dreams. His eyes began to close—

A strange noise off in the distance caused Brutus' head to snap up. He warily looked around. The fire had almost died out and the few remaining coals burned weakly. It was the middle of the night. He must have fallen asleep.

His heart skipped a beat when he heard the queer noise again. He stood, grabbing his sword. "Who's there?"

"Brutus," the voice called to him.

Whoever was calling out his name was deep inside the vineyard, but no one was supposed to be there. His army was camped miles down the road. He had come to spend the night alone, to plan strategy for the ensuing battle. Was this some type of a trick? Had one of Antony's spies infiltrated his camp and now lay in wait for him? He quickly dismissed that thought because, if that was the case, the assassin would have already killed him.

"Brutus." He heard the voice call out again, followed by a deafening silence.

Brutus walked over to the edge of the vineyard. A strong, cold gust of wind blew. He drew his tunic tighter over his shoulders. Slowly, he walked into the vineyard. His legs trembled but he kept walking, following the voice that was calling him.

He was getting closer to the source. The voice disturbed him. It sounded unnatural and a wave of fear shot through him. After about a hundred paces, he stepped past a row of olive trees onto the edge of an open plain.

His heart pounded against his chest and he fought the urge to run. He had found the source—a large, dark figure stood out in the open, directly facing him.

Brutus remained still, waiting for the man to announce his intentions.

When none came Brutus asked, "Who are you?"

The figure remained silent. "I said who are you?" Brutus commanded.

The man still didn't respond, causing some of Brutus' fear to be replaced by a growing anger. He was tired of running.

If this is my death, let it come. I am ready, Brutus thought as he walked closer with his sword raised.

He approached to within ten paces and a strange sensation came over him. It was more an intuition, but something about the man wasn't right. It was almost as if he didn't belong here.

"This is your last warning. Who are you!" Brutus demanded, while grasping the handle of his sword even tighter.

Finally, the man answered, "You already know the answer to your question."

"I am not here to play games. Answer me, or I will kill you."

The man laughed in a deep, mocking fashion. Brutus felt dread rising through him and took a step back.

The man walked a few paces closer, allowing Brutus to get a better look at his tormentor. He was enormous and wore a soldier's outfit of thick chain mail, but there was something about his outfit, his appearance, that didn't seem right.

"Certainly you know who I am, Brutus."

Even though he spoke Latin, there was something unusual, even wrong about his accent. The dialect seemed old, out of place.

The two stood facing each other. Suddenly, disbelief and shock filled Brutus. He recognized the man from a statue in the Forum. He was Lucius Junius Brutus! The man who had overthrown the last Roman King. The man Brutus had falsely claimed to have descended from for all these years. A man dead for five hundred years.

Brutus lowered his sword with the grim realization that no weapon would provide a defense against this. "Are you here to kill me?"

"No."

Brutus shook his head. "You can't be here. It's impossible."

"Is it?"

"You have been dead for five hundred years."

"You have been dead before as well."

Brutus fought the urge to run. "I don't understand."

The apparition narrowed its eyes and said, as if passing judgment from the underworld, "Your time is almost up, Brutus. You have failed, again."

Brutus was paralyzed with fear. "Is there any hope for me?" he asked.

"No. Not here."

"Then why are you here? What do you want with me?"

"To warn you."

"Warn me. About what?"

"I am here to warn you about . . . yourself."

"I don't—" Brutus began but stopped as the apparition laughed again.

It took a few steps closer. They were only feet apart now. Brutus stared into its eyes and thought for a brief second that he might understand, but the feeling was quickly lost as the apparition turned and began walking away.

"Wait!" Brutus yelled, but the apparition didn't heed.

Brutus followed as it walked through an open treeless plain. A stream ran off to his right. Brutus stopped dead in his tracks, confused. Directly in front of the apparition, a dark forest appeared.

He was unaware of any forests in the area. He watched as the apparition disappeared among the trees. He walked up to the edge and stopped, somehow knowing he couldn't enter the forest. He stood and stared into the trees

A wave of terror filled him as he caught a glimpse of his destiny from within the forest. He closed his eyes not wanting to see any more.

"Brutus." He heard his name called from deep within the trees. He began to shake uncontrollably—

Brutus bolted up gasping for air. He was disoriented and it took a few seconds before he realized where he was. He must have fallen asleep by the dying fire with nothing on but his tunic. He couldn't stop shaking then he realized he was freezing cold.

He stood up and began rubbing his arms together trying to generate some warmth. Off, on the horizon, a tiny crest of the sun began to rise. He looked down into the vineyard and then it hit him. The memory of the night came flooding back.

His mind raced as he tried to make sense of it all. It felt too real to have been a dream. He looked down and a chill ran through him. A set of footprints, his footprints, were outlined in the frost on the ground. They led into the vineyard.

He followed them from his campsite through the vineyard and finally out into an open plain where suddenly, the footprints ended.

He looked around in a confused manner then he recalled his dream, this was where the apparition had disappeared into the forest and where he had stopped, knowing he couldn't enter. His mind raced. There was no forest here! He stood frozen for a long time and no matter how hard he thought, nothing could possibly explain what had happened the previous night.

After a long time, Brutus returned to the campsite. There was nothing more for him to do here. He packed up his gear and mounted his horse. He had a last battle to fight.

Chapter 10

The Battle

A cold rain fell from the gloomy skies as Brutus rode hard over the open plains of Philippi. He entered his army's defensive position and guided his horse through a maze of tents, animals, equipment and soldiers.

His first battle with Antony had ended in a stalemate, but Cassius, his loyal brother-in-law, was dead. He had committed suicide after mistakenly thinking that Antony had surrounded his legions.

Cassius' error weighed heavily on Brutus because soon after, Brutus' own legions had rallied and pushed Antony back beyond his original position. Cassius' death was a crushing psychological blow and it pained him to know that Cassius would never see Rome again—all because of him.

Brutus made his way through the mostly sleeping camp, nodding to the few soldiers who were up, sitting idly by their burning fires eating meager rations, writing letters or mending battle gear.

He guided his horse over to a series of small stone buildings serving as his headquarters. A stable boy ran over and grabbed the reigns of his horse. "Go fetch Varro," Brutus ordered. "Tell him to bring the field generals at once."

After Cassius' death, Varro was now Brutus' second-in-command. The stable boy acknowledged the order with a quick nod and ran off.

Brutus entered his headquarters and stripped off his heavy outer tunic. He had thought hard about the speech he was going to deliver to his generals, and he had prayed to the gods that after tomorrow he would be on the way back to Rome.

His officers entered, taking their places at a large round table. When they were all present, Brutus walked around admiring his group of war-tested men. Most of them had been fighting one war or another for the better of twenty years.

He cleared his throat and began, "The final battle is before us, friends. Each of you has sacrificed much. For that, I am eternally grateful. I gathered you here because I have an announcement."

He paused and looked every officer directly in the eyes before continuing, "I wish to attack Antony's forces the day after tomorrow."

His officers remained silent. Finally, Varro stood and spoke, "Brutus, we have the advantage. Winter is setting in. Antony is running low on food and supplies. Why the impatience? We can camp for the winter and attack in early spring, when Antony is weakest."

Brutus had anticipated the question and answered, "Friends, what I owe each and every one of you I could never repay in this lifetime. I speak to you now, not as you leader but as your friend.

"We have come far together. This will not be a decision for me to make alone. It is up to all of us to decide our fate. If it is decided that we stay here for the winter, I will heed your wishes.

"But first." He looked over at second-in-command. "Varro, how long has it been since you've seen your family?"

"Two years, one month and three days."

The generals began laughing. Brutus smiled and walked over to another. "And you, Claudius. How long has it been since you have set foot in Rome? Since you took a true Roman bath? Or spent a day at the theater?"

A forlorn smile overcame the man's face. "It has been more than five years since I have had the pleasure."

Brutus continued on to the next man. "Strato, I remember when we used to go to the gaming halls. You used to beat me every single time." Strato nodded and laughed deeply.

Brutus continued around the table, staring into the faces of his men, noble and honorable men who had sacrificed much.

He came back to Varro and placed a hand on his shoulder. "What Varro says is true. We can fortify our position for the winter and battle Antony in the spring. We will survive, but it will be hard and there are no guarantees. In the spring Antony might be in a weaker position, or he might retreat back towards Rome for fresh supplies and more soldiers. When spring arrives, we might have a slight advantage. But who is to say."

His generals began nodding and Brutus seized the initiative, "But right now! Right here! It is an even battle. If the gods want us to win Rome back, we will."

Brutus paused and took a deep breath. "Friends, I miss Rome. We have all been away too long. It is time to go home or die trying. I leave it to your vote. What shall it be?"

His men looked around at each other in silence. Varro stood, looked at Brutus and announced loudly, "Rome!"

The rest of Brutus' generals stood and began chanting, "Rome! Rome! Rome!"

Brutus drew out his sword and raised it high, "It is settled then. Tomorrow the final battle begins. To the Republic!"

"To the Republic!" the generals shouted back.

Chapter 11

Brutus stepped outside of his headquarters. Low, black clouds stretched across the sky dropping a constant, freezing rain onto the barren plain. A fierce wind blew unabated and it tore through Brutus chilling him to the bone.

Brutus walked over to his horse and stared out at his legions who were awaiting his orders. He mounted the horse cursing the horrible weather because it would make his attack plan more difficult. But, it was too late now. The fight would go on.

His battle plan was simple. On his order, all legions would attack full force straight at the center of Antony's defenses. After the initial attack, Varro would peel off seven legions and two hundred archers and try to pierce through Antony's left flank.

The strategy: create a bulge in Antony's center, thus stretching his outer lines thin as Antony committed more troops to push back the initial attack. Then Varro's legions would be able to break through the weakened left flank. Brutus would then have significant forces in front of and behind Antony, where they could crush him before he had a chance to reorganize or retreat.

If the plan succeeded, Brutus could finally return to Rome. If the plan failed, he was a dead man.

He looked up into the dark sky and turned to Varro. "It is time, General. It has been an honor."

"The honor has been mine," Varro saluted.

Brutus nodded and Varro yelled out the order. The trumpeters blasted their instruments and a mass of soldiers began to move forward. The last battle had begun.

The fighting raged for hours with Brutus riding from legion to legion gathering battle updates from his scouts. The weather had turned even worse with heavier rains and unrelenting winds making their offensive attack even more difficult. With each passing report, Brutus grew more and more impatient.

Time was against him. In order for his plan to work, Varro had to break through Antony's flank quickly because his main force wouldn't be able to sustain the bulge in the center of Antony's line for long. During the initial attack his army had succeeded in creating the bulge, but Varro had not been able to break through Antony's flank.

A scout rode over to Brutus in great haste. The man had wounds in half a dozen places and could barely talk. "Varro urges Brutus to send him more support," he said, gasping for air. "He cannot break through."

"The gods be damned!" Brutus yelled out in frustration. It had to be broken. He maneuvered his horse over to Claudius. "Take four legions and join Varro," he commanded.

Claudius barked the orders to his men. "Claudius." Brutus grabbed him by the shoulder. "If you fail, it is over. We all die."

The General nodded, turned his horse and rode quickly into the heat of battle.

Two more hours passed and even with the rain and wind, the air around Brutus smelled of destruction and death. Late in the afternoon, his most trusted scout arrived from the front. He looked grim.

"Varro and Claudius have failed, Brutus," he reported with tears streaming down his face. "Their legions have been decimated. Antony's forces have cut them off. They're being annihilated."

Brutus exhaled deeply. It was over. There was nothing left to do. He ordered his forces to retreat, knowing most would not be able to.

He led his small remaining group northward. They rode hard until they came over a small hill into a large, open plain. He stopped the group next to a stream.

His personal guard shouted, "Brutus! Why have you stopped? We must go quickly. Antony will not be far behind."

Brutus didn't answer. He got down off his horse and walked to the bank. He stared out at the streaming water. He knew his men were anxious to continue because if they were caught, death was certain.

"Brutus! We must leave now!" the man pleaded. "It is not safe to stay here!"

He turned from the bank and walked back to his loyal soldier. "Gordian, I am sorry. I let you and Rome down."

"You have dishonored no one, but we must leave at once, before it is too late."

Brutus shook his head. "It's too late for me, Gordian. Tell the men to go, but I must stay. I came this far to see that at least a few would escape. I ran away once, but not again. Good luck."

Gordian bowed his head. There would be no further discussion.

Brutus watched stoically as the remaining soldiers rode quickly away. He stripped off his battle gear, walked back to the stream and sat down in the wet grass. He looked around the treeless, desolate plain—how he wished he could at least see the golden sun and blue skies one more time.

Brutus stood knowing his time was vanishing quickly. It wouldn't be long till they found him. He reached inside his tunic and pulled out the coin. He held it in his shaking hands, staring at his portrait. He turned the coin over and ran a finger across the double daggers.

He had been a selfish, vain man—a wasted life. He stood up and pulled out the dagger, the same one he had used to kill Caesar—his father. Raindrops glistened on the blade. Off in the distance, he heard a low roar, hoof beats, thousands, coming fast. A moment later he saw them, Antony's soldiers.

Brutus took one last look into the black sky and spoke up to the heavens, "Father, please forgive me! I betrayed you!"

After those words, Brutus thrust the dagger deep into his heart. He fell to the ground and as his life drifted away, he opened his eyes one last time.

—In front of him stood a dark forest.

Chapter 12

Antony rode over to Brutus' body. He was disappointed the assassin had committed suicide. How he had longed for the pleasure of torturing then killing him. Frankly, he was a bit surprised. He didn't think the coward had the courage or the honor to take his own life.

Antony rolled the body over with his foot. "I hope you rot in your afterlife, Brutus."

He turned to leave but something in Brutus' hand caught his eye. He reached down and picked up the object and laughed. It was the Double Dagger coin. He had melted down thousands of them. It had become, besides killing Brutus, his personal mission to see that every single coin was destroyed. He wanted to wipe out any trace of the man's existence. Antony held it, studying the double daggers.

"Live by the sword, die by the sword. You are truly a cursed man."

Antony looked back down at Brutus' lifeless body. "Remember, my friend. The evil one does cannot be undone. Not even in death."

Antony stepped down to the bank and without hesitation threw the Eids of March coin as far as he could into the dark swirling waters.

BOOK II

Men never do evil so completely and cheerfully
as when they do it from religious conviction.

Blaise Pascal

Chapter 1

1096 A.D. The time of the Crusades

He stood frozen, locked in fear. His heart pounded wildly and his breath came in ragged gasps. An overwhelming sense of panic and impending doom had built into a deafening roar that raged throughout his body. The only reality he could comprehend at the moment was that he was about to die, and the dread he felt was indescribable.

Once again he had descended into the darkness, a place he was certain had to be worse than any kind of hell that might await him after his death. He had been locked in this inferno of suffering many times before, and when the torment was at its absolute worst, it wasn't death he feared, rather the lack of it. At such moments he prayed that there was no afterlife because, maybe in a nonexistence, he could finally find peace.

There had been a time in his past, a place deep in the far reaches of his consciousness, when he thought he remembered an instance of serenity and contentment. But now, that fleeting recollection was a distant memory he wasn't sure ever really existed.

"Goddamn it!" he cursed, as he clenched his fists into tight balls.

The suffering had become too much and once again he had to give into it. He grabbed the wine from the table and drank half the bottle in quick, desperate gulps. Almost instantly, the strong sweet alcohol began to work its magic. He exhaled deeply and could feel his heartbeat beginning to slow. Only after finishing the entire bottle did his breathing return to normal and the all-consuming fear begin to fade.

Michael Claudien opened another bottle and shakily poured the wine into a dirty goblet. He took a long, deep drink. He had learned the hard way that the only cure from such attacks was to completely numb his body with alcohol.

He sat down on a small wooden chair and sighed. The darkness had lifted somewhat, but now, pangs of guilt and self-loathing swept over him as it inevitably always did when he resorted to alcohol for a cure.

He stared intently at a razor sharp dagger lying on top of the table. It would be so easy. A quick swipe across the wrists and he could end his suffering once and for all. He had thought about it hundreds of times but could never muster the courage to do it, and that made him even more despondent.

It was a terrible fate for a man, especially a nobleman, to realize that he was weak and cowardly. But that was Michael's unfortunate lot in life—he was a man of dubious and frail character.

Michael Claudien was born a nobleman, the eldest son of Lord Pierre-Bermond Claudien. His family's estate was situated outside of a town called Vassily, in the Duchy of Upper Lorraine, located in the Northeastern region of the Kingdom of France.

He was a tall man for his day, standing a hair shy of six feet. His frame was of medium build and his dark black hair always lay somewhat askew. Despite the ugliness of his mind, he was a handsome man in a dark insecure sort of way. At twenty-nine years old, Michael was a confirmed bachelor who never intended to marry.

He had had his fair share of women over the years, but since he preferred to remain unattached, most of his love affairs now came from the ranks of peasant women who lived in or around his family's estate.

The main reason Michael preferred these types of relationships was because the lower class women never placed any demands on him. They were fully aware he had no obligations towards them. And unlike the spoiled noble women he had been forced to court as a younger man, these poor maidens were much more appreciative of even the smallest of gifts. It greatly pleased him to watch them squeal with delight when he presented them with small trinkets of his affection.

Michael was even aware of two children he had sired, a girl and a boy, but he had no responsibility or obligation to them because they were born out of wedlock to peasant women. Regrettably, he no longer enjoyed the favors of their mothers, but he did send his ill-begotten children a package of food and clothing during the holidays.

Michael's father severely looked down upon his "liaisons" with the lower class women, but that didn't bother him a bit because it was only one of the many aspects of his life that his father disapproved of.

With every sip of the wine, Michael felt better, though he knew it was only a temporary relief because after the magic elixir wore off, the symptoms would come back in a much worse fashion.

He wasn't quite sure how or when this affliction had begun; only that he had become hopelessly ensnared in a vicious, never-ending circle of self-destruction.

He stood up and walked over to a tiny wooden window cut out of the stone wall of his chambers. He unlatched it and a gust of raw, winter air blew in. He stared down at the empty courtyard, then across his family's estate. The rolling countryside was barren, cold and bleak.

For months a constant veil of gray mist permeated the air, no matter if it was day or night. The horrible weather added to his gloom and despair. It had been weeks since he had glimpsed sunlight, and he began to wonder if the sun had disappeared from this world for good.

Another blast of frigid air caused him to shiver and he quickly closed the window. He was so tired. Tired of everything. And tomorrow—he almost couldn't comprehend it. He was leaving for Constantinople.

"What in God's name have I gotten myself into?" Michael said to himself while sitting back down.

The wine had done its job too well. After two bottles, he was weak and completely drained. He knew it was the tension regarding the upcoming trip to Constantinople that was causing the reoccurrence of his condition. An affliction that had no name, that no one, including himself, could understand, explain or cure.

He still could not fathom that tomorrow, February the Second, in the Year of Our Lord, one thousand and ninety-six, he would leave the comforts of the Claudien estate along with his younger brother, Godfrey, and two peasants. They would set off on a perilous journey over harsh and forbidding lands.

Their mission: travel to the Holy Lands and fight to the death in the name of the one and true, God All Mighty.

The two brothers had accepted Pope Urban's Holy Order to become Crusaders and fight for Jesus Christ. Rather, Godfrey had accepted the calling. Michael had been forced into it. Earlier in the year, the Pope had issued an edict ordering all able-bodied men to set aside their interests and travel to the East to help their Christian brothers—the Byzantines—defend the Holy Lands against incursions from the Moslems and their heretical religion called Islam.

Michael grabbed the large map from the dusty shelf. He unfolded it across the table and stared blankly down at it. How many hours had he spent studying the map, he wondered? A wave of disbelief followed by anger swept over him every time he studied the travel route that Godfrey had carefully drawn on the parched brown paper.

Jerusalem might as well have been on the other side of the world. The holiest of all cities lay almost three thousand miles away, and it would take close to a year to reach it in the best of conditions.

The only consolation Michael could think of was that the route to Constantinople was a well-established one. Pilgrims, merchants and soldiers had traveled the same route for centuries, and it consisted of a network of old roads that had been built by the once invincible Roman Legions—an Empire that collapsed in the West more than six hundred years ago due to political and societal corruption, coupled with constant attacks from barbarians. But, after six hundred years of neglect, the roads were still intact.

Their journey would take them across Northern France to the city of Worms, where they would cross the Rhine River into the fierce tribal lands of

Germany. From Germany, they would follow the trail down the Danube River, through the Kingdoms of Hungary and Bulgaria, eventually crossing into Belgrade. After Belgrade, they would have to traverse the dense and greatly feared Serbian Forest—a forest that had earned a very sinister reputation. Michael had heard countless stories of travelers who entered, never to exit.

He slowly traced the route with his finger. If they managed to emerge from the Serbian Forest, they would enter into the relative safe confines of the Byzantine Territories until they reached Constantinople, capital city of what remained of the Eastern Roman Empire.

Once in Constantinople, the plan was to wait for an army of Crusaders that was also setting off from France, before continuing on to Jerusalem. The army was led by a monk named Peter, who after witnessing Pope Urban's declaration to arms, claimed to have received visions from God commanding him to raise an army and drive the Moslems from the Holy Lands.

In Michael's opinion, Peter was a lunatic. He was a dirty, foul-tempered man whose face resembled a donkey. But, despite his physical shortcomings, the monk had managed to muster a large army by traveling the countryside preaching fire and brimstone sermons about the Moslems.

Peter commanded all who would listen that it was God's will to destroy the Moslems and their religion. Michael saw Peter speak in a small hamlet outside of Vassily, and even he had to admit the ugly monk was highly successful in stirring the crowds into a war frenzy. In Michael's judgment, religious rhetoric was no substitute for fighting ability, even though Peter and his army were certainly full of religious fervor. Michael wasn't sure how that would play out on the battlefield, especially against trained soldiers.

Regardless, it had been decided to set off before Peter and join up with the monk's army after it arrived in Constantinople, then they would travel the last thousand miles to Jerusalem.

It was a plan Michael didn't care for. Despite his serious doubts about Peter, he had pleaded long and hard with Godfrey and his father that they should wait until March and travel with Peter's forces, not only for safety, but for better weather.

His family wouldn't listen. His brother argued that he wanted to get to Constantinople a few months in advance so he could visit all the holy sites in the city. Michael knew that excuse was just a ruse. Godfrey wanted to be able to claim that he was one of the first crusaders to arrive in Constantinople after the Pope's order, and their father was more than happy to support Godfrey when he realized the prestige the honor would carry.

Michael knew from the beginning that his arguments for waiting to travel with Peter would fall on deaf ears. It was a losing battle, so, in the end, he didn't put up much of a fight. Anyway, it was the second part of the journey from

Constantinople to Jerusalem that was, by far, the most treacherous. Even with the accompaniment of Peter's army, they would have to travel through hostile lands inhabited by Moslems, Turks, and God knows what other wretched barbarians. It was this part of the pilgrimage that Michael feared the most.

Their mission was daunting, and with grim realization, Michael understood all too well that if by some stroke of good fortune they arrived in Constantinople alive, they would still have to fight the Moslems all the way to Jerusalem. He had heard countless stories about the fierce Islamic warriors. There was no doubt about the tremendous fighting ability of these savage people.

Michael tried to estimate the odds of safely returning home. First, if by some miracle he made it all the way to Jerusalem in one piece, and then, if he managed to stay alive during their battles with the Moslems, he would still have to travel all the way back to France. The total journey was six thousand miles and would take at least three years to complete.

"What in the hell have I gotten myself into?" he mumbled. It was a suicide mission only a fool would attempt. Michael knew the chances of returning alive were close to zero.

Although he had no desire to embark on the foolish endeavor, he had no choice. A month earlier, in a pomp ceremony that every nobleman, knight, clergyman and peasant in a hundred square miles had attended, the Bishop of Bouillon knighted him and his brother—Crusaders.

In the eyes of those attending, there was no question whether Michael would take the cross and defend God. Anything less and he would be labeled a coward, a heretic.

So, while Michael supported the crusade publicly, he did so only out of family pressure, not because of any idea of personal honor, and certainly not because of a burning desire to serve the Pope or even God for that matter. He had no choice but to go and fight, and since that was the case, he was at least going to try and get something out of it for him.

He had heard unbelievable tales of enormous wealth in the East. Gold, jewels, spices and exotic goods that commanded astronomical prices back in France. Michael's plan was simple. First, he would stay alive by any and all means possible; second, he would attempt to bring back some of the vast wealth the eastern lands offered. If he did survive, he would return to France, buy his own land and leave his family's estate for good.

Michael realized the chances of surviving the crusade, let alone becoming wealthy, were small. But at least his plan was something. It was the last bit of hope that kept him from completely falling off the cliff separating him from the abyss of hopelessness and insanity.

He drained a third bottle of wine and watched in a daze as it rolled off the table and broke on the cold stone floor. This was it his drunken mind surmised, the last night he would spend in the only home he had ever known. He forced himself out of the chair, stumbled over to his small straw bed and collapsed onto it. The wine had performed its magic, as it always did, and now, he could finally get some rest.

As Michael slept, he dreamed. A dream he had had many times. He was at the edge of a dark forest. The forest held a secret—a secret even his sleeping mind knew he must discover if he was ever going to have a chance.

Chapter 2

Michael woke with a startle. "Cursed me," he moaned.

As with most mornings, his room was cold and dank, and he suffered from a pounding head, swollen eyes and an irritable stomach. But today was a morning unlike any other. The fateful day had arrived—Constantinople.

He lay on his back staring up at the cracks in the stone ceiling. There was a large black cobweb in the far corner. How it got there baffled him because after three years, he had never once seen the spider that built it. Every so often, he would knock the web down with a straw broom only to find it miraculously rebuilt the next morning.

"Don't worry, spider," he spoke up to the ceiling. "You're safe now."

Michael grudgingly rolled off the bed while stretching his aching body. He wondered how in hell he was going to ride a horse three thousand miles when he couldn't even find comfort in his own bed.

He hobbled over to the window and flipped the latch. It was just after sunrise. The weather was dismal, again. He looked down at the small traveling party that had already gathered in the courtyard. His brother stood in the middle shouting orders to a handful of peasants loading the last of the supplies onto horses and donkeys.

He stared down at Godfrey with a jumbled mix of brotherly jealousy, angst and affection. His younger brother was a good four inches shorter than him but made up for it with a rock solid physique and an iron constitution. A mop of brownish-yellow hair hung down across his forehead and with his boyish features, he appeared much younger than his twenty-five years.

Godfrey closely resembled their father, in personality and appearance, whereas Michael favored their mother, God rest her soul. It always saddened him to think about her. She had passed away from a stomach ailment when he was seventeen, and there was no doubt in Michael's mind that if heaven really exists, his mother was there among the angels.

He looked over at his father, Lord Pierre-Bermont, who was the exact opposite of his mother. His father was a cold, distant man who never offered a kind word, much less showed any form of affection or love towards him.

As he watched Godfrey direct the peasants, it astounded Michael that no matter what the circumstances, his brother always appeared so sure of himself. A familiar feeling of insecurity fell over Michael. Godfrey was everything he wasn't, or at least that's what their father repeatedly told Michael.

Lord Pierre-Bermond stood next to Godfrey with a proud look on his face. Michael shook his head in disgust. It occurred to him that it didn't matter one bit to the hateful old bastard that he likely was sending his only two sons off to be killed in some meaningless battle on the other side of the world.

His brother and father began to laugh, and in unison, they turned and looked up at Michael's window. Both of their faces took on a hint of displeasure as they spotted him staring down at them. Michael forced a smile and waved, then quickly turned from the window. "Those two self-righteous asses should be going on this trip together," he muttered as he packed the rest of his goods.

He couldn't fight it any longer. It was time to go. He donned his riding gear, gathered his bags and took one last look around his room. He couldn't shake the premonition that he would never see his family's estate or for that matter, France, ever again. He carried his bags down the steep stairs of the manor house and walked out into the courtyard.

It was bitterly cold outside. Dark clouds filled the sky and the air was heavy with mist.

His brother spotted him first and called over, "Good morning, Michael. I'm surprised to see you. I thought you would have run off during the night."

His father chuckled at the barb.

"Very amusing, younger brother," Michael responded, trying to put on a confident front. "As you can see, I am here, and I am ready to battle and die in the name of our ever present, but rather shy and elusive, God Almighty."

"Enough," his father said as he glared at Michael. It was a look Michael had come to know well over the years. It was no secret his father considered him a colossal failure, both as a son and a man. In fact, it wouldn't surprise Michael if his father hoped he died during the crusade. That way, the entire family estate would go to Godfrey.

Michael walked over to his horse and secured his bags to the enormous animal. Percy was a six-year-old heavy horse, and Michael was not the least bit ashamed to admit that he cared more for the moody, insolent beast than he did for his own father.

He could tell Percy sensed something monumental was about to happen, and the horse didn't seem too happy about it. Michael patted the coarse mass of black hair covering his thick neck. The beast's shaggy winter coat was matted and stunk, even though Michael took great pains to see that the horse was well cared for. Percy whinnied loudly while stomping his front right hoof, a habit he often did when he was agitated or bored.

"It's alright, boy," Michael said calmly. If there was one thing he wasn't concerned about in regards to the trip, it was the horse. He knew if any animal could survive the rigors of the journey, it was Percy. The horse had a head the size of a barrel with a massive chest and legs as thick as tree trunks. He was a monster of a heavy horse weighing in at over a ton, and Michael would have bet Percy's strength against an ox anytime.

Michael looked over at the two peasants who would be accompanying them. "Morning, Alberto, Tribert."

"Morning, Sir Michael," Alberto responded while Tribert nodded in his direction.

Alberto was a frail-looking old man who had lost his wife to consumption last fall. The widower had requested to join them on the crusade because he no longer had anyone to keep him here, and he wanted to make a pilgrimage to the Holy Lands to pray for his wife's soul. He had explained to Michael he was certain she had gone straight to hell because of the way she treated him for the thirty years they were married.

Michael watched as the other peasant got onto his donkey. Tribert was one of the stockiest human beings he had ever seen. In fact, he reminded Michael of a human version of Percy. As a small child, Tribert had been kicked in the head by an ill-tempered mule, and, as a result, the poor devil was a dim-witted idiot. Nonetheless, Michael was glad Tribert was accompanying them because he was strong as hell, trustworthy and very amusing, especially after the dullard had consumed a few drinks of ale or wine.

Michael turned to his father. "Well father, I guess this is good-bye."

His father stared at him with a look that was hard to read. He walked over to Michael and hugged him tightly. The unexpected embrace took Michael by surprise. A long-forgotten boyhood desire for his father's love swelled inside of him.

He pulled Michael's head down closer to his shoulder and whispered softly into his ear, "Son, if you do anything to disgrace my family's name, so help me God, don't come home—at least not alive."

With those words, the warm feeling from his father's embrace ended abruptly. Michael pulled away, glaring back at him first with sadness, and then, a rising hatred.

"I love you too, my Lord," he replied sarcastically, holding back the desire to either shed tears or strike him.

Michael climbed onto Percy's stout back, realizing that he no longer had a place on his father's estate.

The rest of the good-byes were bid and the party set off. The journey had begun.

Chapter 3

The Crusaders rode through the countryside at a comfortable pace. Michael casually sipped watered-down wine from a canvas sack in an effort to relieve his pounding headache and jangled nerves.

"How are you doing?" Godfrey asked, sounding almost mildly concerned.

"Terrific, brother," Michael responded in good fashion. With the wine and fresh air, the first hour on horseback was actually somewhat invigorating. The second hour was enjoyable too, but as the third hour passed, he began to grow bored and uncomfortable. His fine spirits were short lived because by the fourth hour and tenth mile of the three-thousand mile journey, his thighs and back began to ache. And by late afternoon, Michael was ready to give up the trip altogether.

As he suffered, his brother happily whistled songs while smiling over at him constantly, no doubt relishing in his discomfort.

Mercifully, the first day's journey ended in late afternoon after traveling about twenty miles. Michael was so exhausted that he didn't even eat. After Tribert pitched his tent, he crawled inside and fell asleep at once.

The first week painfully passed by and Michael's body had yet to adjust to the riding. He was so sore and cramped that he had great difficulty even getting aboard Percy.

But relief, even if it was temporary, was in sight. They were approaching the city of Treves where they had accommodations at an inn for the night. Michael was overjoyed at the thought of a decent meal, a bed and a roof over his head. The sun begun to set as the Crusaders passed through an enormous black sandstone archway that had been built by the Romans hundreds of years earlier. The black gate led them into Treves, a city that had once been an important Roman outpost during the Empire's glory days.

As the Crusaders slowly made their way through the center of town, Michael gawked at the architecture: stores, amphitheaters, public baths and impressive stone buildings lined the city streets. After passing through the main part of Treves they reached the outskirts of the city and found the inn.

Michael dismounted in one quick motion and in doing so, almost fell. His body, from the waist down, felt like it had turned into a block of stone.

Painfully, he began walking towards the inn when he heard Tribert call out from behind, "Why, Sir Michael, you're walking like you have a broom handle stuck up your ass!"

Godfrey and Alberto burst out laughing. Michael felt his neck growing red. "Pipe down you half-wit, or I'll give you a lashing you won't soon forget," he yelled to Tribert.

The half-brained peasant had a confused look on his face. Michael knew the poor bastard didn't understand why he had earned his wrath, so he decided not to give him too bad of a cursing.

But his brother wasn't about to let the fun end. "I think you right about that broom handle, Tribert. It's been stuck there ever since we left the estate."

Alberto continued laughing and Michael glared over at the old man. He refused to be laughed at by common peasants. "Take care of these animals and prepare the quarters for the night," he ordered.

Alberto nodded, and the two peasants began the nightly ritual of quartering the horses and unloading the supplies.

"Come on. I'm hungry," Godfrey grunted to Michael.

They left the servants to their tasks and Michael limped painfully behind Godfrey as they walked over to the inn's entrance. Once inside, a short beefy man rushed over to greet them.

"Ah ha, Lord Claudien sons," he cried out cheerfully while nervously wringing his hands. "My name is Sesto. Welcome to my inn. Have you had a good journey so far?"

"Yes. And we're hungry. Fix us supper!" Godfrey replied dismissively.

Michael shook his head. His brother was such an arrogant bastard.

"Terrific," replied the cherub man, ignoring Godfrey's slight. "Come messieurs," he motioned excitedly. "Follow Sesto. I have supper being made especially for you."

The innkeeper led them down a dark narrow hall into a large room where they were seated at a wooden table in the far corner. The room was empty except for two straggly looking monks seated quietly at a front table.

The innkeeper's teenage daughter, who, unfortunately for her, looked exactly like her father, brought a bottle of wine to the table. Michael grabbed the bottle and poured a generous amount into two cups.

"Brother." He passed the wine over to Godfrey.

Michael raised his cup in a toast. "To our enemies —-may they know we are on our way to destroy them."

Godfrey raised his glass and peered over at Michael somewhat cautiously. "Amen," he toasted.

Michael took a sip. "Not too bad."

"You would say that if it was fortified donkey piss," Godfrey said while simultaneously breaking out in hysterics over his own joke. Michael ignored him and soon was on his second glass of wine.

After a long wait the innkeeper reappeared and Godfrey yelled, "Sesto! Where the hell is our supper?"

Michael shook his head as he watched Sesto rush back into the kitchen. "Do you always have to act like such a pompous ass?"

"What?" Godfrey shot back.

"You heard me, brother. Why do you treat everyone with such contempt?"

Before Godfrey could answer, Sesto came back and put a new bottle of wine on the table.

"A thousand pardons messieurs," Sesto bowed. "Your supper will be out shortly. This bottle is on the house."

Godfrey grumbled as Michael poured himself a new glass and took a long sip of the delightful honey wine.

"Not too bad of wine," he remarked to Godfrey.

"You already said that," Godfrey scoffed.

"Did I?" Michael laughed.

"Are you going to be in an alcoholic stupor all the way to the Holy Lands?"

"Well, I haven't really thought about that," Michael replied sarcastically. "But now that you mention it, yes, I think I will."

"You're pathetic."

Michael smiled. "Why thank you, younger brother. That may be so, but at least I am not a sour old donkey's ass most of the time."

Godfrey opened his mouth to respond to his insult when, thankfully, Sesto's daughter appeared with their supper. The two brothers stopped quarreling and turned their attention to the food. Michael never would have believed that roasted quail could taste so good. The birds had been smothered in boiled onions and the meat was so tender it fell off the bone.

The brothers ate in silence, which suited Michael. After devouring two birds, Godfrey pushed back his plate and stood.

He looked down at Michael. "I am retiring for the night, good brother, and I suggest you do the same. We have a long journey ahead of us tomorrow, and you've had too much of that stuff." He pointed at the wine. "Go to bed."

Michael smiled and raised his glass. "Thank you for your concern, mother. I'll retire when I'm good and ready."

Godfrey shook his head and stormed off. As Michael watched him leave, he was certain there was no chance they would make it all the way to the Holy Lands without one of them killing the other.

Sesto walked over to the table, obviously more relaxed since Godfrey had left. "Was everything satisfactory, sir?"

"Terrific." Michael smiled. The wine and hot food had alleviated some of the pain and stiffness in his body.

"Sesto, my good man, how about a bottle of your best wine."

"Of course," the innkeeper replied before scurrying off to fetch a new bottle.

Soon, he was very drunk and he realized it was too late. He had promised himself he wouldn't get this way, but the damage had already been done. "What the hell," he said to himself, "there's no point stopping now."

"Sesto! Another of your finest," he yelled to the portly innkeeper. The red-faced man hurried away to retrieve another bottle. Michael looked around the tavern with astonishment. Sometime during the night the place had become crowded; he just didn't remember it happening.

The room was filled with a ragged assortment of townsfolk and travelers, although Michael was having a hard time making them out. He was seeing double and could only manage to focus correctly if he kept one of his eyes closed. He put a hand in front of his left eye and stared across to a table filled with a group of four, five, maybe six merchants.

He took a deep breath. The place was disgusting, but he was fully aware that in a short period of time he would probably look back on the inn as a luxury.

He turned his attention to a table of rough looking men who were arguing loudly. An enormously fat blond-headed woman sat between them with a small goat tied underneath her chair. Michael watched as the little beast lay there, happily chewing away at one of the legs of the chair. The woman seemed delighted to drink her ale and watch in amusement as the men fought with one another. It was obvious they were arguing over who was going to receive her favors for the night.

The dirty sots must be pretty desperate to fight over that fat trollop, thought Michael. Even in his drunken state, he would rather spend the night with the dirty goat than with her.

"For you, Monsieur Claudien." Sesto stood over his table with a new bottle of wine.

Michael had forgotten he ordered it. "Yes . . . Yes," he slurred.

Sesto poured the dark red liquid into Michael's glass. Michael took a sip and mumbled thanks. The wine was really taking affect because he now saw three innkeepers standing in front of him.

The innkeeper left and Michael turned his attention to the roaring fire in the hearth. He watched, almost in a trance, as the yellow flames danced about.

Michael knew he should go to bed but he couldn't quite make himself get up. It also didn't help that he had forgotten where his sleeping quarters were located, so he remained in his chair, drinking wine, watching the fire and his fellow travelers.

His thoughts turned to Godfrey. His temperate brother had gone to bed hours ago and it occurred to Michael that he was somewhat jealous of him. At least his younger brother had a mission in life. A purpose.

The only real passion Michael possessed was material wealth, drinking and trying to feel good for longer than two days. He couldn't understand why he was burdened with his condition. He knew he wouldn't drink nearly as much if he didn't suffer from the attacks. Why had God seen fit to give him this affliction? What had he done to anger him so!

Over the years he had tried everything to relieve his mind of its irrational torment. Nothing worked. He had consulted the Bishop of Bouillon who preached to Michael that his problem was caused by his countless sins, and the only way to break the spell was to pray continuously for salvation.

For months, Michael prayed daily and attended church services almost every Sunday. But, he swore off the Church when he became friends with the local priest who was more interested in drinking with him than providing salvation from his ills.

After the Church failed him, Michael enlisted the town doctor in hopes of releasing whatever disease had infiltrated his body, but that was also of no use since the physician's only treatment consisted of bleeding him until he was on the verge of passing out. In the end, the only relief he could find, albeit temporary, was in alcohol.

Michael tried to pour more wine but only a few drops came out. It was past the wee hours and he knew he had to go to bed. God! He was going to hate tomorrow. And in a few days, they would be leaving the territory of France. The thought of entering the lands of the barbaric Germanic tribes sent a chill down his spine.

In his daze, he spotted Sesto and motioned for him to come over. "Help. Help me to . . . ," were the only words he managed to get out.

Sesto appeared to get his point and pulled Michael up from his chair. The innkeeper led him, stumbling the entire way back to his room. Sesto opened the door and nudged him in, but Michael couldn't even make it to the bed. He collapsed on the floor, instantly falling into an alcohol-induced slumber.

Chapter 4

"Where the hell is that no good, drunk brother of mine?" Godfrey yelled over at Tribert, who was busy entertaining himself by throwing rocks at a flock of chickens.

Tribert shrugged then threw a large stone in the direction of the chickens. Godfrey watched as the peasant finally succeeded in hitting one of the chickens. The damn bird began squawking bloody murder as a mass of feathers went flying.

Godfrey shook his head as Tribert began laughing hysterically. "Put those damn stones down, you half-wit," he yelled. "Come on. Follow me."

They went back inside the inn and entered Michael's room. Godfrey took one look at his brother curled up on the filthy floor and shook his head in disgust. "He is truly the son of the Devil."

"Fetch me a bucket of water," Godfrey whispered to Tribert with a mischievous grin. "And make sure it's cold and dirty."

Tribert left the room and quickly returned with a large pail of water. Godfrey grabbed it and tiptoed over to his slumbering brother.

Michael was in the midst of the strange dream. He was alone on a spacious plain. Directly in front of him was a dark, forbidding forest. He was terrified. Next to him, a stream ran and he watched as the water slowly flowed past. He had the sense that no one else existed on earth, just him.

His attention shifted to the forest. He felt like he was being drawn to it, as if the answers he desperately sought lay inside the forest, but he was terrified. He couldn't move. He just stood there staring at it, trying to force himself to walk in. He stepped closer—then instantly he was back in his filthy room as a freezing rush of icy cold water shocked him out of his dream.

Michael felt as if he had been stabbed a thousand times by a hot poker. He jumped up off the floor, rubbing freezing water out of his eyes. He saw his brother and Tribert laughing at his discomfort.

"God Almighty!" he yelled at the top of his lungs. "What the hell is wrong with you!"

"You're late, you no good, filthy drunkard," Godfrey shouted back.

Michael felt woozy and sat down on the straw bed he should have slept on.

The shock of the cold water gave way to a throbbing pain in his head and horrific soreness in his legs and back.

He tried to recall the night before, but was having trouble remembering anything except for the ghastly image of a fat woman's chair collapsing and crushing to death a little goat tied underneath it. The bizarre image made him wonder if the alcohol had finally pickled his brain to the point of no return.

"Godfrey," Michael replied weakly. "I was thinking . . . the animals might need an extra day to recuperate, to get used to the rigors of the trail. Maybe we should leave tomorrow. We don't want to push them too hard."

"You're truly pathetic," Godfrey said. "We'll be leaving shortly brother, with or without you." Godfrey walked out, leaving Michael alone with the peasant.

"Oh Tribert," he moaned. "Please end my misery and just kill me."

"With what?" the imbecile asked.

Through foggy painful eyes, Michael watched as Tribert picked up a chair. "Sweet Jesus, Tribert!" Michael screamed, realizing that the idiot thought he was serious. "I was just joking, you fool. Put that damn chair down."

Tribert looked relieved and set the chair back down. "Can I do anything else for you, my lord?"

"No. No. Just get Percy ready." Michael sighed as he lay across the bed.

His tongue felt like a piece of old leather and his head hurt so bad he thought his brain might explode. After a few minutes of contemplating how bad he felt, he forced himself to get up and gather his belongings. He couldn't go back to his father's estate. He had no choice but to go forward.

Michael stumbled out of the inn, half bent over because his back was killing him from having slept on the hard wooden floor. As he walked outside, he was instantly blinded by bright, piercing sunshine. After months of rain and constant dark skies, it was perfectly sunny and clear.

"I see you have managed to get out of bed," he heard Godfrey call out. "It's a beautiful day isn't it?"

Michael could barely open his eyes. He moaned and staggered over to his horse.

"You'll never learn will you?" Godfrey continued nagging. If Michael could have seen his brother clearly, he would've hit him square across the jaw.

"Here, Michael." Tribert handed him the reigns of Percy.

After three attempts, he managed to climb aboard the smelly beast and the Crusaders set off for the German border.

Chapter 5

Mercifully, as the days passed Michael became less and less sore from the rigors of traveling, although the actual journey had become more treacherous as the lands of northeastern France turned harsh and forbidding.

The Crusaders slowly made their way through heavy forests and along deep gorges. More than once Michael thought Percy had lost his footing, which would have resulted in them crashing down a deep ravine to a certain death.

After another week, the Crusaders left the rugged terrain of northeastern France without incident and crossed over the Rhine River into Germany. After a few days in Germany, the trail became much easier as the landscape grew softer and less rugged. The German Rhineland was rustic and unspoiled, with rolling green hills, and despite his initial fears, the Germans, at least for now, had left them alone.

Michael rode next to Tribert while sipping wine from a small cask. "Here, Tribert." He motioned with the bag. "You want some? I promise not to tell Godfrey."

Michael could tell Tribert knew the bag didn't hold water because he was grinning from ear to ear while enthusiastically nodding his head. Michael looked down the trail. Godfrey and Alberto were riding far ahead, probably having a theological discussion about some dead pope or saint. It seemed that was all they ever talked about.

Michael handed the wine over, and Tribert gulped it down as if it was water.

"Take it easy." Michael laughed at the site of wine pouring out of Tribert's mouth.

Tribert handed the wine cask back. "That's good," he said in a child-like fashion.

"I know." He motioned for Tribert to lower his voice. "Let's just keep this between you and me. All right?"

Tribert nodded his head a few dozen times. "Can I have another sip?"

Michael grinned, and after making sure Godfrey wasn't looking, he handed Tribert the wine.

The Crusaders continued their leisurely travel along a well-kept road that led to the city of Nuremberg. After a few hours, they overtook a small traveling party of religious pilgrims. Michael and Godfrey rode up to a dour-looking man who trailed the group. He wore all black and his appearance was almost frightening. Obviously, he was the man in charge.

"Afternoon, good sir," Godfrey said.

The man nodded back in severe fashion. "Afternoon."

"May I inquire as to where you are headed?" Godfrey asked.

"We are on our way to Nuremberg, then to Regensburg to visit my brother."

"We're headed to Nuremberg as well," Michael said with enthusiasm. "Perhaps we should travel the rest of the way together . . . for safety."

Michael's real interest in traveling with the group stemmed from the sight of a fair-haired beauty sitting atop a chestnut mare. The girl was, without question, the most beautiful creature he had ever set sober eyes on.

The man seemed to be sizing them over. After thinking about the suggestion for a full minute, he answered briskly, "Yes, that would be a good idea. My name is Stephan Berneche."

The proper introductions were made and the travelers moved on. Michael soon discovered that the dour old man was the fair maiden's father, which greatly complicated his plans because he appeared to be a very religious, stern sort of a man. The two parties rode together for a couple of hours while Michael waited patiently for the right time to approach the fair girl.

Finally, he saw an opportunity and slowly rode over to her.

"Hello, my lady." He bowed his head. "Let me properly introduce myself. I am Michael Claudien."

She smiled warmly. Michael couldn't believe his eyes; the young pilgrim was even more beautiful up close. She had long brownish-blond hair, beautiful milky skin and a pair of the biggest, bluest eyes he had ever seen.

"I'm Jessica," she said in a soft, feminine but sweetly innocent voice.

"Jessica," Michael repeated aloud. "What a lovely name."

She giggled. "Thank you."

"I understand you're traveling on a religious pilgrimage?"

"Yes, we are traveling to the city of Regensburg. My father's brother is a priest there. We are going to visit his church."

"Then we have something in common," he responded slyly.

"And what is that?"

"My brother and I are also on a pilgrimage. We are traveling to Constantinople, and then on to Jerusalem."

Her eyes grew wide. "Are you one of those Crusaders I have heard about?"

"Yes. I have taken an oath to carry the cross for Jesus Christ," he boasted. "We are going to kick the cursed Moslems out of the Christian lands for good."

Michael smiled and then added for good measure, "We want to make the

Holy Lands safe for pretty young Christians like you."

He was trying his best to impress her because he didn't have a lot of time. They would be arriving in Nuremberg in only an hour or two, and after tomorrow, they would go their separate ways.

She rubbed the mane of her horse and blushed. "I have heard my father talk about Pope Urban and his speech calling for a Holy War, but I have never met a Crusader in person. You are indeed brave men. We should consider ourselves lucky that you are willing to fight for us, and our God."

"Well, the Lord has called us," Michael said with a mischievous grin. "Alas, it is our duty."

Jessica's father suddenly turned on his horse and glared at Michael with a disapproving look.

Michael waved at him and said to Jessica, "It doesn't look like your father approves of us talking."

She rolled her eyes. "He says that most men are animals, and believe me, he does his best to keep me away from them. He preaches endlessly that unmarried daughters should remain virgins until they receive the sacrament of Holy Matrimony."

Michael almost fell off his horse. Jessica was an un-blossomed rose. He knew then and there that he had to have her. Her father turned around and, again, glared at him with a scowl. Michael would have to lay the groundwork and fast, because it wouldn't be long before the old codger rode over to break up their little chat.

Michael grabbed his satchel and took a long pull of the wine. Here goes nothing, he thought, as he gazed over at Jessica and said, "The Apostle Paul said that virgins are blessed creatures of God and that there is no glory greater than to give thyself to a man answering the Lord's call."

"Apostle Paul said that?" she asked with a hint of skepticism mixed with amusement.

"I've read it in the Bible."

"Where?"

"I believe it was in, ah, I think the book of Revelations," he replied, doing his best not to laugh.

She grinned slightly and Michael couldn't tell if she was playing along or actually thought he was telling the truth.

"Maybe we can take a walk later tonight?" he asked.

Jessica looked ahead in her father's direction. "I don't think my father would approve."

Michael groaned but he wasn't going to give up that easy. "What he doesn't know won't hurt him," he whispered over to her.

She looked back at Michael. He knew this was it. Please God he prayed.

Just this once. Please grant me this favor.

She smiled somewhat mischievously. "We are staying at Saint Sebald's Church. Meet me behind the rectory after the moon is full."

Michael spirits soared. "I look forward to it, my lady." He bowed his head slightly and nudged Percy up ahead deciding not to push his luck any further. He rode up to his brother and Jessica's father.

"Sir Berneche," Michael greeted the man in an innocent voice.

Jessica's father nodded in a grumpy fashion. He appeared to be in his fifties and was a tall, lanky fellow with long silver hair that curled out from underneath his hat. He was a mean looking cuss, and his face looked like he hadn't smiled in at least forty years.

"You have a lovely daughter, sir," Michael said, instantly regretting his foolish statement.

"Yes, Jessica is a sweet, blessed child," Berneche began in solemn manner that quickly turned disagreeable. "And I have sworn to God that if any man was to lay a hand on her before the sacrament of marriage." He stared straight at Michael. "I'll kill the rascal with my bare hands."

Michael chuckled at the threat. "But sir, isn't one of the Ten Commandments, 'thou shall not kill'?"

"That is correct, son," Berneche shot back, "but the good book also says an 'eye for an eye'. So God would expect me to take retribution on anyone who sins upon her."

"Amen," Godfrey interjected, obviously trying to defuse the situation.

Antagonizing Jessica's father was definitely not in his best interest, so Michael drifted back to ride with Tribert the rest of the way to Nuremberg.

Much to his chagrin, in his excitement to talk to Jessica, he had left one of the wine sacks with Tribert. The brainless peasant was now drunk as high heaven, and Michael had to spend the entire way to Nuremberg making sure Tribert didn't fall off his horse. He had enough to worry about, and didn't need to get in a row with Godfrey over Tribert's drinking, especially with the delightful possibility of meeting Jessica later that night.

The group arrived at Nuremberg late in the afternoon and the travelers bid their good-byes and parted ways to attend to their quarters for the night. The sun began to set and as nightfall overtook the sky, Michael's anticipation over his late night meeting with Jessica grew to a fevered pitch.

As was his custom, Godfrey went to bed shortly after dinner, while Michael decided to take a walk before his rendezvous with Jessica. At the appointed time, he made his way over to the church's rectory.

He hid behind a large bush, just in case Jessica's father decided to make an appearance. He was a man Michael definitely didn't want to tangle with—you could never be too careful with religious zealots. Half an hour passed, and then an hour. His once soaring spirits began crashing as it appeared the lovely Jessica was not going to show.

With a heavy heart, Michael started to leave when he heard the rectory's back door crack ever so slightly. In the moonlight, he saw the lithe form of Jessica as she snuck out.

"Thank you, God," Michael whispered as he stared up at the night sky.

Jessica spotted him and tiptoed over. "Sorry. I couldn't get away," she whispered.

He began to say something but she put a finger to his lips and led him behind the church. The moon was full, and for this time of the year, the temperatures were mild. Michael couldn't believe his good fortune.

Finally, when they were out of sight of the rectory, she relaxed and said bashfully, "I'm glad you waited for me."

"I'm glad you came." He held her hand and looked into her eyes as they stopped in front of a group of trees. "You know, Jessica, I may not make it back in my fight for God."

Jessica squeezed his hand tightly. "Oh, don't say that, Michael. You are fighting for Jesus. He will protect you."

"I know God is on our side, but still, men die fighting His battles."

He slipped his arm around her, and Jessica moved closer towards him. They walked out into a large meadow and Michael heard the gentle trickling of a stream off to his right. The sound almost reminded him of his dreams.

It was now or never. He turned to face her. "Jessica, both of our journeys are dangerous ones. No one knows what tomorrow will bring." He paused and looked up at the large yellow moon in dramatic fashion. "It would be a shame if we didn't love one another while we had the chance."

He pulled her tightly towards him and kissed her deeply. After a brief hesitation, she responded enthusiastically to his advance. Before he knew it, they were on the ground feverishly groping, kissing and tearing at each other's clothes.

In no time they had stripped off all their garments and at the edge of a meadow under full view of God, Michael and Jessica made love the way the good Lord intended. After their magnificent union, they lay on their backs, blissfully gazing up at the heavens.

"The stars are so beautiful tonight," she said.

Michael ran a hand through her thick hair. "Yes, they are."

"Do you ever wonder what happens to your soul when you die?" she asked.

He turned towards her. "I try not to give it much thought. I have enough problems here on earth."

She laughed softly. "I believe everyone has different paths they can take in life. People should pay attention to their actions and especially coincidences. It matters more than most people think."

"What do you mean, 'coincidences'?"

"Things always happen for a reason, Michael."

"And if you choose the right path, where will that lead you?"

"There." She pointed up at the stars. "Eventually, after many lives here on earth, it leads you there."

Michael stared up at the stars and thought it was a queer notion for a young girl to have. "You believe that people come back again after they die?"

"Of course," she answered without hesitation. "What do you think happens?"

Michael laughed nervously. "I don't know. I'm just trying to make it till tomorrow."

Jessica rolled over towards Michael and kissed him lightly on the lips. She looked into his eyes. "You have the blackest eyes I have ever seen."

He gently stroked her cheek and thought about what she had said. In certain moments in his life he had felt as if he had lived before. Maybe it was the dreams.

"Tell me what those dark eyes see?" she asked.

"I see a beautiful woman."

She smiled. "You know what black eyes like yours mean?"

"No."

"You are an old soul."

"Is that good or bad?"

"Only you would know," she answered as she rolled over on her back. "It's getting late, Michael, I have to go."

Reluctantly, Michael stood, then pulled Jessica up. She was so beautiful standing there naked. He hugged her tightly, one last time, savoring the feel of her body. They dressed and the two lovers walked back to the rectory holding hands in the moonlight.

They stopped just outside the rectory's door. Michael kissed her on the cheek. "Good-bye, my darling," he said, disappointed in the realization that he would probably never see her again.

She hugged him tightly. "Good-bye, Michael. Maybe I'll see you in the stars some day."

He smiled. "If I ever get there."

She squeezed his hand, then opened the door and disappeared inside. Michael slowly walked back to his quarters, reliving each second of the magical night, and the more he thought about it, the more it seemed that Jessica had a lot of experience to have been a virgin. She had gracefully performed acts that he was almost certain most virgins wouldn't know about.

He stopped in his tracks as a new thought occurred to him. Maybe, she wasn't actually a—

Chapter 6

The journey continues…

Almost two months had passed since the Crusaders departed their father's estate, and now they were leaving Germany for the Kingdom of Hungary. Michael rode in agony, but not from the pains that had afflicted him in the beginning of the journey. It had been a fortnight since his nighttime rendezvous with Jessica, and he had developed a bad rash in his groin. He didn't think much of it at first but after three more days, the itching had become unbearable, and riding Percy all day long was becoming next to impossible.

The warmer weather should have been a blessing but it only added to his misery, and as much as he tried to hide it, his discomfort was obvious.

"What the hell is wrong with you?" Godfrey finally asked after listening to his moaning for the better part of an hour.

"My balls and hammer itch so damn bad . . . it feels like they are on fire."

Godfrey looked at him with disgust. "Sweet Jesus! You're a mess. Do you have a rash?" he asked impatiently.

"Yes, a bad one at that. It must be from the riding and the warmer temperatures."

Godfrey pulled the reigns of his horse and jumped off. "Get down," he commanded.

"What for?"

"Just get off the damn horse."

Michael gingerly dismounted Percy.

"Pull down your breeches," Godfrey ordered, as Alberto and Tribert walked over to see what the delay was about.

Michael looked over at the peasants. "What in God's name for?" he protested.

Godfrey glared at him leaving Michael no choice but to follow his brother's directive. He reluctantly pulled his clothing down to his ankles and stood there in humiliation as Godfrey and the two peasants inspected his privates.

After a few moments he heard Alberto snicker, and Godfrey responded with an air of indignation, "Just what I thought."

"What? What is it?"

"Whatever bordello you visited back in Nuremberg, the whore you slept with gave you a nasty case of crotch lice and who knows what else."

"Dear Lord," Michael exclaimed in embarrassment and shock. He was stunned. His beautiful, sweet Jessica, not only wasn't she an un-blossomed flower, but she had left him a painful, itchy reminder of their brief but unforgettable tryst.

He angrily grabbed his breeches and pulled them up. The pain and humiliation he now felt from the constant itching completely eliminated the joy of the once magical night.

He now wished he had heeded her father's warning not to partake of the forbidden fruit—fruit that already had too many bites taken out of it.

The Crusaders set off again and Michael suffered in silence. He knew his righteous brother loved the fact that he was being punished for his ill-discretion.

Mercifully, after two more painful weeks, they arrived in Vienna and Michael found a doctor who prescribed an ointment that helped relieve the itching. The messy lotion stunk to high heaven, but it was a godsend to finally be able to sleep through the night without scratching. The relief of the ointment actually brought Michael more pleasure than his one night love affair with the little Jezebel.

The third month of the journey passed and much to his disappointment, Michael had yet to acquire even one piece of wealth; but the thought of Constantinople and the riches it held kept his dreams of treasure alive.

The Crusaders trudged on, and without fanfare they crossed a large stone bridge taking them over the Danube River into Belgrade. The Bulgarian city was a dirty, overcrowded place, but after months on the road, Michael was thrilled to be back in a city again. And, much to his delight, there were plenty of places for him to get into trouble.

The plan was to rest for a week and restock their supplies before making the final push to Constantinople. After securing their quarters, Michael took a walk through the streets.

He thought about paying a visit to one of the many houses of female companionship, but with the curse of Jessica still fresh in his mind, he decided to pass on the idea.

Instead, he settled on a tavern, figuring that the worst thing he would suffer from the next morning would be a hangover. And since he didn't have to travel the next day, a few dozens drinks were certainly in order.

As he walked through Belgrade's streets, it dawned on him that the further he got from France, the better he felt. The unexplainable bouts of impending doom and mental anguish that had afflicted most of his adult life seemed to have greatly diminished. He had had some minor attacks along the way, but much to his surprise and immense relief, his problem had remained hidden.

He spotted a drinking establishment and Michael walked into the tavern hoping to enjoy a nice evening. The tavern was a big, dark paneled room with a few old tables, and a large bar that stretched along the far wall where a couple of patrons sat drinking and talking.

Michael ordered ale from a toothless bartender, and took a seat on one of the stools. He cautiously took a sip of the drink and was pleasantly surprised by the taste. The ale was heavier and more bitter than he was used to, but nevertheless, it was delicious. He ordered a second, and took a closer look at his surroundings.

All the tables were empty except for a group of men playing a game with a pair of dice. Judging from the shouts after each roll, Michael knew that money was involved. After downing a few more drinks, he decided to see if he could get in on the action. He ordered a round for the players and walked over to their table.

"Good evening, gentlemen," he said to a motley group of Bulgarians. The gamblers responded with nothing more than a few grunts. The bartender brought over their free drinks and set them on the table. The men began drinking and didn't even bother to thank him for the free drinks.

"What are you playing?"

"Bones," answered a haggard looking old man with a large black patch over his left eye. He was almost as tall as Michael, and his crinkled face told the story of many years spent in harsh environments.

"Ah, a wonderful game," Michael responded cheerfully, hoping for an invitation.

None came, and he realized he would have to ask for the right to play.

"Do you kind gentlemen mind if I join the game?" he asked cautiously. "I have a little money I could afford to part with."

The Bulgarians started conversing with each other in their native tongue. Michael picked up foreign languages quickly but he had no idea what they were saying. He stood uncomfortably as the gamblers argued amongst themselves.

The old man with the eye patch turned towards him. "My friends don't like Gauls."

Michael shrugged. He wasn't going to argue with them and he turned to leave.

"Hold on," the old man replied. Michael turned back. "Just because they don't like you, doesn't mean they don't want to take your money."

He pointed to an empty space at the table. "Please, join us. My name is Dragomir Radoslav." He motioned to his friends, "and their names are not important because, not only do they not like Gauls, they don't speak your language."

It was not exactly the welcome Michael had hoped for, but at least he was in the game.

"Honored to meet you," he responded to Dragomir. "My name is Michael Claudien."

He pulled out a small satchel containing his silver coins. Wisely, he had left his gold with Godfrey, where at least he knew it was reasonably safe.

One of the Bulgarians handed Michael the dice and he proceeded to win on his first roll. A strong feeling overcame him that tonight was going to be his lucky night. The dice rolling lasted late into the night and Michael's earlier intuition proved fateful. He was having an unbelievable run of luck that was almost too good to be true.

Unfortunately, his new Bulgarian friends were not as pleased as he was, and he could tell they were beginning to get upset about their losses. Michael knew he had to be careful. He didn't know anything about these rough-looking men except that they outnumbered him four to one.

As any gambler knows, losing money is easy, but winning in a strange city against hostile players and leaving with one's health still intact was a much more difficult proposition. He knew he would have to play the situation just right, or he might find himself beaten to a pulp in some dark alley, or worse. He had learned the hard way that when gambling with strangers, it was all right to win some of their money, but not all of it.

He called for a new round of drinks, hoping the free alcohol would cheer the Bulgarians up. However, after the drinks were served, Michael knew he would have to do more. The group was getting surlier with each toss of the dice.

Over the next hour, Michael gave back a quarter of his earnings, which helped to put the Bulgarians in a better mood. And after losing a couple of more rolls of the dice, he figured it was time to try and exit the game.

"Well, gentleman," he announced while standing up from the table. "I have enjoyed playing with you." He glanced at Dragomir, hoping to get his approval since he appeared to be their unofficial leader. "I have to take my leave, as I have a busy day tomorrow."

Dragomir translated his words to the other men, and a round of evil scowls were directed towards Michael. He knew they wanted him to stay and continue playing, especially since he was on a losing streak.

Dragomir looked at him with an expression that was hard to read, but it made him nervous none-the-less. "You have won a lot of money from us, my good friend. Why don't you stay and play a little longer?"

Grunts of agreement came from the other players which surprised Michael because he had been under the impression from Dragomir that the other men didn't speak French.

He sighed, while peering around the tavern trying to judge whether he could make a run for it. But it was too late. The Bulgarians had slyly moved behind him, cutting off his only escape route.

He stared into Dragomir's single eye. "It seems I have no choice."

"Don't say that, Michael," Dragomir replied. "We are civilized people. I tell you what, we'll even call it a night if you so desire, but first, you'll have to buy something from me to at least make things somewhat equitable."

Dragomir pulled a leather satchel from his belt and dug inside. He grimaced as he pulled out a strange looking coin. He held it directly in front of Michael's face.

"You won our money fair and square," Dragomir grunted, "but we have families to feed, debts to be paid."

He handed the coin over to Michael. "I'll make you a deal. Buy this coin from me and we'll call it a night."

Michael took the coin hesitantly, and for some reason he remembered Jessica's strange statements about the stars, coincidences and rebirth.

He studied the coin more closely. "What's this?" he asked, wondering what in the hell he had gotten himself into.

Dragomir smiled shrewdly. "It's a coin from Rome's glory days."

Michael knew he was about to get taken but there was nothing he could do about it.

"It's actually a very famous and valuable coin," Dragomir continued. "It was minted by Brutus. The man who assassinated the mighty Caesar."

Dragomir paused and leaned closer. "I have been told that Brutus was actually Caesar's son."

Michael looked at the double daggers on the coin. Suddenly, he felt strange, almost out of place. He shook off the odd sensation because he had an intuition that if he didn't agree to Dragomir's offer, he would end up like Caesar.

He had to play the game. "How much do you want for it?" Michael asked, knowing he was about to give up his hard earned winnings in exchange for a single old coin.

Dragomir thought for a second. "I could probably get a lot more than I am going to ask, but ever since I came into possession of that cursed thing it has done nothing but bring me bad luck. I'll let you have it for, say, ten Bezants."

Michael sighed. That was almost all of his winnings. Dragomir stared intently at Michael as he mulled over the proposal.

"That's strange," Dragomir suddenly blurted out.

"What?"

Dragomir smirked and pointed to the portrait on the coin. "You have quite a resemblance to Brutus."

Michael stared at Brutus, which despite the age of the coin, was detailed and clear. He studied the portrait of Caesar's assassin and an eerie feeling came over him. He felt as if he knew the man, yet, that was impossible. Brutus had died more than a thousand years ago.

"Interesting," Michael replied, stalling for time.

Old Roman coins were pretty commonplace, but he knew that some were indeed valuable. He had never seen a coin that commemorated the assassination of Caesar.

Michael sized up Dragomir's offer. If he accepted the deal, he had some fun, won a little money, and owned a famous coin which he guessed he could always sell later, but more important than all of that, he would probably get out of the tavern without further incident. All in all, it wasn't too bad of a deal, especially considering the circumstances.

Michael nodded to Dragomir. "All right. It's a deal." He pushed across the Bezants. "But tell me why you think the coin has brought you so much heartache."

Dragomir face dropped. "Do you really want to hear my story?"

"Yes."

Dragomir sipped his drink and sighed. The other men at the table abruptly got up and left.

Michael looked inquisitively at the old man. "They've heard the story," Dragomir replied. "A Turk gave me this coin."

Dragomir lowered his head while mumbling something in Bulgarian that sounded like expletives. He stared back at Michael. "The Mohammad worshiping infidel told me that the coin was found in an old, dried up riverbed west of the city of Philippi. A bit of history for you Michael, Philippi is the city where Marc Antony defeated Brutus. Brutus retreated to the river outside of the city after his defeat, and that was where he fell on his sword after he knew all was lost."

Dragomir paused and drank the rest of his ale before continuing, "Originally, the coin was found by a Persian then it was passed on to an Arab rug dealer. The Arab was a greedy, unscrupulous man who had made many enemies in his travels. On the way back to Syria, his caravan was ambushed by Turkish thieves.

"Normally, the Turks would have just taken all of his goods and left the caravan alone, but not this time. Unfortunately for the Arab, the leader of the Turks had been double-crossed by the Arab in a previous business transaction, and the Turk was known for his hot temper and lust for revenge."

Michael stared at the coin uneasily.

"You know what they did to the Arab?"

Michael shifted uncomfortably in his chair and then shook his head.

"They tied him to a pole and made him watch as they raped, then slit the throats of his wives and daughters. His women were lucky compared to the torture they saved for him. After being forced to watch the horrible murders of his family, the Turks cut the rug trader down and rolled him up inside one of his carpets. Then they tied it off with ropes so he couldn't escape. And there, they left him to rot in the desert."

"That's nice," Michael said.

Dragomir laughed. "I didn't tell you the best part. The Turks are very peculiar about revenge and when they desire it, a simple, quick death is not to their liking. They rolled the Arab carpet dealer up with swarms of maggots, worms, fire ants and lizards."

Michael grimaced as Dragomir smiled broadly. "If he was lucky, he would have suffocated after a day or so."

The Bulgarian burst out in a high pitch laugh. "On the other hand, if he was not so lucky, he might have lived for a while. And that meant he was slowly eaten alive by the vermin."

Michael couldn't imagine a worse death. "How did you hear of this story?"

Dragomir pointed at the coin in Michael's hand. "That coin you bought from me was stolen from the Arab by one of the Turkish robbers."

Dragomir once again swore in Bulgarian. "I was at a market in Erdine when I ran across the Turk in a business transaction. I should have known the sneaky bastard was up to something. See Michael, the Turks believe that if they have a cursed object in their possession, they simply cannot throw it away; rather they have to pass it on to someone else. After we had haggled over a price for my goods, the Turk gave me the coin supposedly for bargaining with him in good faith."

Dragomir lowered his head. "It was a trick. Regretfully, I accepted his gift. I can still remember the smile on his face as he gave me the coin. That son of a whore knew it was cursed."

Michael watched as the Bulgarian's eyes betrayed a feeling of immense pain and sorrow. Dragomir wearily added, "It has brought me nothing but bad luck ever since."

He pointed to the patch covering his left eye. "After I left Erdine, I went on to Constantinople to trade the rest of my tin for spices and silk. As in years past, I dealt directly with the Emperor's Trade Minister, a more devious and vile man there is not." Dragomir looked away before adding softly, "He was married to a sweet, beautiful woman named Eudoxia."

Dragomir's voice faded and his features relaxed a bit. Michael wasn't sure what to make of the unexpected display of emotion.

Dragomir continued in a saddened tone, "We had grown quite close over the years."

Michael now understood the nature of his emotions—Dragomir had feelings for the minister's wife.

Dragomir tugged at his eye patch. "During that trip, Eudoxia and I spent more and more time together, and we knew we couldn't be separated any longer.

We made plans for her to escape her husband and return with me to Belgrade.

"Alas," he sighed deeply. "Her husband discovered our plans. Before we could flee, I was taken prisoner by the Emperor's Guard. They threw me in a dungeon underneath the royal palace. You know what the guards called the dungeon?"

Michael shook his head.

"Hell. They called it Hell. For two months I sat in a hideous little cell and witnessed things you should pray you never see in your lifetime."

Dragomir suddenly lifted the large patch revealing the monstrosity that used to be his eye. Michael tried his best not to gag at the sight.

"The Emperor's torturer stuck a flaming hot poker into my eye while Eudoxia was forced to watch. I was thrown back into my cell where I teetered between life and death for weeks. By some miracle, I survived, and for some reason, the Emperor must have taken pity on me. After three months in Hell, I was released. I returned to Bulgaria broke, half blind and without Eudoxia."

He pulled the patch back down over his eye and stood up from the table. "Michael, even though you are a dirty Gaul, I am going to give you some advice. Sell . . . or get rid of that coin as soon as possible. It is cursed. It always has been."

Michael stared at the double daggers on the coin and strange thoughts began racing through his head. When he looked up, the Bulgarian was gone.

Chapter 7

Michael turned back and watched as Belgrade disappeared from view. Thank God, this was it. The last leg of the journey—Constantinople was now within reach. He had grown weary of the endless miles and couldn't wait to finally reach the "Queen of all Cities," and see for himself if the stories of Constantinople's magnificence were true.

The plan was to stay in the city until Peter's forces arrived, probably in another two months then, they would depart for Jerusalem.

The weary band of Crusaders followed the downward slope of the Bulgarian steppe, and after a few days of easy riding they unceremoniously entered the relative safety of the Byzantine territories. As they progressed over the open lands, the sun grew larger and hotter with each day. Michael's satchels now carried water instead of wine, although he still had a few bottles stashed away in case of emergencies.

Michael looked over at his brother with a surprisingly warm feeling. "We're getting close," he said.

"I know." His brother looked over with a smile.

Michael knew that they both were surprised at how well they had gotten along, especially during the latter part of the trip. Despite their vast differences, they were still brothers and Michael supposed nothing would ever change that.

"I have enjoyed riding with you," Michael said with a hint of amusement. "You haven't been as big a pain in the ass as I thought you would have been."

Godfrey took the barb with good humor and a smile spread over his face. "To be honest with you, Michael, I didn't think you would make it this far. I thought for sure you would have drunk yourself into a stupor and quit long ago."

"What me?" Michael gave his brother a sly grin.

Godfrey returned the smile. "What's that necklace you're wearing?" He pointed at Michael's chest.

Michael touched the Brutus coin at the end of the necklace. Before they left Belgrade, he had a jeweler attach a bracket around the coin, and he now wore it as a necklace.

"It's a good luck charm," Michael answered. "I won it playing bones. The coin was minted by Brutus after the assassination of Julius Caesar."

Godfrey looked dubious. "Brutus?" he said skeptically. "Brother, you would be advised to forget such charms and rely more on faith and God. You should wear the cross of Jesus Christ, not some pagan coin."

Michael laughed. "Maybe you're right," he replied, realizing that some things would never change between them.

The gentle lands of the Byzantines passed quickly and the anticipation of reaching the most famous city on earth grew to a fever pitch.

Before Michael left France he had learned from the local priest quite a bit about the Byzantine Empire and its historic capital city. Constantinople could trace its roots back to 657 BC when the city, Byzantium, was founded by a group of nomads from Argus. For the next thousand years, the city experienced many cycles of wealth and power as well as poverty and insignificance.

But the city's cycle of boom and bust all changed in 330 AD when the Roman Emperor, Constantine the Great, decided to rebuild the legendary city and make it the new capital of the Roman Empire. Not only did Constantine transfer the center of the Roman Empire to the East, but he also cleared the way for Christianity to become the major religion for the entire Western World. As a result, the final grandeur of Constantinople was born.

Constantine intrigued Michael. The man was complex and full of contradictions. He was a self-proclaimed emissary of God and the teachings of Jesus Christ; yet he practiced many pagan rites and even refused to be baptized until he was on his deathbed.

On the battlefield, Constantine routinely spared the lives of his enemies, only to turn around and murder members of his own family including his oldest son and a wife.

As Michael thought about the contradictions in the great Roman leader, his mood turned serious. Despite his many doubts about the journey he had never questioned Godfrey about it.

"Why are we doing this?" Michael blurted out, knowing that his brother probably wouldn't understand the question.

Godfrey looked over at him. "You know why."

"No, I really don't."

"To fight for God," Godfrey answered quickly.

"Well, who are the Moslems fighting for then?"

Godfrey's face looked perplexed. "Who cares who those dirty savages are fighting for, they're probably fighting for the Devil," he snorted.

"But the Moslems believe in one God as well. Do you think God would look favorably upon his children murdering each other, all in his name?"

Godfrey glared at Michael then grinned. "Older brother, you never cease to confound me." He struck his horse and rode up to join the peasants, obviously not wishing to discuss the subject any further.

As the miles passed, Michael knew they were getting closer to Constantinople because the road had widened significantly and it had become clogged with merchants, peasants, pilgrims and soldiers.

It was a clear, sunny day and Michael was riding in the lead when he passed through a thick outcrop of trees and over a small hill. Suddenly, like a magnificent oasis in the middle of a desert, the "Queen of Cities" appeared.

"Constantinople!" Michael shouted back to the others.

Godfrey rode up to him with a big smile and the brothers kicked their horses, galloping as fast as their large horses would go to get a better look at the amazing sight. When the horses tired, they pulled over to the side of the road and gazed out at the beauty and enormity of the city.

Godfrey made a sign of the cross and began reciting the Lord's Prayer. Even Michael bowed his head out of respect for such an awe-inspiring site. Like Rome, the city was situated among seven hills; but unlike Rome, it was almost completely surrounded by the sea providing for a natural defense.

Directly in front of them lay the western side of Constantinople. It was the only part of the city not situated on the sea, but it was protected by a massive stonewall built by the Emperor Theodosius. The wall stood at least fifty feet high and stretched in all directions as far as the eye could see.

"I don't think any army could breech that barrier," Godfrey said.

"None have so far." Michael whistled. "Can you believe a million people live inside that fortress?"

Godfrey shook his head. "A million people—I bet there are not even a million people in all of France."

Alberto and Tribert joined up with them and the Crusaders nudged their horses forward, slowly riding down the gentle landscape leading to the city. They passed through clusters of small villages whose inhabitants tended crops and made their living selling goods to the citizens of Constantinople.

And as they got closer, the enormous protective wall seemed to grow larger. Billowing guard towers rose out of the top of it and they soared high into the clear blue sky. In front of the wall was a wide ditch filled to the top with oily water. Large pieces of debris floated on the water making it impossible for any army to cross.

The Crusaders crossed over a heavily guarded wooden bridge and finally, after months of travel, they passed through the gates into Constantinople. Michael could hardly believe it. The first leg of their journey was over. The tired brothers secured their lodgings. Now, finally, they would have some time to rest, explore and enjoy one of the greatest cities in the world.

Chapter 8

Michael spent the entire first week in Constantinople walking the streets and exploring. The grandeur of the city surprised him more and more with each day. It was clear the designers of Constantinople knew what they were doing because, despite the city's vast size, it was easy to get around, and the layout served to highlight the natural beauty of the area.

After passing through the front gates of Theodosius' Wall, a large brick-paved street ran all the way down to the sea on the eastern side of the city. A second, much smaller wall, built by Constantine the Great, was inside the main entrance. And, after passing through it, the bulk of the city spread out across the horizon.

Once in the main section of the city, a multitude of avenues flowed off from the central thoroughfare. They were lined with buildings of all shapes and sizes; and scattered among the commercial buildings were tall residential brick houses with high, open balconies.

Despite the large population, the city was clean, contained a vast number of open spaces for parks and lavish gardens and was relatively free of crime.

In keeping with old Western Roman traditions, public baths were everywhere, but even more numerous than the baths were the churches. Constantinople was a religious city and it was obvious the Byzantines took their Christian beliefs seriously.

Michael was on one of his daily expeditions when he walked past a building called a hospital. He had been told it was a place where people with illnesses or diseases could go for treatment. There were also orphanages, shelters and Godfrey told him that no citizen ever went hungry while inside the city.

Michael was on his way to the eastern edge of the peninsula to view, what he had been told, was one of man's finest architectural creations—the church of Hagia Sophia. The church was almost six hundred years old, and even though he was not religious, Michael decided to visit the famous church. He came to the rise of a large hill and there it stood—the Hagia Sophia. Behind it, the blue waters of the Sea of Marmara stretched as far as he could see.

He stood and stared. The square church was built in typical Greco-Roman style with a massive golden dome sitting atop the church and four tall spires soaring high into the sky. The church sat on a huge estate filled with dormitories, offices, galleries, residences and shrines.

The bright spring sun was high in the sky and the sunlight reflected brilliantly off the church's golden dome. The whole area seemed to have a magical quality to it, like Constantinople itself.

Michael entered a large basilica adorned with murals of saints, apostles and other divine figures. It led out to the main floor of the church, and it was the single largest room he had ever been in. The area for mass alone stretched more than three hundred feet. He stared upwards. The cathedral's dome soared to a mind staggering height of two hundred feet, and the entire ceiling appeared to be coated in pure gold. Four stone columns supported the enormous weight of the dome with silver arches at both ends of the ceiling.

After touring the church, Michael spent the rest of afternoon exploring the courtyards and gardens. There was so much to see and before he knew it, the afternoon had turned to early evening. He had one more place he wanted to visit before the day was done.

Michael left the church and walked to the eastern side of the city. He walked over to the seawall and gazed out at the sparkling blue water that stretched in all directions.

The Sea of Marmara rose out of the south with the mighty Bosporus leading across the harbor of the Golden Horn over to the mysterious and forbidding continent of Asia.

He glanced over the edge of the wall and became dizzy. It was a long, long fall down to the rocky shore below. He understood how the city had prevailed for so long against the mightiest of invaders. The city was impregnable.

As he stared out at the deep blue waters, Michael thought about the circumstances that had led him here. He had been sent here to kill, and for why? He still didn't understand why God had created such beauty in this world, equaled only by the destruction that man seemed to cause. He contemplated the question for a while before realizing the answer lay beyond his understanding. He hopped down from the seawall and headed back to his quarters.

Chapter 9

On the way back home Michael stopped at the gardens of the Acropolis. He sat on one of the many marble benches lining the pathways and watched as people came and went on their daily business.

He noticed that as a whole, the Byzantines were a handsome, regal people. The men were tall, dark skinned and refined, while the women possessed beautiful olive skin, delicate features and stunning eyes. Michael must have fallen in love at least a hundred different times, but he hadn't dared approach any of the women, especially after the horror story Dragomir had told back in Belgrade.

"That crazy Bulgarian," he mumbled, while looking at the Brutus coin. "Some curse."

In fact, ever since he had come into possession of the coin, things had been going pretty well. He laughed. Maybe it took a curse to counteract his personal demons.

As he sat in the gardens, Michael spotted people of all nationalities— Syrians, Bulgars, Kurds, Arabs, Jews, fair-haired Scandinavians, Germans and Slavs, all of whom had free run of the city.

The only requirement necessary to get by in Constantinople was to practice Christianity and speak Greek. He could fake the first well enough, and one of the few advantages he had over his brother was his ability to speak other languages. Greek had always come easy to him.

But, getting by in Constantinople, and being accepted, were two different things, as Michael quickly discovered. Foreigners, especially Europeans, were tolerated, but not well liked. The Byzantines were not deliberately rude. They were just cold, and for the most part, ignored the Europeans all together.

A tall man in a splendid red robe appeared out of nowhere and approached Michael with a big smile on his face. The sleeves and neck of his silk robe were adorned with shiny emeralds and dazzling red stones that Michael believed must have been rubies. The man stopped right in front of Michael and peered down at him. He had long, dark hair and was very handsome in a soft, almost feminine way. He carried an air of high standing and nobility.

"A Gaul?" he asked fluently in French.

"Yes," Michael answered, somewhat flustered. "How did you know?"

The man smiled broadly and sat down next to him. His pale green-blue eyes stared intently at Michael. The color of the man's eyes was very unusual because most Byzantines possessed dark brown or black eyes.

"We have many visitors to our fine city," he said, "and, over the years I have come to be able to recognize where a person hails from simply by studying their posture."

"Are you telling me, good sir, that you can tell a person's country just by how they carry themselves?"

"Indeed, it is true. Take your countrymen for example. I knew you were a Gaul because your head is held high, but your shoulders slump as if they are carrying a sack of rocks upon them."

"And that is a trait of Gauls?" Michael asked.

"It is when they visit Constantinople."

Michael began to wonder if the mysterious Byzantine was having fun at his expense. The man once again smiled broadly, displaying a perfect set of white teeth.

"Let me properly introduce myself. I am Prince Nicephorus Melissenus, younger brother of Emperor Alexius—King of the Byzantine people."

The pronouncement shocked Michael and he couldn't form any words with which to reply. For a week he had tried in vain to engage any Byzantine in conversation, and now, when someone finally speaks to him, it was the Emperor's brother.

After a moment he finally stammered, "I am Michael Claudien of Vassily, France. It is my honor to meet you, Prince Nicephorus."

The Prince bowed then said, "Now back to my trick. Tell me if this is untrue. You are a proud man and believe that your country is one of a noble and honorable people. Is that correct?"

Michael shook his head in agreement.

The Prince spread out his arms. "That is why you hold your head high in Constantinople, to compensate for your feelings of subordination and astonishment that there is a society far greater than yours." He pointed at Michael. "And that is also why your shoulders slump."

Suddenly, Michael felt as if his shoulders really were slumping. He was unsure how to respond to Nicephorus. What he had first thought was a compliment, now appeared to be a back handed slap in the face.

"You still don't believe me about my talent?" Prince Nicephorus asked in good humor.

"My good Prince," Michael answered, deciding not to be offended, "of course I believe you."

Nicephorus laughed warmly. "Watch, I will demonstrate."

He stared at the mass of people passing through the gardens. "There." He pointed to a hulking man who had just entered the gardens. "He is a German. See how he walks very upright with his chest sticking out and a scowl on his face."

Michael stared at the man.

"Watch his strides." Nicephorus pointed, "See how big they are?"

"Yes, but how does that tell you he is German?" Michael asked.

"The Germans are unrefined warriors. They are different from your countrymen because they believe in strength, not nobility. The Germans know and accept that they are culturally inferior to the Byzantine people, and unlike the French, they don't care. So they take great pains to display their strength in the way they carry themselves; their strength, of course, being pride and fierceness."

The man walked to within earshot of them and Nicephorus called out in German, "Good morning my fair friend. Welcome to Constantinople."

The man grunted and replied huskily, "Thank you, Prince. You have a very strong city."

Nicephorus turned back to Michael grinning. He pointed to the Brutus coin hanging from his neck.

"That's an interesting coin. I know a thing or two about coins. It looks like an early Roman coin, back when the capital used to be in Rome."

"You are right." Michael took the necklace off and handed it to Nicephorus. "It's called the Double Dagger Denarius. It was minted by Brutus, commemorating the death of Caesar."

Nicephorus studied the coin intently and nodded. "Yes, I thought I recognized the portrait. Do you wear the coin because of your resemblance?"

"Pardon me?"

"The assassin, Brutus, he looks like you. Are you also an assassin Michael? Should I be worried?"

Michael smirked. "No, I am just a Crusader for God. Nothing more."

"Well then, maybe you were a Roman in a previous life." The Prince handed the coin back. "Where did you get it?"

"I won it playing bones."

"Bones. Are you really sure you won it? You're aware that Brutus killed his own father. An unforgivable sin."

"Yes," Michael answered, surprised the Prince knew the history. "At least that is what the Bulgarian who gave me the coin said."

"Well, Michael, do you think it is an eternal sin for one family member to kill another, even if his actions are justifiable?"

Michael was taken back by the question. Was the Prince asking if he thought Brutus's actions were acceptable? He answered carefully, "I guess it depends on the circumstances."

"I like your coin, Michael. Perhaps one day I will come across one just like it . . . to add to my collection."

Nicephorous stood from the bench and looked down at Michael. "Join me for dinner tonight at the Royal Palace. It has been a while since I dined with a noble Gaul. You can update me on the happenings of your fine country."

Michael was floored but managed to reply, "It would be my honor, Prince Nicephorus."

Nicephorus bowed. "Excellent. Go to the main entrance of the estate and the guards will escort you in." With those instructions, the Prince turned and left.

Michael looked at the portrait of Brutus on the coin, and the more he stared at it, the more he did notice a resemblance between himself and Brutus. It was just a coincidence, he thought, as he slipped the necklace back on and left the gardens. He couldn't wait to tell Godfrey that he had been invited to the Royal Palace by the Emperor's brother.

Chapter 10

Michael approached the entrance of the Palace grounds with a rush of nervous excitement. A fierce-looking group of Imperial Guards stood in front of the iron gate adding to his already jangled nerves. The soldiers wore a complete body suit of polished silver armor with the royal family's purple and red crest prominently displayed on the breastplate. Michael timidly approached the soldiers. One of the guards stepped forward and thrust a very sharp lance directly at his chest. Michael stopped dead in his tracks.

"Michael Claudien?" the guard barked in a heavily clipped accent.

"Yes."

The soldier held up his hand then motioned with his lance. The gate opened and Michael followed him onto the Palace grounds.

Michael followed the guard through a maze of residences, offices, churches, and palaces. They passed by a large fenced-off section containing a huge number of wild animals. He spotted elephants, zebras, lions, monkeys and many exotic animals he didn't recognize.

"Are all those animals for food?" he asked, somewhat bewildered by the sight.

"It's called a zoo," the guard answered, with his back still towards Michael. "The animals are appreciated, not eaten."

Michael frowned. He had never heard of such a thing. He followed the soldier past an enormous marble bath and through an exotic flower garden. A large fiery red moon rose over the horizon and Michael felt butterflies dancing around in his stomach.

Once through the gardens, the soldier walked to the entrance of a large building next to the main Palace and motioned for Michael to enter.

Michael walked though the doorway and into a small foyer where he was immediately greeted by a servant cloaked in finer garments than his own. The servant bowed and in fluent French replied, "Prince Nicephorus is expecting you."

Michael followed the servant through a large hall lined with marble statues of the royal family. It spilled out into a cavernous room with a high vaulted ceiling decorated with beautiful frescos. Michael saw the Prince lying on a pile of large cushions with a dozen scantily dressed women standing at attention around him.

The Prince stood up with open arms. "Welcome, Michael Claudien."

Michael walked over and bowed deeply. "Prince Nicephorus. I want to thank you for your invitation to join you tonight. I brought you a token of my appreciation." He handed the Prince an ivory cross. "The cross was designed by a master craftsman in my hometown. I hope you enjoy my small gift."

Nicephorus smiled warmly. "Thank you. I will put it in the Royal Cathedral so all can see that the French are true believers of Jesus Christ."

Nicephorus pointed towards Michael's chest. "Still wearing your Brutus coin?"

Michael laughed. "It's good luck."

"Come, sit down." Nicephorus gestured toward a set of plush pillows.

Michael sat and immediately one of the comely servants rushed over and served him a glass of a wine.

"To your good health and fortune," Nicephorus toasted.

Michael raised his glass and took a deep drink. It was the sweetest, most full-bodied wine he had ever tasted. He felt a warm glow as the liquid slid down his throat and into his stomach.

"This wine is delicious."

"It comes from the countryside outside of Florence. My family owns a large vineyard. I don't know much about the process of winemaking but I am told the agreeable taste has something to do with the soil and the climate in that region."

Michael took another sip. "I believe this is the finest wine I have ever tasted." He knew it was going to be hard to control himself with wine tasting this delightful.

Without instruction, another woman brought a large platter of olives, roasted stuffed peppers, smoked fish, figs and plums. As the sweet haze of the alcohol overtook Michael's body, it became obvious that his earlier pledge of sobriety wasn't going to work, especially since every time his glass became half empty, it was quickly filled to the top by one of the attentive servants.

Michael looked around the room. "Prince, is it just the two of us for this entire feast?" he asked, wondering if other members of the royal family would be joining them.

"Alas, it is just the two of us. The Emperor is too busy running his empire to dine with his only brother."

Michael noticed a tone of animosity in the Prince's voice and he made a mental note not to bring the subject of the Emperor up again. As more and more wine flowed, the splendid evening passed too quickly.

After the main course was served, a group of dancers and musicians entertained late into the night. The strange, enchanting music coupled with the erotic rhythms of the lithe dancers gave Michael a feeling of pure contentment.

Finally, the last of the musicians bid farewell and the Prince stood. Michael was still lounging on his pillows with a feeling of pure satisfaction.

"Thank you for a most enjoyable evening, Michael," he said. "As it is so late, it would be my honor for you to spend the night on the grounds. I have taken the liberty of preparing quarters for you." A devilish grin came across the Prince's face. "The women will escort you."

Michael looked over his shoulder and saw three very beautiful young women standing behind him. They grabbed his arms and pulled him up to his feet; then they wrapped their arms around him, began giggling and led him out of the room through a series of darkly lit halls. They entered a candle-lit room where a steaming hot bath had been drawn. Michael stood at rigid attention as the exotic women slowly began to unclothe him.

He was far too intoxicated and far too happy to be embarrassed at his nakedness. He just hoped everything would work properly later on because he had a titillating intuition that the bath was not going to be the end of his night.

Michael sat atop a horse watching a battle rage in front of him. Death and destruction surrounded him. A feeling of doom filled him with anguish.

He knew the battle was lost and turned to flee—

Michael jerked awake in a dark, strange room. A few moments of panic passed before he realized he was on the palace grounds. He lay back down thinking about the dream. He had been leading an army into battle. A war that was lost. He had awakened as he turned to flee, but Michael had an intuition that if the dream had continued, his escape would not have lasted long.

He took a couple of deep breaths, figuring he must be growing anxious about the trip to Jerusalem. As the cobwebs cleared out of his head, the memory of the three women and their special talents brought a smile to his face, quickly replacing the fear of his dream. Never in his wildest fantasy could he have imagined a night like last night. The memory was such a pleasurable thought that he barely noticed the throbbing of his temples. He started to drift back to sleep when he heard a soft knock.

"Yes," Michael called out. A young boy appeared with a cup of tea and some biscuits on a gold serving plate.

In perfect French, he said, "I have been sent to escort you off the estate. Prince Nicephorus apologizes for not seeing you this morning but he has some affairs to attend to. Please enjoy your tea, then we will leave."

Michael drank his tea and dressed. He summoned the servant who led him off the palace grounds. As he slowly walked back to his humble quarters in the city, he couldn't wait to tell Godfrey about the night.

Chapter 11

The weeks drifted by and Michael kept his mind off leaving Constantinople by exploring every inch of the magical city. His only disappointment was that he had not heard a word from Prince Nicephorus since their night together.

He had greatly enjoyed the Prince's company, not to mention the luxurious trappings that went along with it, and he wondered if he had done something to insult the Prince. Maybe he should have given him the Brutus coin? After all, the Prince had shown interest in the coin and was a collector.

But just when he thought he would never hear from the Prince again, a courier arrived with a letter requesting his attendance at the Royal Palace for an afternoon banquet. Michael's spirits soared.

The day of the banquet arrived and once again Michael was led through the grounds by one of the Imperial Guards. But this time, much to his growing excitement, he was directed to the main Palace. They entered the enormous building and he followed the guard down a wide marble hallway. The ceiling of the hall was adorned in solid gold with colorful mosaics of saintly figures staring piously down at him.

They passed the Emperor's Great Hall. It was obvious from the room's splendor that this was where Alexius entertained envoys from around the world. Michael peaked into the room and was immediately awestruck by the Emperor's throne—it was a sight to behold. The throne was elevated on a large tiled stage and on each side of the arm rest, life-sized solid gold lions stood at attention. Their massive necks were adorned with diamond and emerald collars.

A sharp crack made Michael's head snap back out of the room. The Guard glared at him and motioned with his lance for him to catch back up. Michael was led to a large ballroom where the festivities were already in full force.

Hundreds of lavishly dressed people filled the hall. A servant quickly appeared and handed him a glass of wine. He slowly made his way though the crowd, admiring the people and trying to keep an eye out for Nicephorus. Finally, after a second glass, he spotted the Prince in the back of the room talking to a contingent of well-dressed men. Judging by the expressions on their faces, it didn't appear to be an enjoyable conversation. Michael decided to wait before approaching Nicephorus to offer his greetings.

He continued to survey the room. Banquet tables were filled with every delicacy imaginable: large oysters, squid, giant prawns, boar meat, fish eggs, olives, tantalizing fruits and many items that he didn't even recognize. The jewels worn by the women were breathtaking. It wouldn't have surprised Michael if there was more wealth in this one room than in the entire Kingdom of France.

He turned back towards Nicephorus and watched him angrily wave his arm in a gesture of dismissal causing the group of men to quickly disperse. Michael walked over, hoping the Prince was not in too foul a mood.

"Prince Nicephorus." He bowed. "Thank you so much for your kind invitation."

Fortunately, the Prince instantly recognized him and the scowl left his face. He smiled brightly. "If it isn't my favorite Gaul. I hope you have been well?"

"Very well, thank you."

"Sorry I haven't gotten in touch sooner, but I have been very busy with some family matters."

"That's quite . . ." before Michael could finish, the dull roar from the festivities halted. Michael turned to see what had brought on the sudden silence.

In grand style, Emperor Alexius strode into the room followed by his wife and teenage daughter. The crowd began to clap and bow enthusiastically as the royal family slowly made their way through the throng of delighted guests.

"They make a stunning illusion don't they Michael," snarled the Prince.

Michael turned towards Nicephorus, not sure how to respond. Nicephorus glared at Alexius, and in the Prince's eyes Michael saw pure hatred.

"All families have their illusions, Prince," Michael answered carefully.

Nicephorus' eyes darted away from his brother and once again his face revealed the handsome, fun loving man Michael had first met.

"Maybe we have more in common than you think," Nicephorus said.

"We do?" Michael asked.

"Well, you told me of your brother and your relationship with your father."

Michael tried hard to recall the conversation. Obviously, he must have mentioned it at some point in his drunken stupor the night they had dined together. Hopefully, he hadn't bored the Prince with the whole sordid story.

Nicephorus motioned for a servant to refill their glasses. "You know why Alexius is emperor and I am not?"

Michael shook his head, although he knew the reason. A common practice in both France and the Byzantines was that the line of succession always started with the oldest son, no matter if it was to rule an empire, or inherit a peasant's hut.

Nicephorus drank the wine then continued, "It isn't because he is more intelligent, stronger or braver than I am. Alexius was born sixteen months earlier, and that is why he rules the greatest Empire in the world, while I can only watch from afar, wasting my time on trivial bureaucratic matters."

"If you were emperor," Michael cut in, "I have no doubt the Empire and its citizens would be extremely prosperous."

The Prince grunted, "Come, I will introduce you to my brother and his family." Just before they got to the royal table, the Prince turned to Michael and said, "Afterwards, we'll leave this boring event and have some real fun."

The Emperor looked up as Nicephorus and Michael approached. He didn't appear all that happy to see his brother.

"Alexius," the Prince announced. "I would like to introduce you to the nobleman, Michael Claudien, of France."

Michael bowed. "Emperor Alexius—" he struggled to find the right words. "I am honored to be a guest in your magnificent city and palace."

Alexius looked at Michael with a bored expression then said sarcastically, "A Crusader?"

Michael wasn't sure if the Emperor was making a statement or asking a question. "Ah, yes, I am leaving for the Holy Lands once Peter's forces are ready."

"Good," Michael heard the Emperor's daughter sneer. "You Crusaders cause nothing but problems."

Michael looked over at her in dismay.

Alexius held up his hand. "Excuse my daughter, Crusader. She does not understand the ways of Europeans."

Alexius gestured towards the teenage girl. "I would like to introduce you to my daughter, Anna, and my wife, Irene." Both women nodded slightly but remained silent.

"Come now, my sweet Princess," Nicephorus responded. "Don't be so hard on the Crusader. It was your father who requested their help in the first place."

"Yes, that is true," Alexius interrupted, "but I asked for warriors. Not a group of misbegotten, misbehaving peasants. My city has been invaded by these uncivilized rascals like a swarm of locusts destroying everything that lies in its path."

Michael knew there was some degree of truth to the Emperor's comments. The fifty thousand men that followed Peter to Constantinople were, indeed, mostly peasants with no training or fighting ability; and there had been plenty of ransacking along the way. Michael had heard numerous stories including one about a band of Norman Crusaders who had raped and pillaged everything in sight, all the way to Constantinople.

But, even with the unfortunate transgressions, Michael was shocked by the resentment displayed by the royal family. The Crusaders had traveled halfway around the world with a common purpose of fighting and destroying the

Moslems—sworn enemies of both Europe and the Byzantine Empire.

Michael stood uncomfortably. The tension around the table was obvious and at this point he just wanted to leave the banquet.

He bowed with formality. "It has been nice to meet you Emperor Alexius, Lady Irene, Princess Anna. I hope that when we arrive in the Holy Lands and defeat the Turks, it will make up for the some of the problems and mistrust we have caused."

The Emperor chuckled in a mocking fashion and turned away indicating that their conversation was over.

"Emperor." Nicephorus also bowed. He gave Michael a curt nod and said softly, "Follow me."

They left the palace in silence and walked though the grounds of the estate with a small group of the Prince's entourage following closely behind.

"Pardon my brother and his family," the Prince finally said. "They can be overbearing and snobbish, especially that little brat, Anna."

Michael wasn't quite sure what to say. It was obvious that Alexius resented the Crusaders and there certainly appeared to be no love lost between him and Nicephorus.

"That is quite all right. I know the Emperor is in a difficult situation and has a lot on his mind."

Nicephorus shrugged and picked up his pace. They approached the front entrance, the gate was opened and they walked out into the city.

"Where are we going?" Michael asked, happy to be off royal grounds.

"The Hippodrome," the Prince announced loudly.

Michael's mood brightened immediately. The Hippodrome was the last major sight that Michael had yet to visit and it was the one he wanted to see the most. It was a large outdoor stadium that showcased the Byzantines favorite pastime—chariot racing.

As they approached the stadium, the crowd grew thick, and there was an energy and a buzz of excitement in the air. Vendors lined the streets selling all kinds of food, wine and even little souvenir chariots.

Michael followed Nicephorus through throngs of Byzantines and into the giant circular stadium. They took their seats in the royal box, which naturally, had the best view. Michael guessed there must have been forty thousand people packed into the stadium.

"Why is everyone wearing either blue or green?" Michael inquired.

"Well, in Constantinople, when it comes to chariot racing, you either support the blues . . . ," Nicephorus took out a large blue scarf, raised it high in the air and shook it wildly which caused a loud roar of approval from part of the crowd.

He lowered the scarf and turned to Michael, "Or you support the greens.

And while sitting in this box, you support the blues."

Michael laughed. "Blues it is. How many races are there?"

"Tonight, there will be twenty-five."

"Who's the favorite?"

"You Crusaders," Nicephorus retorted in good humor. "The blues are going to crush them."

As they watched the first set of races, Michael nibbled on pickled eggs, smoked salmon and clams while washing it all down with a fruity white wine. The races had not begun well for the blues with their drivers losing the first two races.

Before the start of the third race, Nicephorus turned to Michael and said to him in a serious tone, "So, Crusader, I guess you will be leaving shortly?"

"Yes, I suppose I will." He had been trying not to think about leaving Constantinople for the dangerous lands of the Moslems and Turks. The very thought of it filled him with anxiety and dread.

The more time Michael spent in Constantinople, the more doubts he had about the Crusade. He hated to admit it, but the Emperor was right about Peter's army. It was no army at all, and Michael seriously wondered if he was being led to a slaughter.

He had brought the subject up with Godfrey a number of times but his brother had scoffed at him, arguing endlessly that it was God's will and that the Almighty would be with them once the fighting began.

"Why leave?" the Prince asked, interrupting Michael's thoughts.

Michael looked back at Nicephorus. "I don't know. I guess I have to."

"Why?" Nicephorus asked again.

The thought of not going on to Jerusalem had never really crossed Michael's mind. He knew if he managed to survive the journey, which was doubtful, he would never return to his family's estate. So why was he risking his life for his family's honor? He certainly wasn't doing it because he believed it was God's wish.

Nicephorus casually picked at a bowl of grapes and replied nonchalantly, "Peter's ragtag army is going to get slaughtered by the first group of Turks it meets, and Alexius doesn't care one bit. He has actually come to hate you Crusaders more than the Turks or Moslems."

Michael was shocked by the frankness of the Prince's words.

Nicephorus continued, "I am telling you this for your own good. If I were you, I would stay here in Constantinople. I will make sure that you have adequate quarters and employment. I could find you a position, maybe in capacity of the administration of my affairs."

Michael was taken back by the Prince's offer. Could he stay in Constantinople? The thought made him delirious with excitement.

"I am grateful for the offer, Prince. I will seriously consider your most gracious proposal," Michael replied.

"Good." They toasted their wine glasses and turned back to the chariot races.

The blues staged an impressive comeback and ended up winning a total of fourteen races which seemed to put Nicephorus in an exceptional mood.

Afterward, Michael bid the Prince good night and returned to his quarters. All he could think about was Nicephorus' offer to stay in Constantinople. His only dilemma—he would have to tell Godfrey.

Chapter 12

"But Godfrey, you don't understand," Michael pleaded. "Peter has no army! He commands no battle-tested soldiers. His fighters are nothing but malnourished peasants. It will be a bloodbath, and part of that blood will be ours! Don't be a fool, brother!"

Godfrey looked irritated but he replied in a calm manner, "It is our duty to serve God. The Lord will be with us, Michael. Have some faith for once."

"Faith!" Michael yelled. "Have you gone insane! That dirty monk is a stark raving lunatic! He doesn't have the ear of God. We'll be led straight to our deaths. I've been told by people that know. The Turks have amassed a sizable army in Nicea."

He lowered his voice. He had to convince his brother of the futility of their mission. "Godfrey, they are waiting for Peter's army like a pack of hungry vultures. And let me tell you something else, brother, Alexius is not going to help at all."

"To hell with Alexius," Godfrey rebutted. "I doubt he is a true believer anyway."

Godfrey looked at Michael with disgust. "I know you have been corrupted by your new friends, but we have to go to Jerusalem. We took an oath in front of our father, and more importantly, in front of God."

Michael walked over to his brother and placed a hand on his shoulder. "Godfrey, I'm not going."

"What!" Godfrey swung his fist and forearm up, knocking Michael's arm away.

"You heard me," Michael repeated. "I'm not going."

"You would turn your back on God and disgrace your family's name?"

"There is no honor in dying for a worthless cause."

"That's what you think this is?" Godfrey spat. "A worthless cause?"

Michael remained silent.

Godfrey pointed at him. "You're a coward. You promised me you would be with me to the very end. I need you."

His brother's words came as a shock. He needed him? He had expected Godfrey to be angry, but not this. He didn't know what to say, but it still didn't change anything. Michael had made up his mind—he was staying in Constantinople.

"Brother, if you want to die, that's your decision. You don't need me for that."

"Yes, I do," Godfrey said softly, turning his back on Michael.

"Listen," Godfrey replied with his back still turned. "We are both aware of your problems with our father. And I know we have had our struggles as well, but despite our differences, we have always been there for each other when it truly mattered. Is that not true?"

Godfrey turned around and pointed at Michael's chest where his necklace hung. "Don't betray me like Brutus betrayed Caesar. It's a mistake you can't afford to make."

Michael felt a sense of doubt beginning to grow. He had never heard his brother speak like this. Suddenly, he wasn't so sure about staying in Constantinople. He had been convinced that his decision was the right one, but now, he had doubts.

"Godfrey, I—"

Godfrey held up his hand. "Michael, don't make your decision now. Think about it. That's all I ask. Father won't live forever you know. We can work out our differences."

Michael nodded weakly and watched as Godfrey left. He sat down in a chair and sighed deeply. He was confused and desperately wanted a drink, but he knew he mustn't. He needed to think this through clearly.

He sat for a moment in frustration, then pounded his fists on the arm of his chair and yelled to the empty room, "I've got to get the hell out of here!"

He walked over to the gardens of the Acropolis to think. He sat on his favorite bench next to a large water fountain.

He was deep in thought when a young woman sat down next to him. He looked over and was shocked to see that it was Anna, the emperor's daughter who had brazenly insulted him at the royal banquet.

He studied her face. She was beautiful. Her soft olive skin, high cheekbones and large brown eyes gave her a stunning appearance. She turned and started at Michael. He looked away. After her last slight, he wasn't going to give her the pleasure of acknowledging her presence. Finally, she broke the uncomfortable silence and said, "So Crusader, I suppose you will be leaving our city soon?"

Michael wasn't in the mood to be talked down to, especially by a snotty young girl. He didn't care whether she was nobility or not.

"No, my Empress," he answered stiffly. "Nicephorus has requested that I stay in Constantinople and assist him with his administrative affairs."

Anna laughed then said bluntly, "Nicephorus wants to be emperor. I would be careful if I were you, Crusader. My father's brother has an agenda that you are not fully aware of."

With those words, Michael realized he was now treading in dangerous waters. He remembered the look of hatred in Nicephorus' eyes for the Emperor and his family.

"If what you say is true, why doesn't your father do something about it?"

"What makes you think he hasn't?" she answered calmly.

Michael remained silent, realizing it was best to choose his words very carefully from this point on.

Anna continued, "My father sent me to talk to you because of your relationship with Nicephorus. I would like you to answer a question, and answer it honestly."

Michael was growing more nervous by the second. It was evident he had gotten himself caught in the middle of a royal feud, and both sides probably considered him an expendable pawn.

"What is your question?"

"Has Nicephorus given you any indication of any plots against the Emperor?"

Anna's question was asked so casually Michael couldn't tell if she was serious or not. One thing he had learned about the Byzantine people was that they were masters of illusion and trickery. Michael knew he was now part of a dangerous game that could end badly if he didn't play things carefully. He reached inside of his shirt and pulled out the Brutus coin. He handed it to Anna.

"What's this?"

"Are you familiar with the story of Brutus and his role in the assassination of Caesar?"

"I know the history. We are Romans after all."

"Well, Empress, this coin was minted by Brutus after the death of Caesar. I guess it is true . . . ," he stared out over the gardens before looking Anna directly in the eyes. "Sometimes, your worst enemies are those that are closest to you."

Anna stared at the double daggers. "What does that numeral I stand for?"

"Aah, you are very observant. It's a mintmark. It signifies that this coin was the very first one minted. Supposedly, it was given to Brutus and he carried it until his death. I've been told that the coin is cursed and that bad things befall people who have it in their possession."

"Well, if you continue to associate with Nicephorus, bad things will befall you." She handed the coin back to Michael.

In spite of his initial dislike for the Emperor's daughter, his instincts told him that Anna's intentions were noble and she was just trying to protect her family.

Michael looked her in the eyes. "I have been placed in an untenable situation. I can promise you this. If I become aware of any plot against your father, I will try and make you aware of it. That I promise."

"How?" she asked.

"I will tell you. And if I cannot personally warn you, I will give you a sign."

"A sign?"

"Nicephorus has an appreciation for coins. He told me he collects them. If I can't warn you myself, I will give the coin to the Prince. If you find Nicephorus in possession of it, then you will know that he means to betray your father."

Anna stood up from the bench. "Very well, Crusader. My father sent me because he trusts me. Now, I'm putting my trust in you. I will take your word and promise no harm will come to you, as long as you keep your word."

Michael nodded and watched her walk out of the gardens. He sat there a long time before leaving.

Chapter 13

The call to arms that Michael had been dreading finally came—Peter's army was set to leave Constantinople in three days. Despite Anna's warning, Michael had been spending most of his time drinking and gambling with Nicephorus so he wouldn't have to face Godfrey. However, the more he was around the Prince, the more Michael began to notice a change in the Prince's disposition.

Nicephorus seemed distant and short-tempered. Trips to the Palace grounds were not as fun as they once had been and an air of tension hung over everything. But despite Nicephorus' erratic behavior, Michael still enjoyed the Prince's friendship, especially the luxury that went with it. And, despite Godfrey's words and his own doubts about leaving his brother, he still planned to remain in Constantinople after Peter's army left. It was the perfect opportunity for him to get away from his father and live the type of life he had always dreamed about.

Michael sat in his quarters waiting for Godfrey to return so he could tell him his decision. Complete annihilation awaited Peter's army outside of Constantinople's walls. Godfrey was a full-grown man. If he wanted to get himself killed, that was his decision. Why should he have to suffer the same fate?

Godfrey entered the room and greeted Michael sarcastically, "No games with the Prince today?"

"No," Michael said.

"Do you have something to tell me?" Godfrey asked, breaking the cold silence.

"I'm not going to Jerusalem."

Godfrey acted as if he didn't hear Michael's words and replied confidently, "As you know, Peter's army is leaving in three days. I know you'll end up making the right decision. You wouldn't abandon your brother, or your God. When we finish up the last part of our adventure, we'll return home heroes and make things right between you and father."

"Godfrey," Michael began, but his brother wasn't going to listen to him. Godfrey waved his arm and left the room.

Prince Nicephorus sat alone in the dark room. The General of his personal guard entered and bowed.

"So, the plan is in place?" Nicephorus asked.

"Yes," the General responded. "The Emperor is so desperate to get the stinking Crusaders off his lands that he has promised to send his Royal Guard to escort them across the Bosporus to Nicea. That is when your brother will be most vulnerable."

"How long will his Imperial Guard be gone?"

"It will probably take two weeks to get to Nicea and back." The general laughed. "Unless they have too much fun watching the Turks slaughter the Crusaders. What about the Gaul?"

"He will serve his purpose when the time comes. This is the opportunity that I have waited my entire life for. The Kingdom will finally be mine. Prepare your men."

The General bowed. "It is done."

Michael paced restlessly. He hadn't slept well for weeks. Even with a heavy dose of wine fortification, he hadn't been able to get more than a couple of hours of sleep at a time; and when he did, he was tormented by strange dreams. He felt completely exhausted but after his brother and the Crusaders left, he would start to feel better.

He stood on top of the western wall and stared down at the mass of Crusaders gathered outside the city. Their families, animals, carts and equipment created an unwieldy clog of humanity and confusion.

Michael hadn't intended on watching Peter's army depart, but, in the end, he couldn't help it. He had to see them leave; and then, maybe, it would bring some closure.

He couldn't help but wonder if he was making an awful decision. The only reason he would even consider going to Jerusalem at this point was his brother, and it tortured him that in Godfrey's one moment of need, he was abandoning him. Was he betraying his brother?

"God forgive me," Michael said up towards the cloudless sky.

He watched solemnly as the peasant army slowly started moving forward. Thankfully, in the mass of people and animals, he didn't spot his brother. After about an hour of watching the exodus, Michael turned to leave but a group of stragglers caught his eye. He walked back over to the edge of the wall and looked down.

At the end of the line was Godfrey. He was on his horse looking back towards the gates of the city. The army had moved on and yet Godfrey, with Tribert and Alberto at his side, had held their ground. A pang of sadness shot through him when he realized that Godfrey was waiting for him.

He knew he should turn and leave but he couldn't take his eyes off his brother. He felt a lump grow in his throat. Then Godfrey looked in his direction and the two brother's eyes locked on to each other. They both remained motionless for a long moment. Finally, Godfrey violently pulled the reigns of his horse and rode off to rejoin the army.

Michael watched Peter's army disappear over the horizon. Only when the last Crusader had vanished over the hill leading to the Bosporus—only then did he turn and leave. Godfrey was gone, and Michael knew he would never see his brother again.

Chapter 14

Michael's hands trembled as he opened the note from the Prince. He began reading—Peter's entire army had been massacred. Godfrey was dead.

Michael's vision narrowed and his heart began pounding. He stumbled over to a chair gasping for air, he felt his chest starting to squeeze tight and panic seized him. He grabbed a bottle of wine and drank most of it directly from the bottle.

After consuming almost half the wine, he regained some control and continued reading the note. It informed him that a week and a half after the Crusaders had departed Constantinople; a large contingent of Turks outside of Nicea fell upon them. The Crusaders were taken by surprise and didn't have a chance.

Michael had betrayed his brother—a fact that he would have to take to his grave.

At the end of the note, the Prince offered his condolences and bid Michael to please join him at his quarters later in the evening.

Michael made his way to the Palace grounds with a heavy heart. He stared up at the giant yellow moon and intense sadness swept through him. He wondered what he had expected because he had known the minute that Godfrey left that he was doomed.

Michael had become a familiar sight to the guards and they let him pass. He made his way over to Nicephorus' quarters and upon entering, ran straight into a group of heavily armed soldiers.

His heart skipped a beat. The Prince's entire Guard was with him and they appeared nervous and agitated.

He saw the Prince and greeted him, "Nicephorus, thank you for your condolences." Michael bowed hesitantly.

Nicephorus pointed at him and sneered, "Seize the Gaul."

A pair of guards sprang upon him and grabbed his arms. A chill ran through his body. "Prince, what is the meaning of this!" Michael yelled.

Nicephorus didn't even look at him but addressed his general instead. "Alexius' guard is due back any day."

The General nodded. "Tonight is it. There is no going back."

Nicephorus finally looked at Michael. "Congratulations."

"For what?"

"For murdering the Emperor."

Michael felt his stomach turn. "What in the hell are you talking about?"

Nicephorus smiled as he walked towards him. "Well, I can't very well let the good people of Constantinople think that the Emperor's own brother assassinated him, now can I? Unlike your culture, Michael, we are a civilized people. Byzantines would never stand for it. And that is where you come in. You are the assassin who murdered Alexius."

Michael glared at him with contempt and he could only think of his own brother. He felt his knees buckle but the soldiers held him up.

"No one will believe it," he said weakly.

"Oh, a few will have their doubts but it will make perfect sense to most. Think about it. The Turks slaughter your brother. The Emperor knew about the ambush all along, but did nothing to help the Crusaders. You wanted revenge for your brother's tragic death. You have access to the Palace grounds through our relationship. Trust me, my dear Gaul, the story will be believed by those who matter."

Nicephorous whispered something to one of the soldiers then grinned back at him. "I'll see you later, Michael."

Michael watched him leave with his General.

The soldiers bound and gagged him leaving him on the floor with guards posted around him. Hours passed before he was stood back up and led through a dark tunnel that ran underneath the grounds of the estate. When they exited the tunnel he was thrown into a covered cart. He could do nothing but lay helplessly, all the time thinking that maybe he deserved what was happening to him.

After a long, bumpy ride, the cart stopped. Michael was pulled out by his legs and thrown onto the ground.

Nicephorus stood over him. "Untie him," he ordered.

The soldiers cut his bindings and took the gag out of his mouth. He was yanked up to his feet, and even though it was nighttime, he instantly recognized where he was.

"Why are we here?" Michael asked, although he already knew the answer.

"Because, Michael," Nicephorus said, "after you murdered the Emperor, we chased you to the wall where you jumped to your death. It all makes sense now, doesn't it?"

His fate had been set, that much Michael was sure of. "Is the Emperor dead?" he asked.

"Not yet. But he will be after we are finished with you."

Nicephorus walked directly up to him and placed a hand on his shoulder. "Now, Michael, I want you to go quietly. You know how much I hate bloodshed.

Don't make me take you to Hell, to the torturer. You don't want to have a thousand cuts."

The mere mention of the torture made Michael's blood curdle. He couldn't allow himself to be brought to the dungeon beneath the Palace. There were worse things than death.

He stood helplessly staring at Nicephorus. In his eyes he saw the same look of hate as the night of the banquet when he talked about Alexius.

"Did you plan this all along?" Michael asked calmly.

Nicephorus laughed and spread out his hands. "What, did you really think I craved the friendship of a dirty little Gaul?"

The soldiers began to laugh. Michael looked down at the coin on the end of the necklace and he thought about Dragomir. The Bulgarian had been right all along. The coin was cursed.

The soldiers pushed him towards the seawall. "Get on top of the wall, Michael," Nicephorus ordered.

Michael climbed up onto the seawall and stared over the precipice. Even though it was late at night, the moon was full and he could see down to the rocky bottom far below.

He turned back around to Nicephorus. "You're no emperor, Nicephorus. You will only end up disgracing your people."

"Any other final words, Michael?"

Michael pulled the Brutus coin from around his neck. "Will you at least grant me one wish?"

"Maybe."

"Here, take the coin. It doesn't need to go to its death because of me."

Nicephorus smiled. "How gracious of you, Michael. I'll add it to my collection."

Michael threw it down to him. Nicephorus caught the coin and put the necklace on. "See, I'll even wear it proudly. After all, it would be fitting to wear the coin of a man who failed in his attempt to take over Rome. But, I can assure you Michael, that won't happen to me. I will wear it as a reminder that I succeeded where Brutus failed."

Despite the fact that he knew he was going to die, Michael smiled. "I hope the coin will bring you good fortune, Prince Nicephorus."

"Don't worry, it will. After all, I am no Brutus."

Michael turned back around and looked out over the harbor. The moonlight reflected brightly off of its smooth calm waters. What a magnificent night to die he thought as he stepped off the wall and into the abyss.

As the ground rushed up towards Michael, something unbelievable happened—the rocky shore transformed itself. Instead of rocks, Michael was falling towards the forest he had seen so many times in his dreams.

As he rushed towards the trees, it amazed him how many thoughts a man could have with only seconds to live.

The last thought Michael had before his death was that he was finally going to learn the secret of the forest.

Chapter 15

The man, formerly known as Prince Nicephorus, let out a horrific wail of unimaginable terror, pain and despair. He had been chained upright to a wall for days, or at least that is what he thought, as time no longer had any meaning. Every second had become a lifetime of unfathomable pain and suffering. But his mind was able to comprehend one thing—he knew where he was; in the Emperor's torture chamber called Hell.

As he slipped back into semi-consciousness, the events of how he arrived in Hell played out in his mind, over and over. After the Gaul had been disposed of, Nicephorus and his soldiers returned to the royal estate to kill Alexius. He entered the grounds through the front gate while his soldiers used the secret tunnel in order not to draw unnecessary attention.

The plan was to meet up at the Emperor's Palace where they would sneak into his chambers through another secret entrance. Then they would assassinate Alexius and later blame it on Michael.

After entering through the gates, Nicephorus had spotted Anna off in the distance. At the time he had thought it unusual that she was out so late, but it didn't matter because he was going to kill her too.

He remembered Anna pointing to the coin on the necklace and yelling, "Nicephorus, don't you realize that today isn't the Eids of March?"

She began to laugh in a mocking tone and ran back into the palace. He didn't have time to fool with her at the moment, so he had let her go and entered Alexius' palace.

He met up with his soldiers. Everything was going according to plan until they entered the outer room of Alexius' quarters. The Emperor's Imperial Guard appeared out of nowhere. Nicephorus knew instantly he had been tricked and was doomed.

His soldiers threw their weapons down and begged for mercy. There would be none. One by one, his soldier's had their throats cut. Nicephorus could only watch in horror, wondering what his punishment would be.

 A blood-curdling yell made him regain consciousness. It took a few seconds for his mind to register that he was the one yelling. The torturer had returned and applied his devices. Every nerve, every tissue in his body exploded in excruciating pain, a feeling he never knew could exist. He screamed louder as the agony multiplied, but he knew there would be no relief.

The torturer moved away and Nicephorus fell back into a pain-induced semi-consciousness and to his memories of the night. He remembered, after all of his conspirators had been slaughtered, only then did Alexius come forward. Alexius refused to hear his pleas and only responded by handing him a dagger.

Why! Why couldn't he have done it and spared himself all of this. He was a coward. His brother had given him a choice, a way out, but he was too weak; and now he was in Hell.

In his tortured delirium he heard someone approaching.

"Uncle," he heard a female voice say. He couldn't see who it was because both of his eyes had been put out, but he recognized the voice. It was Anna.

"You don't look so well, Uncle," she said to him. "Looks like you have got yourself in a bad situation."

"Is Alexius coming? Please, Anna. I beg you to get him for me."

He heard her snicker. "No, he refuses to see you. You are already dead to him."

"How? How did he know?" he muttered.

She laughed. "You are unbelievable. Well, since you asked, Alexius long suspected that you would try and steal the Empire from him. He also knew that you would consider him most vulnerable when his Imperial Guard had dispersed to Nicea with the Crusaders. He kept his best soldiers hiding inside the Palace in case you tried something. But in the end, it was your friend, the Gaul, who gave your plan away."

"The Gaul. But how?"

"You are so predictable, Nicephorus. I went to see Michael Claudien and from his comments I was able to put the last piece of the puzzle together. When I saw you at the gates, I knew for certain that you had come to try and kill Alexius."

"But how?"

"The coin. You were wearing the Brutus coin."

Nicephorus moaned loudly. "Please Anna, take that cursed coin off me. I don't want it upon my body when I die."

He heard her laugh again. "Uncle, they took the coin from you the first night you were here."

"I beg you," Nicephorus whimpered. "give it to Alexius, He won. I lost. He should wear the coin as an honor of his victory over me."

"That is the difference between Alexius and you. You are a greedy fool, and Alexius knows the power of curses and fate. He has already sent the wretched coin back to France. He doesn't want the cursed thing in the city, or even on Byzantine land."

"Anna," Nicephorus pleaded. "Please, I am begging you, kill me. Don't make me suffer anymore. I am sorry. I truly am."

"Uncle, you had a choice. And this is what you chose."

"But I didn't know it would be like this."

"You talk too much for a dead man," she said.

Once again, Nicephorus heard the heavy footsteps of the torturer approaching.

"No!" he yelled.

His head and jaw were violently grabbed and his mouth forced open. He felt a quick swipe and his mouth filled with a warm liquid. Then the pain came. He tried to scream, but now, Nicephorus had even lost the chance to even beg.

As he lost consciousness, he prayed for death and a chance to be reunited with the French Crusader in hell.

BOOK III

Hence it is no accident that the first cultures
arose in places where the Aryan,
in his encounters with lower peoples,
subjugated them and bent them to his will

Adolph Hitler

Chapter 1

Paris, France
June 1940

The cold, dreary rainstorms plaguing the French skies during the last few days had finally subsided, much to the relief of Colonel Maxwell Von Studt. He never quite understood why, but ever since he was a young boy, he had a propensity of growing severely agitated, even depressed, during bad weather.

He stared up into the clear blue sky. The large yellow sun brightened his disposition, almost as much as the sight of German soldiers freely patrolling what used to be the French capital city of Paris. Colonel Von Studt sat alone at an outdoor table of a Parisian café savoring the victories of the German army. He peered down the tree-lined Champs-de-Elysees with an overwhelming sense of pride and achievement. His thoughts turned to his mother. She would have been so proud of him. He wished she was still alive to see all that Germany, led by the Nazi party, had accomplished.

He watched as a group of SS soldiers, dressed in their customary all-black uniforms, marched down the center of the street in a perfect formation. The sight of the soldiers made him nostalgic because these were the types of men his mother told him stories about. She never bothered to read him fairy tales or typical children's books. Instead, she told grand stories of legendary men, men of action, men of war, brave and mighty warriors called by names such as, Xerxes, Genghis Khan, Hector, and Alexander the Great.

He distinctly remembered his mother's favorite story. The epic tale of Hannibal of Carthage and his mighty army that succeeded in crossing the Alps with a herd of elephants to attack the Romans in Rome itself. As a child, he would beg his mother to tell it, over and over again.

Unfortunately, colorful stories and the exploits of ancient generals didn't sit too well with his strict Catholic father. Von Studt's smile disappeared as he thought of him.

His father was a cold-hearted bastard who ruled his family with an iron fist. He was a strict disciplinarian who never hesitated to use his fists as punishment. As a child, his mother had repeatedly warned him that their stories were meant for their ears only, but he slipped one day and his father gave not only him, but his mother a brutal beating.

He didn't mind being punished. Punishment was something he had come to expect; but it made him physically sick to hear the wails of his mother from behind the closed bedroom door.

Von Studt clenched his fists as he recalled one morning in particular. He remembered sitting at the breakfast table, one eye closed shut, and the other, black and bruised. His rear end hurt so bad he could barely sit. He stared at his father across the table, who sat there reading the newspaper as if he didn't have a concern in the world, as if he hadn't just beaten his wife and son senseless. When his mother came out of the bedroom to make breakfast, her face was so badly swollen and bruised he had burst out in tears. The sight of her had made him so sick—he jumped from the table and barely made it to the bathroom before throwing up.

Von Studt could still almost feel the anger building up inside of him until he thought he might explode. He had wanted to smash his father's face in, but he was just a child. All he could do was return to the table in silence with hate burning inside of him.

Later that day, he received another beating from his father after getting expelled from school for the entire term. He had gone to school and had taken out his pent up rage on the class weakling, beating the boy severely, the whole time wishing it was his father. Every time his fist crashed into the crying boy's face, he swore that one day he would repay his father for what he had done to his mother.

But it was a promise he hadn't been able to keep. When he was eighteen, both his father and mother were killed in a fiery collision when a truck driver blindsided them in their small automobile. The truck driver got off with only a small fine. He later learned that both the driver and the judge were Jewish.

A loud explosion followed by a short burst of gunfire brought Von Studt back to the present. He looked down the avenue. Paris had been secured but a few insurgents still had to be flushed out. He carefully swirled the wine in his glass then took a sip of the strong dark liquid.

"Delicious," he said, then laughed as it occurred to him that making wine was, perhaps, the only thing the French were good at.

He turned back to the café, abruptly motioning to a frail, nervous waiter. Von Studt pulled a cigarette out of its pack and placed it between his lips. He watched with amusement as the Frenchman scurried over to his table and pulled a scuffed silver lighter out of his dirty black vest. He tried, with trembling hands, to light Von Studt's cigarette and after three tries, finally succeeded.

Von Studt took a deep drag and dismissed the waiter with a wave of his hand. He exhaled a large stream of smoke, watching it rise quickly before disappearing into the air. He stared back down the Champs-de-Elysees and marveled at how well Germany's war plans had progressed.

Like a set of children's dominoes, the enemies of the Third Reich were falling, one after another, after another. In less than a year, the German war machine had swept across the northern part of Western Europe, conquering Poland, the Netherlands, Luxembourg and Belgium.

A new military tactic called the Blitzkrieg was largely responsible for the decisively quick victories. The maneuver entailed the integration of tanks, air support, artillery and infantry to create a highly destructive army that moved with lightning fast speed. The world had never seen such tactics before.

Von Studt believed the surprise attack against France would have made even Hannibal proud because the German Panzer tank divisions and infantry units had done what was thought impossible. They had cut a swath through the dense Ardennes forests slicing into France over a border that was believed impenetrable.

"The French," Von Studt uttered with contempt. He stared over at the waiter who immediately looked away. What a cowardly lot. To have given up their capital city without even a fight proved to Von Studt that the whole nation consisted of nothing but disgraceful cowards.

A loud roar came from overhead. Von Studt gazed skyward as a squadron of Messerschmitt 109's flew directly overhead. He flicked a cigarette ash onto the ground and smiled. Soon the entire country would be under German rule; and then it would be on to Britain.

Von Studt raised his glass towards the sky. "Heil Hitler."

The toast was well deserved. To have accomplished so much with so few casualties was indeed a remarkable achievement. Only thirty-five thousand brave Aryan soldiers had been killed during the initial phase of the war, deaths that were unfortunate, but expected, even necessary to achieve the final solution.

Von Studt had no doubt that his fallen brothers would be deeply appreciated when the master plan was complete and the pure bloodlines took their rightful place as rulers of the world. He believed this with all his heart.

Colonel Maxwell Von Studt was a leading member of the Schutzstaffel or SS, the elite paramilitary organization originally formed to serve as Hitler's bodyguards. Over the years the SS had turned into something much more important, much more powerful than just bodyguards. The organization was responsible for the rise and success of the Nazi party. Although Heinrich Himmler was the leader of both the SS and the Gestapo, Von Studt was the Fuhrer's closest confidant and advisor. It was his job to keep an eye on Himmler, Goerhing and the others. In effect, he answered only to one person, and that was Hitler.

Von Studt's relationship with Hitler had begun in 1931 when they both were imprisoned in Landsberg on trumped up political charges. It was during this time that they became comrades with many shared beliefs.

Von Studt helped Hitler write *Mein Kampf: My Struggle*, a book that laid the foundation for the Third Reich. But what Germany and the rest of the world didn't know was that *Mein Kampf* was just the first book in a series of three. Hitler dictated the second book to Von Studt shortly after their release from prison, and it had yet to be published. Hitler planned on making it public only after Germany had succeeded in conquering all of Europe, which in Von Studt's estimation was only a year or two away. To Von Studt's knowledge no one else had read the second book except for Heinrich Himmler.

The second book was titled *Mein Urspruenge: My Origins*. It gave a detailed account of the cosmogony—the beginning of the universe, the history of earth and the rise of civilization. More importantly, it discussed The Order, and the emergence of the pure bloodlines, the Aryans.

Mein Urspruenge was much more philosophical and scientific than *Mein Kampf*. *Mein Urspruenge* explained that a spark of energy erupted at such enormous temperature and velocity that it tore the fabric of time and space thus creating the foundation for all life in the universe. The book theorized that all energy in the universe moved according to laws established during the first nanoseconds of the initial expansion—creating matter and antimatter particles.

These two opposing but equal forces were destined to spend the rest of eternity fighting for dominance, which explains the duality of the universe. Without destruction there cannot be creation. Without death there can be no life. Even the basic human emotion of happiness could not exist unless there was also suffering.

Von Studt looked back over at the defeated-looking French waiter and saw in his miserable face pain, suffering and humiliation. But without the Frenchman's misery, Von Studt knew he would not be experiencing the happiness, joy and power that presently coursed through his body and mind.

How clear it was to Von Studt that the universe and man thrives only because of the doctrine of "survival of the fittest." And it was a battle that had been occurring since the planet was created, just as it had on millions of other planets in galaxies throughout the universe.

A feeling of pride filled Von Studt. He felt privileged about his place in The Order and to know what so few did about the true history and origin of the human race.

According to *Mein Urspruenge*, earth was first populated eons ago from the DNA of aliens known as the Annunaki. The genetically engineered race of humans they created were called Aryans. According to The Order's doctrine, two species of humans populate earth: the Aryans, the superior race; and everyone else, who evolved from apes over tens of millions of years.

It wasn't until the rise of the Trojan Empire in the thirteenth century BC that the Aryan bloodlines had become strong enough to unite as a force capable of ruling the world. The Trojans were the First Reich or Empire, but their dynasty did not last long as its capital city, Troy, and many of its Aryan descendants were slaughtered by the Greeks during a decade long battle.

A few powerful Aryans did manage to survive the carnage, including Aeneas, who sailed to the barbarian shores of Italy. In Italy, the Aryans regrouped and through the ages the bloodlines grew stronger and stronger until a twenty-five hundred year period, or Second Reich, almost succeeded in its ultimate plan.

The Second Reich began with the Roman Republic in 750 BC, and grew stronger until it became an Empire after the death of Julius Caesar. Despite what modern history books teach, the rule of the Romans continued in Constantinople with the Byzantines, down through the reign of Charlemagne and the Holy Roman Empire until its collapse in 1806 with the resignation of Francis the Second.

But now, once again, the bloodlines had reorganized, grown stronger, more powerful; and this time, Von Studt had no doubt that The Order's ultimate plan would finally be achieved. And it was Adolph Hitler who had been chosen to lead them to the final phase.

This was the point where the second book ended, with the rise to power of Hitler, the Nazi Party and The Order. Von Studt speculated that Hitler's third book probably detailed how the world would function under the rule of the Third Reich. The last book had been completed after Hitler's rise to power, and much to Von Studt's disappointment, he had not seen a single word. All Hitler would tell him was that when the time was right, he would get his chance to read it.

Von Studt finished his wine and set the glass on the table. It still astonished him that ten years ago he was rotting in prison, and now, he was sitting outside of a café on the Champs-de-Elysees in German occupied Paris.

He thought back to his time in prison. Despite the harshness of captivity, it was one of the most rewarding times of his life because he learned so much from Hitler. They had served only nine months of their five-year sentences. During that time, Von Studt listened, studied and memorized the creation, as well as the history and reasons for The Order.

Hitler displayed such an unwavering belief in both his and The Order's destinies, and had such specific plans to achieve them, Von Studt believed, without doubt, Hitler would not be denied.

After their release from prison, a bloody insurgency followed and Hitler rose to power in Germany. Now, Hitler and his Nazi party commanded the mightiest country the world had ever seen. But, just as important as Hitler's ascension to power, The Order had grown cohesive and strong. There were many followers, waiting in every country around the world for the day when the Third Reich ruled the world. Von Studt felt a chill run down his spine as he imagined the entire world kneeling down to Hitler and The Order.

A column of Panzers slowly moved down the avenue. East Europe and Britain were next and Von Studt believed they would fall as fast as the others, especially since there were so many sympathizers in those countries. Men who were patiently waiting until The Order came to their rescue and restored what should have taken place millenniums ago.

But even with his supreme confidence, Von Studt knew they had to be careful. Treachery was all around them. Hitler repeatedly warned his officers that there would be traitors among the chosen, and those traitors would stop at nothing to see the Third Reich fail.

After all, it had happened before. Both the First and Second Empires had crumbled from within; but Von Studt had taken an oath that he would die before that happened. The Third Reich was going to last a thousand years, then the pure bloodlines would be merged with the Annunaki in glory, and Von Studt would be part of it all.

He flicked the cigarette onto the ground and watched as a group of infantry soldiers crossed the wide avenue toward him. As they approached, he recognized the battle emblem on their sleeves. They were riflemen from a division commanded by Heinz Guderian.

Guderian. Von Studt shook his head in disgust. He was certain the man was an imposter who had infiltrated the German army to act as a saboteur. Von Studt thought Guderian looked too much like a Jew to be a true believer, and Guderian's recent actions only strengthened Von Studt's intuitions.

Guderian had been a vocal opponent of Hitler's plan to attack France, and repeatedly argued that the German army was not prepared for such an invasion. Guderian even went so far as to suggest that they could suffer defeat at the hands of the French if the Panzer units got bogged down in the Ardennes Forest.

Of course, Guderian hadn't been the only opponent to Hitler's invasion plans. There had been others—men that Von Studt knew would have to be taken care of later. That was the most important part of his job within the Reich—he took care of problems.

The soldiers strode confidently over to Von Studt with their rifles pointed at him. A fair-haired soldier stepped forward. "Your papers!"

Von Studt studied the baby-faced soldier who still had pimples on his cheeks. He couldn't have been older than twenty. Von Studt smiled. It didn't bother him that the soldier was questioning him in such a manner. After all, the soldier was just doing his job. Due to the nature and secrecy of his position, Von Studt often dressed in civilian clothes, and today he was wearing a dark brown suit.

However, it did irritate him that the soldier thought he might be some disgusting Frank. Von Studt was proud, even vain regarding his appearance. He had thick black hair, cropped short with dark black eyes. The rest of him was pure Aryan. He was tall, athletically built, clean-shaven with a solid jaw and an aquiline nose. The women he had courted all told him he was a handsome man; and they implied he was handsome in a somewhat dangerous, forbidding way.

Von Studt ignored the soldier's command and pulled out his lighter. He lit a cigarette and took a deep drag, exhaling the smoke directly in the soldier's face.

The soldier stuck his rifle into Vons Studt's chest and shouted, "Your papers, now!"

Von Studt pushed the barrel of the rifle away and replied calmly, "Do I look like a filthy Parisian? Or perhaps you think worse of me. You don't think I am a Jew, do you?"

The soldier lowered his gun slightly. "No, of course not," he replied hesitantly, obviously realizing he might be making a mistake.

He looked around at his comrades for guidance and after receiving none, continued in a more measured tone, "We are under orders to secure the area. I need to confirm your identity—if you don't mind."

Von Studt raised his hand. "Of course not. I am well aware of your orders." He pulled out his papers and casually tossed them to the young soldier.

He watched in amusement as the soldier's eyes grew wide, after all, Adolph Hitler had personally signed the documents. The young soldier's disposition quickly changed from one of confidence and power, to one of uncertainty and weakness. Von Studt loved playing this game. He loved watching submission, especially when people discovered who he was.

"Colonel Von Studt." The soldier saluted briskly. Upon hearing his name the other soldiers quickly snapped to attention.

The soldier handed back his papers and identification card. "I apologize for the misunderstanding, sir. Please forgive me."

Von Studt stared into the eyes of the young soldiers who, like the French waiter, were doing their best not to look him directly in the eyes. He didn't blame the soldiers for not recognizing him by appearance. His position and duty to Hitler kept him in the shadows; and even though most Germans didn't know what he looked like, all knew his name and reputation. Von Studt relished seeing fear in other people's eyes, even if it was from other Germans.

"That is quite all right," he finally replied. "What is your name, soldier?"

"Gotthard, sir. Rifleman Joseph Gotthard."

"Well Gotthard, perhaps you can help me. Can you tell me how far the Louvre is from here?"

"No sir, I—"

"Colonel." One of his fellow soldiers stepped forward. "The museum is down the Champs-de-Elyees, just around the corner from the Arc De Triumph."

"Would you care for us to escort you there, Colonel?" Gotthard asked.

"That's unnecessary. Please carry on with your orders."

The soldiers saluted and just like the Parisian waiter, they hurried off, leaving Von Studt to ponder with pleasure why he always seemed to have that effect on people. Everyone always appeared relieved to be leaving his presence.

He looked at his field watch. It was a quarter-till-five. He still had over an hour before his meeting with Hitler who, earlier today, had triumphantly marched under the Arc de Triumph and into Paris as a conqueror.

Chapter 2

Von Studt left the café and walked down the sidewalk to the front of the Louvre. The centuries old museum was a magnificent sight. He had been told that *The Mona Lisa*, one of the most famous and priceless paintings in the world, was inside. Von Studt could have cared less about the painting or any of the other treasures. He only wanted the Brutus Double Dagger coin.

His fascination, a near obsession to possess the Double Dagger coin, had started early in his life. Ever since he was a child, he had been enthralled with the Roman Empire and its history, especially the violent era when Julius Caesar ruled. He had read every book he could find on the subject.

One day, he came across a book chronicling famous Roman coins and the history behind them. He remembered turning the large pages with a sense of awe, but when he came to the picture of the Double Dagger coin, it took his breath away. He was only twelve at the time and he remembered sitting at the kitchen table staring at the coin for hours.

He knew then that he had to find a way to own the coin, and not just any Eids of March coin. He had to possess the one minted for Brutus and inscribed with the Roman numeral I. He didn't understand why, but he felt as if he was the rightful owner of the coin.

His quest had caused him to spend endless hours over the past ten years trying to locate the coin. A year ago, he received the break of a lifetime from a German spy embedded with the French Ministry of Culture. The spy had seen the coin at the Louvre, and after grilling him about it, Von Studt was positive that it was the one he was after.

He checked his watch. He would have to wait until tomorrow to retrieve the coin. He flagged down a transport vehicle carrying a group of soldiers and, after showing them his identification, hitched a ride. Five minutes later, the vehicle pulled over to the curb outside of Hitler's hotel.

He walked up to the entrance. The soldiers raised their rifles at him. Von Studt pumped his right hand straight out. "Heil Hitler."

The soldiers lowered their weapons and returned the salute. He wondered as he watched them return the "Heil Hitler" salute if they would be impressed to know that he was the one who had created it while in prison. It had been used by Romans to salute Caesar. Symbolism and adherence to old traditions was important to Hitler and Von Studt knew it would only be a matter of time before the whole world knew of the salute's significance.

The guard quickly checked Von Studt's identification papers then motioned with his rifle for him to pass. He walked through the ornate foyer of the magnificent hotel and had to admit, despite the moral and character weaknesses of the French, they at least had exquisite taste in architecture.

Large gold chandeliers hung down from the towering marble ceiling. Beautiful statues, vases and paintings lined the walls with exquisite Oriental carpets covering the floor. The hotel was completely devoid of Parisians and was now staffed and run by German officers.

He walked to the front desk and saluted the officer. "Colonel Maxwell Von Studt," he announced in a brisk military tone. "I am here to see the Fuhrer."

The staff officer stood a little more rigid after hearing his name. "Colonel, just one moment please." He picked up a black phone and mumbled something into the receiver.

"The Fuhrer is in the penthouse suite on the top floor. The elevator is over to you right."

"Thank You."

Von Studt left the desk, passed through two more checkpoints, and then was escorted by a pair of armed guards to the top floor. He was excited. He hadn't seen Hitler since Berlin and he couldn't wait to congratulate him on the tremendous victory. They stopped in front of the penthouse door and one of the soldiers knocked briskly.

"Codeword," a voice asked from behind the door.

"Palladium," answered the lead soldier.

Von Studt smirked. The Palladium was a powerful ancient symbol to both the Trojan and Roman cultures. The legendary Trojan War hero, Aeneas had saved the Palladium after the Greeks stormed Troy during the Trojan War, and had brought it with him to Italy. Both the Trojans and the Romans believed the Palladium gave their Empires its strength and power.

The door opened. Standing in the entrance to the penthouse was Heinz Linge, Hitler's long time manservant. Linge was a dingy, feminine man standing no taller than five foot three. Von Studt thoroughly distrusted him, but despite his recommendations, the Fuhrer refused to release him.

"Colonel." Linge gestured for him to enter.

Von Studt brushed by the servant without acknowledging him. He entered the spacious penthouse and walked over to a row of large windows overlooking Paris. The Eiffel Tower stood out against the blue sky off in the horizon.

Von Studt took his hat off and set it on a coffee table. He ran a hand through his short thick hair and whistled. "Some view, huh, Linge?"

"Can I get you something to drink, Colonel?" Linge asked, ignoring his question.

Von Studt would have liked nothing better than to pummel the man right this instance. "No," he replied while lighting a cigarette.

"Very well." Linge nodded. "The Fuhrer will be out momentarily." Hitler's servant disappeared, and Von Studt sat down expecting to have to wait.

Despite his adoration and unconditional loyalty to the Fuhrer, he felt Hitler's personal habits could be somewhat disconcerting. Hitler habitually slept quite late, took lunches lasting hours and dined sometimes as late as ten o' clock in the evening. He loved movies, and Von Studt had known him to watch as many as three or four movies in a sitting, no matter what sort of turmoil was occurring around him. Hitler could also be temperamental, sometimes to the point of childishness, and much to Von Studt's annoyance, he was never on time.

Twenty minutes and three cigarettes later, Von Studt finally heard the back bedroom door open. He stood and watched as Adolph Hitler marched out wearing a gray three piece suit. He looked happy and relaxed.

Von Studt saluted. "Heil Hitler."

"Maxwell." Hitler walked over and affectionately clasped him on the shoulder.

The Fuhrer pointed out towards the city and with great pride in his voice said, "Paris is ours."

Von Studt studied Hitler's face as he stared out the window. The Fuhrer was a slight man in height and build, standing a good four inches shorter than him. Hitler kept his dark brown hair cut razor-short along the sides with bangs that swept down across his forehead. Years ago he had grown a brush mustache for reasons Von Studt suspected were to take attention away from his rather broad and un-Aryan nose.

Hitler turned to face him. "It is a truly amazing sight, isn't it?"

"Yes, it is. But did you ever have any doubt that this day would come?"

Hitler laughed heartily which surprised Von Studt because Hitler was generally a humorless man, not prone to those types of expressions or emotions.

"No, I never had a doubt. But to think back—ten years ago we were in prison." He paused. "And now—"

Hitler walked up to the window and placed his hands on the glass. Von Studt knew Hitler was prone to sentimental streaks at times and he suspected that was the case now. He remained silent as he watched Hitler stare out at Paris, a city and a country now fully in his control.

The Fuhrer turned back from the window and faced Von Studt. "I have a very important mission for you, Colonel. I want you to fly to Malta for a meeting with the Knight."

Von Studt's pulse raced and his knees almost buckled. He couldn't believe it! It was the opportunity of a lifetime. He was going to finally meet with the head of The Order, the only man in the world more powerful than the Fuhrer.

Hitler continued, "He has a message that's too important to trust to any other form of communication. Anyway, I think it's time for you to finally meet him."

Von Studt bowed his head. "Thank you for putting your trust in me for such an important mission."

Hitler waved his arm dismissively. "Maxwell, the battle has just begun. We have a long way to go to achieve our ultimate objective. Your trip is paramount to the success of our next stage. Take every precaution."

Von Studt nodded. "I understand."

Hitler lit a cigarette. "A Swiss cargo plane will take you to Malta the day after tomorrow. When you return to Paris, report directly to me. Is that clear?"

"Yes."

"One other thing." Hitler dug inside of his coat pocket and pulled out a clear capsule with a large pill inside of it. He handed it to Von Studt.

"It's Zyklon B—Cyanide. Upon ingesting it, you will be dead within minutes. We can't take any chances."

"Of course."

Von Studt had taken an oath to die for Hitler and The Order if necessary, and there was no doubt in his mind that if he was faced with that choice, he wouldn't hesitate to ingest the poison.

"It's just a precaution," Hitler added. "If you happened to be caught by the wrong people, you'll be glad you have it. After all, there are worse things than death."

Von Studt tucked the cyanide into his coat pocket.

"So Maxwell, have you had any luck in finding your Roman coin?" Hitler asked, changing the subject.

"I am going to the Louvre tomorrow. It may take me a while, but I'll find it."

Hitler smirked. "Sometimes I wonder about your obsession with the Roman Empire, especially that Dagger coin."

"I like the history," Von Studt interjected. "We have to learn from the past if we are going to build The Third Reich into an Empire that surpasses the Romans."

"Colonel, it has occurred to me more than once that your insistence on attacking France as soon as we did could have been just a ruse so you could have an opportunity to retrieve your little treasure."

Von Studt laughed. "Might as well kill two birds with one stone."

Linge reentered the room. "Sorry to interrupt, Fuhrer," he spoke to Hitler without looking at Von Studt. "I was to remind you of your other appointment."

"Ah, yes. Thank you, Linge." Hitler turned towards Von Studt. "Your orders are clear."

"Yes, Fuhrer. I won't let you down."

Hitler nodded. "Have a safe flight and I'll see you when you return."

Von Studt saluted and the two men shook hands. He left the hotel in elation. In two days, he would meet the most powerful man in the world, but tomorrow, he would finally retrieve the Double Dagger coin.

Chapter 3

He stood in a large open field. A stream ran along the side to his right. Instinctively, he knew he had been here before. Many times. He stared straight ahead at the dark forest. It stretched out in front of him as far as he could see in either direction, like an army of soldiers standing guard.

He felt his legs move him forward. His heart pounded. The closer he got, the greater the fear and anguish. He was close now, almost to the edge. He could hear the forest calling him as it always did. He was torn between wanting to find out what awaited him on the other side of the trees, and his fear. He was afraid that if he entered, he could never come back out.

He stepped closer to the trees. He had been in this exact spot hundreds of times, but now, for the first time, a sense of inevitability came over him. Slowly, he reached out and placed his hand onto the black bark of a large tree.

Instantly, his body stiffened and began to shake violently as if he was being electrocuted, but instead of electric volts: visions, memories, experiences, thousands, maybe millions of them, streamed through his mind. He saw his mother laughing, his father hitting him, figures cloaked in tunics hiding in the shadows, a platoon of soldiers dressed in strange primitive uniforms, an empty treeless plain, a bloody dagger, the Eid of March coin, huge stone buildings, a great wall overlooking a foreign sea, and a darkness within the forest that could only mean . . . death.

He saw everything, yet understood nothing. He tried with all of his strength to pull his hand from the tree as the visions, memories, raced throughout his mind. He felt as if his body could explode any second, and he screamed as he had never screamed before —

Von Studt violently jerked awake. He was soaked in a cold sweat. The sheets were tangled in a mass around him and his body felt as if it had been beaten with a metal pole. He forced himself to sit up. The torment was unbearable and he cried out as intense pain shot through his body.

Bit by bit, the dream came back to him. He had touched the tree and had seen what? What had he seen?

He rolled over and stared out of the hotel window. It was early and the sun had just begun to rise over Paris. Von Studt sighed heavily, still trying to catch his breath and ease the pain.

He forced himself out of bed. "God damn it!" he swore.

His legs wobbled beneath him as he walked over to the window. What was the meaning of the dream? He had had the dream hundreds of times going back to his early childhood, but this time was different. He tried to remember what he saw, what he felt when he touched the tree, but it was just a jumbled haze of incomprehensible bits of images, feelings and memories. Was he losing his mind?

He looked out of the hotel room window, down at the streets of Paris. He took more deep breaths trying to shake off the sense of doom that the dream had left. What he saw and felt after touching the tree was hard to comprehend. It was like fragments or pieces of a puzzle. The dream had left him confused, unsure. But he was certain about one thing—it meant something important.

He poured himself a glass of brandy and drank deeply. "It's just a goddamn dream. It means nothing," he tried to reassure himself.

Von Studt turned quickly from the window remembering with pleasure that today was the day he would finally take possession of the Brutus coin.

He took a cold shower, shaved, and with a little help from a large measure of brandy, began to feel better. Once outside the hotel the sense of impending doom that the dream had left began to fade. It was a beautiful day and the fresh air made him feel better, more relaxed, and seemed to clear his mind.

He could have commandeered a vehicle to take him to the Louvre but he preferred to walk. The citizens of Paris were also beginning to wake to a new day. Von Studt noticed more and more Parisians venturing out into the streets, no doubt accepting their fate of German rule.

After a brisk twenty-minute walk, he arrived at the Louvre. Much to his surprise, after pulling on a few doors, he found one unlocked. He had been prepared to break in but some incompetent Parisian must have left the door open by mistake. He walked into the cavernous main entrance with his footsteps echoing loudly throughout the building. There was not a single person in sight. His spy had given him vague information as to where in the museum the coin would be stored but the building was much larger than he anticipated. He needed someone to help with his search.

Von Studt walked down a darkened hallway off the main entrance. A series of offices stretched out on both sides. One by one, he peered into the rooms. All were empty. About halfway down the hall, he noticed a small patch of light coming from underneath one of the doors at the very end of the hall. He walked down and looked through the office's small window. Much to his surprise, sitting behind a large metal desk, was a bespectacled old man studying a large stack of documents.

Von Studt didn't bother knocking. He opened the door and entered. He stood in the middle of the room and almost began laughing. The old man didn't even notice he was there. Von Studt watched in amazement as the man continued reading his papers, totally oblivious that someone was standing only a few feet away.

Von Studt coughed. It startled the old man who looked up quickly. The two men stared at each other for a few seconds, neither saying a word.

Finally, the old man said in a rattled tone, "I'm sorry. We are closed for the day. Please come back later."

Von Studt smiled. The French have such a sense of humor. Von Studt was dressed in a dark suit instead of his black SS uniform. He figured the old man probably thought he wanted to tour the museum. He slowly approached the desk.

The old man's eyes darted nervously about and he asked, "How did you get in?"

"One of the front doors was open," Von Studt answered in heavily accented French.

The man looked at him suspiciously after hearing his accent. "Damn it! I told the custodian to make sure all the doors were locked. We are closed today. In, ah . . . light of the circumstances."

Von Studt stood over the frail man. "Who are you?"

"I'm the museum's head curator, and I must ask you to leave. I have a lot of work to do. Items to be cataloged."

Von Studt laughed. These Parisians never ceased to astound him. A centuries old enemy had just overthrown the man's city and country, and all he cared about was his precious artifacts.

The curator stood up. "I will show you the way out."

The curator never saw it coming. As he walked past, Von Studt punched him in his kidney so hard that it caused him to drop to the floor. Von Studt stood over him as he writhed in pain, desperately gasping for air. The old man's face began turning a deep purple.

"Shit!" Von Studt knelt down and straightened the man out onto his back so he could get more oxygen into his lungs. "Breathe," he said calmly. "Breathe."

At last, the curator gasped as air rushed into his lungs. "That's better. Inhale. Exhale. Slowly. The pain will go away."

After a few minutes the old man's face had almost returned to its normal color. Von Studt lit a cigarette, annoyed at himself for having acted so irresponsibly. He needed the man, and killing him certainly wouldn't help. He dropped the lit match on the curator's chest and sat down in a chair behind the desk. He waited patiently for another ten minutes before the curator finally caught his breath enough to sit up.

Von Studt stood up from the chair and walked back over to the fallen man. "Sorry, Mister Curator. I thought I might have killed you." He grabbed the old man by the lapels and gently helped him up from the floor. He carefully sat him back in his desk chair.

Von Studt squatted next to him so that they were at eye level. The old man's eyes registered pain and fear making Von Studt feel ecstatic, alive. "We have some work to do, Mister Curator. I need a bit of your, eh, how do we say, professional assistance."

"What do you want?"

"Just one small item, that's it. You'll hardly even miss it."

"Who are you?" the curator asked.

"That's not important. What is important is that I get what I have come for. If you help me, I promise no harm will come to you or your museum."

Von Studt picked up the documents that the old man had been reading and casually tossed them into a wastebasket next to the desk.

"On the other hand, if you try to deceive me and don't help me find what I have come for, I will send a squadron of SS soldiers to confiscate every artifact in your museum. And I will make you watch as your precious collections are carted off to Germany. Then, I will burn your museum to the ground with you inside of it. So what do you say good chap, will you help me?"

The curator winced. "Find something? I don't understand. All the items in the museum are property of the French Government."

Von Studt had lost his patience and shouted in the face of the curator, "What goddamn universe do you live in! The French government no longer exists! You no longer exist! The country of France is now owned by Germany!"

He stabbed the curator hard in his chest with two of his fingers causing the old man to cry out once again. Von Studt fought his growing urge to kill the man.

He took a deep breath and said in a more patient tone, "I own you. I am being very reasonable with you, but I am losing patience. I have come for the Double Dagger Denarius. The Eids of March coin. I want it and I want it now! Do you understand?"

The curator tried to say something but began sobbing.

"Shut up before I hit you in your other kidney."

Even with the threat, the man would not stop crying. Von Studt was close to the point where he could not be held accountable for his actions. He had been more than reasonable.

"Maybe you will understand this then." He pulled the Lugar out of its holster and in one quick motion slammed the butt of it directly into the man's ear. The curator screamed and collapsed back onto the floor. Von Studt instantly felt better as blood began to pour out the side of the curator's head.

"What is wrong with you?" Von Studt asked. "Your miserable country has let an invading army capture its capital without even a fight. You should be out in the streets trying to kill Germans. Instead, you're doing paperwork. What the hell did you think was going to happen when the Nazi's took control of Paris?"

"I—"

The curator still couldn't formulate a sentence so Von Studt kicked him in the ribs. "Tell me! I would like to know how cowards think."

"I know where the coin is," the curator finally gasped. "I will show you. Please. Please don't hurt me anymore."

Von Studt smiled. "That's a good fellow. See, I can be a reasonable man."

Once again, he helped the curator stand up. Von Studt waved a finger in his face. "Now show me the coin. And if you try to trick me, I will kill you in such a slow agonizing way, you'll think what just has happened to you was child's play."

The curator nodded and led him out of the office. The man must have suffered a concussion from the blow to his head because Von Studt had to practically carry him up three flights of stairs. He led Von Studt down a hallway lined with priceless paintings of the old masters—Van Gogh, Monet, Goya, Degas and Cezanne.

Von Studt had no interest in the paintings. Others would come later to take them back to Germany. Von Studt only wanted the coin.

They turned off the main hall into another dark hallway. The curator stopped at a door and pulled out a set of keys. After fumbling around for a second, he managed to unlock the door. He flipped on the light and looked back at Von Studt.

"We keep our coins in here when they're not on display."

Von Studt cautiously peered in. The room was small. A long metal table sat in the middle. The only other piece of furniture was a small desk sitting in the corner. Next to the desk was a large, black safe.

The curator pointed. "The coin you want is locked in the safe."

"Open it."

The curator hobbled over to the safe and knelt down. He began twisting the dials then with a click, the safe opened. Von Studt stood directly over him, mostly to make sure he didn't try anything foolish, like pulling a gun on him.

Von Studt stared inside the safe. There must have been thousands of coins, all cataloged and arranged in neat order in wooden boxes. The curator reached in and pulled a small box from the back.

Von Studt grabbed the box from him. "It's in here?"

The curator nodded. Von Studt took the box over to the table. He had dreamed of this day for so long. His hands actually trembled as he opened the lid.

The sight took his breath away. Staring back up at Von Studt were two double daggers—one on each side of the liberty cap. Underneath the daggers ran the inscription, Eid Mar, and next to the inscription, the Roman numeral I.

He had finally found it! The first Double Dagger Denarius minted for Brutus.

Von Studt smiled as he took the coin out of the box. A strange feeling surged through his body as he held it in his hands. He felt as if the coin had been waiting for him, waiting for its rightful owner to take possession of it. He studied the daggers and the portrait of Brutus. A sense of satisfaction and joy welled inside of him.

"How long has the coin been here?" he asked the curator.

The curator shrugged and sat down on the edge of the desk still breathing heavily. "I don't know. It's been here as long as I have worked here."

"How long's that?"

"Thirty-two years."

"What else do you know about the coin's history?"

The curator sighed and wiped a line of sweat off his forehead. "It was rumored that Napoleon stole it from a Moscow coin gallery during his invasion of Russia in 1812."

"Russia," Von Studt replied in amazement. He couldn't take his eyes off the coin.

"What else?" Von Studt asked. He felt as if he needed every possible piece of information regarding the coin's history, its life.

The curator hesitated and then replied, "Fewer than fifty are known to exist, but this one is the most valuable and most important. The coin is in remarkable condition. Almost mint condition, but our staff numismatist has told me he can't scientifically explain the perfect condition of the coin."

"What do you mean?"

"Even though it is silver, there should have been some wear on an object that is almost two thousand years old. But the coin is nearly perfect, as if it was minted yesterday."

Von Studt gestured for him to continue. The curator pointed towards the coin. "See the numeral I next to the inscription."

"Yes."

"Ancient sources say that Brutus had that numeral inscribed into the coin to signify that it was the first coin minted."

Von Studt closed his eyes visualizing Brutus. He felt like—he could almost feel what Caesar's assassin had felt.

He opened his eyes and said to the curator, "This was Brutus' coin. He kept it till his death."

"I have given you what you came for. Will you leave now?"

"Yes, Mister Curator. I will be leaving now. As a matter of fact, I have an important trip. I am going to Malta tomorrow. I'm going to meet The Knight."

The old man looked at him with confusion and pain. Von Studt carefully placed the coin back into the box and pulled the Lugar back out.

"No!" the curator pleaded as he stumbled back against the safe. "You promised me no harm if I gave it to you. Please! Don't . . ."

Von Studt laughed. "I think the Louvre needs a change in management."

He pointed the Lugar at the man who had begun to whimper. Normally, he would take his time torturing him but he couldn't fool around any longer. He really did have to get going. Von Studt pulled the trigger. The shot echoed loudly and the curator fell back against the safe, clutching his stomach. Thick dark blood oozed from between his fingers.

The curator looked up at him with such a mix of emotions that it almost unsettled Von Studt.

"Why?" he wheezed. "You got what you came for."

Von Studt smiled down at him. It amazed him how most people in the world just didn't get it. "That's just the way it works, my good man."

The curator cried out in agony. Von Studt had witnessed plenty of stomach wounds before and he knew being shot in the stomach was probably one of the most painful, agonizing ways to die. He tucked the coin case inside his jacket and turned to leave.

"Please," the curator pleaded, "please don't leave me here like this."

Von Studt stopped. For some reason he had a change of heart. It was untypical of him, but maybe he would show some mercy after all. He pulled his Lugar back out and aimed it at the man's head. "If we ever meet again, my good friend, remember that I took pity on you and saved you from a lifetime of suffering and pain."

"No, I won't, you Nazi bastard!" he spat in Von Studt's direction, "because you'll be rotting in hell!"

Von Studt shook his head and pulled the trigger. He watched in gruesome fascination as the curator's head exploded in a volcano of grayish-red gore.

He stared for a bit at the carnage he had wreaked then tucked the Lugar back inside his jacket and said aloud, "I wonder what got into him. I was only trying to help the man out, show him a little mercy. Oh well, what can you do."

Von Studt walked out of the Louvre whistling a boyhood song his mother used to sing to him. He went back to the hotel to finish the last minute arrangements for his trip to Malta. As he walked down the Parisian sidewalk packed with German soldiers, a feeling of invincibility filled him. It was, as if, the Double Dagger coin now completed him.

Chapter 4

The Swiss cargo plane had been airborne for two hours and except for the two Luftwaffe pilots, Von Studt was the only passenger. He sat in the large open hold, strapped to a hard metal seat.

He stared out of the tiny window as the plane flew over the Southern Alps. White tipped mountain peaks jutted high into the sky. He watched as the right wing dipped suddenly. The plane shook violently and he grabbed the edge of his seat. He had been warned to expect turbulence due to the unstable air in the mountain passes, but this was ridiculous.

Von Studt reached inside his jacket and pulled out a large flask. He took a long pull of the strong whisky, inhaling deeply as the magic liquid flowed down his throat into his belly. He took six more deep drinks then closed his eyes, praying that he wouldn't dream about the forest. Despite the heavy turbulence, he drifted off to sleep, and awoke only when he felt the hard bump of the wheels touching down. He was in Malta.

He stared out of the window as the plane taxied down the runway and made its way over to the hangar. The only activity he saw in the entire airport was a herd of scraggly goats milling about in a grassy field.

Von Studt unlatched his harness, grabbed his bag and made his way over to the cargo door. The plane abruptly stopped and he stood there anxiously for a few minutes until the cargo hold was opened. He was too impatient to wait for a ladder. He jumped down onto the tarmac while shielding his eyes from the bright sunlight.

When his eyes adjusted, he saw a man dressed in a brown monk's tunic walking towards him.

"Colonel Von Studt," the man replied in broken German. "My name is Ignia. I am to escort you to the Fort Saint Angelo. Please follow me."

Von Studt followed the monk through the hangar to a waiting car, a brand new black Rolls-Royce. Ignia whisked them through the Maltan countryside at a high rate of speed. The island was a rocky, picturesque place. He saw more animals than people and except for a few old cars and an occasional tractor, the island looked as if it probably hadn't changed for hundreds of years.

But Von Studt hadn't come to Malta to admire the scenery. He was here to fulfill a secret mission for the Fuhrer, and in doing so, gain more insight and knowledge about The Order.

After a twenty minute trip, the Rolls came over a steep hill and on top of a rocky promontory, sticking out into the Grand Harbor, was the massive stone citadel, the headquarters of The Order, Fort Saint Angelo. As they got closer, Von Studt estimated that the wall surrounding the castle had to be at least fifty feet high with a twenty foot wide moat directly in front.

Von Studt broke the mutual silence and said to the driver, "That is quite a Fortress."

Ignia nodded his head. "The castle has stood for ages. It was extensively rebuilt by the Knights of Saint John in 1530."

"Has the wall ever been breached?" he asked.

The monk looked back at him in the rear view mirror with a wry smile on his face. "No. The closest it ever came to being breeched was during the great siege of 1565. Seven hundred knights with five thousand men defeated more than thirty thousand Turks after a five months siege."

Von Studt shrugged. In 1565 the castle was probably impregnable, but not today. Give him three Panzer tanks and he could destroy the entire castle within an hour.

They approached a large iron gate guarded by soldiers dressed in elaborate, almost ancient looking, military uniforms. The scene looked straight out of the middle ages. The men were tall, dark skinned and they all wore a light suit of armor with a purple and red shield covering the breastplate. On top of their heads were bright hats with plumes of peacock feathers sticking out of the back.

The Rolls was immediately waved through and it crossed over a stone bridge through the castle's wall. The car approached another series of gates and once again they were cleared through by another series of guards. The Rolls pulled down a circular gravel driveway and halted in front of the castle. A tall thin man dressed in a black tuxedo stood at attention outside of the castle's entrance. He walked over to the car as Von Studt was getting out.

"Colonel Von Studt," he announced in a friendly manner. "Allow me to introduce myself. I am Werner Johanssen."

The two men shook hands.

"I am the Knight's concierge. I trust you had a good flight?"

"It was fine. Thank you."

"Excellent. Welcome to Saint Angelo. I will escort you to your room. I'm sure you need a little time to freshen up."

Johanssen took his bag from him. "The Knight is expecting you for dinner at six. Until then, I am at your disposal. Please follow me."

Von Studt followed Johanssen up the giant brick stairs and into the castle. If he thought the castle was big from the outside, the sheer opulence of the interior left him speechless.

The entrance hall was practically as large as any building he had ever been in. The domed ceiling rose seventy-five feet and it was adorned with solid gold moldings. He followed Johanssen through a maze of hallways, rooms, and stairwells, all exquisitely decorated with expensive furniture and priceless artwork.

Johanssen finally stopped in front of a large mahogany door. He pulled out a single large key and opened the door. "I hope your quarters are satisfactory."

Von Studt looked into the spacious, eloquently decorated room. "It's fine. Thank you."

Johanssen set his lone bag down next to the bed. "If you need anything, dial 315. I will meet you back here at five-to-six to escort you to dinner."

Von Studt nodded and watched as Johanssen disappeared down the long hallway. He walked over to a large window and pulled open the curtains. His room was near the back of the castle and he had a spectacular view of the Grand Harbor.

A bottle of wine sat on a table in front of the window. Von Studt opened it and poured himself a large glass. He stared out at the estate which stretched as far as he could see.

He took a sip of the sweet, luxuriant nectar and whistled as it washed gently down his throat. "Damn, that's good stuff."

He walked over to a massive bookcase lining two entire walls, and slowly ran his hand along the books. There must have been thousands of books packed onto the shelves that ran from the floor all the way to the top of the fifteen-foot ceiling. The books looked ancient. He pulled one out from the shelf and blew a fine layer of dust off the spine.

When was the last time anyone had read one of these things? The book was bound in thick, hard leather, and the pages were stiff, worn from the passage of many, many years. He flipped through the old book. Von Studt was proud that foreign languages came naturally to him. He could speak German, French and English fluently, and could also manage to get by in Italian and Russian.

But the words in the book were unlike any he had ever seen. They seemed to be some strange mix of Egyptian hieroglyphics and Hebrew. Perhaps the books were written in some ancient language that no longer exists. He pulled a few more of the books out and they all were written in the same strange language.

After a while Von Studt grew bored paging though the indecipherable books and returned them back to their spots on the bookcase. If he got the chance, maybe he would ask the Knight about it later. Von Studt changed into the only other outfit he had brought, and waited for six o' clock.

Chapter 5

At precisely five-to-six, Von Studt heard a polite knock. He opened the door and Johanssen stood there, still dressed in his black tuxedo.

"Colonel." He motioned for Von Studt to follow him.

They walked a great distance through another confusing array of halls and passages. They came to an open, sparsely-decorated hall, and stopped in front of a room that appeared to be a small study.

Johanssen showed him in. "The Knight will be down shortly. Please make yourself comfortable."

Johanssen disappeared again and Von Studt nervously paced the floor. He had no idea what to expect of the Knight. He had never seen a picture of the man and he deliberately tried to clear his mind of any preconceived notions regarding him. Some things were best to be experienced first hand.

However, there was one thing Von Studt was certain of, although the Knight was not a president, a dictator or a king, his rule and influence stretched from continent to continent. He was perhaps the greatest puppet master the world had ever known. Even the President of the United States didn't know that many of his own decisions were shaped by a man most of the world didn't know existed—a man who lived on a tiny island in the middle of the Mediterranean Sea.

Unlike Von Studt's meetings with Hitler, the Knight did not keep him waiting. A few moments after Johanssen left, a tall, distinguished looking man wearing a plain purple robe entered the room. Von Studt's heart skipped a beat.

"Colonel Von Studt," he said in perfect German. "It is nice to finally meet you."

His accent surprised Von Studt. The Knight sounded as if he had spent his entire life in Berlin.

The Knight wore a brown pair of sandals and, except for a dark red sash around his waist, wore no other garments or jewelry. He seemed to be in his late sixties and appeared to be in excellent shape. He had thick silver hair with sharp, alert facial features.

The Knight walked over with his hand extended. Von Studt grasped it. "My Knight, it is an honor to meet you."

Von Studt had never knelt to anyone, including Hitler, but the Knight gave off such an aura of power and knowledge that he felt almost compelled to show his servitude to the man. Before Von Studt realized what he was doing, he had knelt on one knee and began kissing the Knight's hand.

The Knight motioned for him to rise. "Please Colonel, call me Damascus. Formalities are not necessary here."

Von Studt rose. The two men were about the same height. The Knight had lively, clear gray eyes but a very un-Nordic, rather thick nose, and very dark skin.

"Your presence here puts you at a level that very few people will ever achieve," the Knight said.

"I am here to serve you and The Order."

Damascus smiled. "We all serve The Order." He touched Von Studt on the forearm. "Come. Let us enjoy dinner first. Then we will have our discussion."

As if he was eavesdropping on their conversation, Johanssen arrived and announced, "Gentlemen. Dinner is served."

"After you, Colonel." Damascus gestured.

Johanssen escorted them out of the study, down another series of hallways and into a small dining room. The room had a low ceiling and was dark. Almost every inch of wall space was covered with paintings of medieval battle scenes. A small fire lit up the far end of the room, and the only other light came from candles sitting on the dinner table.

"I like to use this room when I am entertaining small numbers of guests. I think it is more comfortable, more intimate than sitting in the formal banquet room," Damascus said while motioning for Von Studt to take a seat at the table.

Von Studt sat down and a waiter, dressed in a white tuxedo, appeared with a bottle of red wine. After pouring each man a glass, Damascus raised his glass, "To the success of Germany and The Order. Our fates are intertwined."

Von Studt raised his glass. "To The Order."

Both men took a sip of the wine and the Knight said, "So Colonel, Adolph has told me you have quite a fascination with Ancient Rome."

"Yes, it was quite a fascinating period. Ever since I was a boy, I have read everything I could find about the Roman Empire. I also collect coins from the same period."

"Any of importance?"

Von Studt beamed. The Knight obviously was a man who shared his same passion for the Roman Empire.

"Yes, as a matter of fact." He reached inside his suit jacket and pulled out the Double Dagger coin. He stood up and walked over to The Knight's chair.

"I believe you know a little about this coin. The Double Dagger Eids of March coin struck by Brutus after the assassination of Caesar."

Von Studt handed the coin to the Knight and returned to his chair. He watched with pride as the Knight moved a candle closer and intently studied the coin.

After a few moments, he looked up at Von Studt with astonishment. "It is magnificent. I have come across references to this coin many times in my readings but I can't believe I am actually holding it." The Knight looked back down at the coin.

Von Studt smiled even more broadly knowing the Knight had seen and understood what made this particular coin so special. "It is magnificent. Isn't it?"

"Unbelievable. I really can't believe it exists," Damascus exclaimed.

"I spent three decades trying to find it. Finally, I tracked it down. It had been in the Louvre for decades. The only Double Dagger coin ever minted with the numeral I, given by Rome's mintmaster directly to Brutus."

"Absolutely astonishing." The Knight handed the coin across the table to Von Studt.

"You know, I have quite an extensive library of ancient manuscripts from both the Greek and Roman cultures. Perhaps on another trip, when we have more time, we can discuss our passions."

"I would like that very much. And I meant to ask you Damascus, the books in my bedroom. What language are they written in? I have never seen anything quite like it."

The Knight stared over at him with a strange expression. He didn't reply and Von Studt began to feel tense. Had he asked an inappropriate question?

Finally, Damascus smiled, but it was a cautious smile, a smile Von Studt had learned to recognize. It was a smile of deceit.

"Those books are written in an ancient language that no longer exists—a language that dates back before even the Trojan War. The books are priceless. They . . ." Damascus paused as a waiter entered the room with the first course.

The plates were set and Damascus began eating without finishing his sentence. Von Studt wondered if he was hiding something. Much to Von Studt's disappointment, the books and Double Dagger coin were not discussed any further.

The rest of the meal passed with the conversation centered almost entirely on Germany's recent military victories and its war campaign. After dinner, Damascus led him to a library where they sat by a roaring fire. A servant brought out cigars and a snifter of cognac.

"I suppose, Colonel, you would like to know why you have flown all this way."

"The Fuhrer said you had a message for me to bring back to him," Von Studt replied while lighting his cigar.

Damascus lit his cigar and blew out a large stream of smoke before taking a drink of his brandy. He turned towards Von Studt. "Do you believe in fate?"

Von Studt wondered if he was being tested. "Yes."

"Good. Because to move to a higher level within The Order, this can only be achieved through one's increased knowledge and understanding. That is it. No elections, no tests, no awards, no ceremony. Only when fate and those with higher knowledge believe you are ready, only then can it happen. Bloodlines and knowledge are the true keys—the only things that ultimately matter.

"I know your bloodlines run deep, but your knowledge of The Order, its reasons for existing, its ultimate purpose, is still quite limited."

Von Studt felt his heart pounding inside of his chest. Was he going to learn something of great importance and meaning?

The Knight continued, "But I think your fate is about to change. The Order is made up of hundreds of thousands of pures. Some don't even know they are part of The Order, not yet, at least."

The Knight raised his finger and then added, "That is how we have managed to exist for all these millennia. You have served us well over your lives and it is now time for you to take the next step. It is important to remember . . . we do not recognize one through pomp and ceremony, but only through increased knowledge. Your actions and place are known and will always be known. So, all I will explain to you at this time is the message I want you to give Hitler, and what it means."

Damascus stood. He walked over to the fireplace and threw his cigar into it. He turned back towards Von Studt.

"Sometime in late 1941, the Japanese will attack America at Pearl Harbor in Hawaii."

The declaration shocked Von Studt. Was it possible? How could the Knight possibly know this?

"After which," Damascus continued, "the United States Government will declare war on both Japan and Germany. The Japanese attack will be known in advance by certain high ranking United States officials, but they will do nothing to stop it."

A thousand thoughts ran through Von Studt's head. Did the Knight actually infer that officials within the United States Government, quite possibly the President, knew about Japan's intent to attack the United States? And they weren't going to do anything to stop it?

The Knight must have noticed the confusion on his face. He smiled broadly. "There is much you do not know or understand. Have you ever heard of the Architeuthis dux?"

"No. I don't believe I have."

"Most people haven't, which is why it is the most mysterious, elusive animal in the world."

"Mysterious?"

"Yes, the Architeuthis dux is one of the largest animals on the planet. It can grow as long as seventy-five feet."

"Seventy-five feet," Von Studt repeated, trying to think of an animal that big.

The Knight nodded. "Only the blue whale is larger. And yet, almost no one in the world has ever seen it. But I assure you it exists. The animal is the giant ocean squid. It stays far below the surface of the ocean, hidden. In its kingdom, it is the most feared predator around. The Order is like the giant squid. It stays hidden, out of sight, but its power is far reaching. And just like the giant squid, our tentacles are spread throughout the world.

"There is little doubt that the United States will ultimately defeat Japan, but this battle will serve two purposes for us. First, it will eliminate the Japanese as an economic and military power; but more importantly, the Pacific front will weaken the United States enough that they will be forced to abandon their European war efforts. Eventually, they will have to sue for peace. Then, the initial phase of the plan will be complete. Europe will be united under one rule and after the next election in the United States, America will be led by individuals who, shall we say—are quite sympathetic to our causes."

Von Studt nodded in understanding.

It all made so much sense and for the first time in the night, he heard Damascus' voice take on a hint of emotion. "It is then that The Order will emerge from the depths of its hiding place. The world will be forced to kneel to our rule. That is the message I want you to take to Adolph."

The depth of the Knight's message left Von Studt in awe. It was complex, a stroke of pure genius. "I will give Hitler the message," he replied.

Damascus drank the rest of his brandy then added, "You'll be escorted to the air field and flown back to France tonight."

"It is an honor to serve you, Damascus."

Damascus shook his hand. "Because of men like you, Colonel, The Order will succeed this time. The world will be ours."

Von Studt watched with a feeling of belonging as Damascus left the room.

Johanssen entered with his bag. "Colonel, your plane is waiting."

Chapter 6

APRIL 21, 1945— Five years after Germany invaded France and Von Studt's return from Malta.

Von Studt stared out of the restaurant's window while sipping stale, bitter coffee. The sky was an ugly dark gray, and even the light rain that fell took on a dirty grayish hue.

His coffee was cold but it didn't matter. Nothing did, now. Germany and the Third Reich had been defeated. He reached inside his jacket and pulled out the case. He took out the Double Dagger coin and held in his hand. "Even you have failed me," he spoke to the coin.

It was agonizing to think that the coin that had once meant so much to him had also lost its power—just like Hitler, Germany and The Order. He rubbed the double daggers somehow wishing it would rekindle the magic the coin once held but he knew it was too late, far too late. He looked at the portrait of Brutus and wondered if SS Colonel Maxwell Von Studt was marching down the same path of self-inflicted destruction.

As Von Studt stared out of the window, the sight of the defeated-looking German people huddled against the cold wind, depressed him even more than the gloomy weather. He watched a woman in a shabby black overcoat walking down the sidewalk towards the café. Her head was tucked low as she tried to shield herself from the biting wind.

As she passed the window in front of him, for the briefest moment their eyes met. In them, Von Studt saw defeat and despair. He had seen that look before. The woman had the same expression of hopelessness as the French people did after Germany had taken Paris. He couldn't understand where it had gone so wrong.

Von Studt could hardly believe almost five years had passed since he returned to Paris to give Hitler the message from the Knight. Everything at the time had gone perfectly. The initial phase of the final solution and the thousand-year rule had proceeded exactly as planned. The air attacks against London had severely demoralized the Brits. The southern part of Russia had fallen and the United States was preoccupied with its Pacific war against the Japanese. Field Marshal Rommel, with Italy's help, had secured Northern Africa; and the final solution to get rid of the Jews had been successfully implemented.

Then inexplicably, Nazi advances abruptly stopped, and by mid-1943, the tides of the war had begun to go against Germany. First, Northern Africa was lost. Then, Russia had pushed Germany completely across the border. The losses from these campaigns were staggering, and 1944 brought even larger defeats.

The United States had staged a massive attack at Normandy, and their troops were advancing the western battle lines into Germany. And to make matters worse, the Russians were pushing just as hard. The eastern front had collapsed and Germany's forces were in full retreat.

The last time he had met with Hitler, the Furher looked twenty years older than his fifty-five years. He could hardly believe the transformation that had taken place in just a year's time. Hitler's skin had taken on an almost grayish color. His eyes were glassy, almost as if he was continuously medicated, and worse of all, he acted completely paranoid, almost delusional most of the time.

Von Studt sighed as he thought back to the explosion that had occurred at The Wolves Lair—Hitler's Prussian headquarters. He looked at his watch and it dawned on him that the assassination attempt took place exactly six months ago, almost to the hour.

A bomb had been planted in a briefcase hidden underneath a table where Hitler sat. Four of his staff officers were killed but miraculously Hitler escaped with only minor injuries.

After the assassination attempt, Hitler's mental and physical health took a turn for the worse. Hitler blamed Von Studt for the attempt, at least to the extent that Von Studt should have been aware of it and done something to prevent it. Their relationship had seriously soured since then, and there had been times when Von Studt seriously thought his life was in danger.

After the failed assassination attempt, thousands of men, regardless of their guilt, were executed. The preferred method of killing: hanging by piano wire, or in some cases, forced suicide. But the worst fate was left to those who were carted off to slow, miserable deaths at one of the concentration camps. Even the German war hero, Field Marshal Erwin Rommel, was not spared. He took poison to save his family from being executed.

The Third Reich had imploded upon itself.

Von Studt drank the rest of his coffee only out of habit, while pondering his fate. Germany had lost the war. If he survived the coming battles against the Russians and Americans, he had no doubt that he would be executed for war crimes.

A haggard looking waitress stopped by the table and refilled his coffee without uttering a sound. Von Studt watched her walk away.

"It is time," he replied. He had been preparing for this possibility for almost a year now. He owed it to The Order. He must survive to carry on the bloodlines and what knowledge he had gained.

He had spent months establishing an escape route that would take him to South America. The trip would be dangerous, filled with great risks, but he had absolutely nothing to lose. If he stayed here, he would die one way or another. Everything was in place. He would leave Germany the day after tomorrow.

But first, there was one last bit of business—a meeting with Hitler and his few remaining officers. The meeting was scheduled for tonight in Hitler's underground Chancellery bunker. Von Studt desperately didn't want to attend but he had no choice. He couldn't even fathom what Hitler wanted to discuss. The man was now so unstable that anything was possible.

He picked the coin up from the table and placed it back into its case. It would be the only possession, other than his guns and gold that he would take on his voyage out of this hell.

His spirits brightened as he reminded himself that his current situation was similar to that of Aeneas who had escaped the carnage of Troy and carried the Palladium to Italy to begin anew. Maybe this had been the master plan all along. Maybe he was the chosen and, like Aeneas, he would escape and bring the Double Dagger coin to South America. There, he and The Order would start over.

Chapter 7

Von Studt chain-smoked cigarettes as every fiber in his body screamed for him to run, to get out of Hitler's bunker. But all he could do was sit there, waiting for Hitler's dismissal. Two servants entered the small dining room and without speaking began clearing the dishes from the table.

Around the circular table sat what was left of Hitler's closest confidants. No one spoke. They only listened to Hitler's incoherent babble. The tension in the room had become unbearable. And to make matters worse, the underground bunker was hot, and the air was stagnant and polluted from all the heavy smoking. Von Studt felt as if he was suffocating.

Hitler rose. He was pale. Sweat glistened on his face, and his right hand shook violently.

"Failure," he replied softly while looking downward.

Von Studt watched as the other officers looked around at each other, obviously thinking the same thing as him. The man they had trusted their lives and futures to—had gone insane.

Hitler began to walk around the table. "Each one of you has failed me, some more than others. The blame of The Third Reich's defeat lies solely among the men in this room."

Von Studt lit another cigarette. He only had two left in the pack.

Hitler suddenly began screaming, "The Third Reich has been defeated! The Order crushed!"

Von Studt watched as Hitler's face lost its pale white color and turned a deep crimson red. "There are traitors, cowards in this room. Men, who from the beginning, were set on sabotaging us."

Von Studt inhaled deeply, trying to get some fresh oxygen into his lungs. Hitler looked directly at him and what Von Studt saw sent a chill through his body. In Hitler's eyes, Von Studt saw complete emptiness. The man had simply ceased to exist.

"There is a Brutus seated at this table," said Hitler as he paced around the outside of the table. He stopped directly behind Von Studt's chair. Von Studt resisted the urge to turn and face him. He could feel beads of sweat running down his back. He wiped his brow as his heart hammered inside of his chest.

"Colonel Von Studt."

He felt Hitler's hands on the back on his shoulder and it was all he could do not to jump out of the chair and run out of the bunker.

"Yes, Fuhrer," he replied, still with back to Hitler.

"Why don't you tell all of us the story of Brutus since you know it so well."

A chill ran down his spine. "Furher, I . . ."

His chair was violently spun around. Hitler grabbed at the inside of his jacket and pulled out the case holding the Double Dagger coin. He opened it, holding out the coin for everyone to see.

"Why don't you tell us the history of this coin—a coin that you take such great pleasure to carry with you at all times."

Von Studt's mind raced. Hitler was a madman. Was this some type of a test, a trap? Had he been singled out to be a final scapegoat?

He had no choice but to answer, "It is the Eids of Mar coin. It is nothing but a memento, a good luck charm. The coin means nothing more."

"And who minted this coin?" Hitler asked.

Von Studt winced. "Brutus."

Hitler looked out at the other officers. "Brutus. A man who committed the most egregious acts ever. A man who betrayed Julius Caesar. A man who betrayed the Second Reich."

Hitler's hands now shook uncontrollably. No one in the room made a sound. "Caesar was not murdered by one of his country's enemies. No. He died at the hands of one of his own. A man he trusted."

Hitler looked down at Von Studt and pointed an accusing finger in his face. "Et tu Brute!" he shouted in Latin, then followed in German, "and you Von Studt. After everything I gave you. You repay me by stabbing me in the back."

"This is madness!" Von Studt yelled. "Your accusations are false. Everyone in this room knows it!"

He began to rise but was pushed back down by Hitler. A soldier guarding the entrance rushed over with the barrel of his rifle aimed directly at his chest.

"Is that so? Let's ask them. Who here would like to defend the Colonel?"

Hitler threw the coin down onto the table and spun Von Studt's chair back around so that he was now facing the officers again. He saw hatred in their eyes, not necessarily for him, but for the position they were now all in. Predictably, no one came to his defense, and Von Studt realized that he might be the first to die in this room, but every man here was doomed.

"You have all failed me." Hitler pointed to each officer. "But none like Brutus." He returned his attention to Von Studt. "It saddens me to realize that the man I trusted and gave everything to—is a British spy."

Von Studt felt a wave of anger and desperation rise in him. "Fuhrer, I protest. This is—"

A crushing blow hit the back of his head, followed by an explosion of pain, then blackness.

The throbbing that ran from the base of his skull through his temples and into his eyes brought him back to consciousness. Von Studt didn't know how long he had been out. He tried to move but couldn't. He looked down and saw his wrists and ankles bound to the chair. After a few confusing moments, he remembered the dinner, Hitler and his absurd accusations.

As his mind processed what had happened, Von Studt knew he didn't have to worry about escaping to South America any longer. He would never leave the bunker alive. After a few minutes his vision cleared and he saw that he was alone in the room except for a soldier sitting in a chair by the doorway with a rifle pointed at him.

He stared at the young man's face and spoke softly, "Get out of the bunker the first chance you can. You'll die if you stay here."

The soldier, who looked more like a boy, didn't respond, but Von Studt saw uncertainty in his face. "It's too late for me. Get out. I promise you. You don't want to be here when the Russians arrive. At least out there, you have a small chance of living."

The soldier began to say something but stopped as Hitler entered the room.

"You may leave," Hitler snapped.

The soldier quickly glanced at Von Studt with a look of what appeared to be gratitude. Hitler approached the table and picked up the Double Dagger coin. He waved it in front of Von Studt.

"You've gone mad, Fuhrer," Von Studt said.

"I am mad, you say?" Hitler began laughing hysterically. "Is that so? Well, I think it is the other way around, Maxwell. I cannot believe how naïve and stupid men like you are. To actually believe in some kind of master race, that your bloodlines are superior to others."

"What the hell are you talking about?" Von Studt demanded.

"Here." He placed a one-page document in front of Von Studt's face. It was dated January 30, 1933—the date Hitler became chancellor of Germany.

"This is my third book. The one I promised I would let you read one day. Go ahead. It is very short—only one page long."

Von Studt began reading. It was simple a communiqué from an individual named Joseph Weinstein acknowledging that one hundred-million Reichmarks had been wired from the Swiss bank, Banque Cantonale de Geneve, to the Reichsbank for further credit to the account of the Nazi Party and Adolph Hitler.

"Finished?" Hitler asked.

"Yes. So what," Von Studt replied, not sure what the memo was supposed to mean.

"You see, Maxwell, *Mein Kampf*, the history of The Order, the Third Reich, the Aryan race—all of that was nonsense. A smokescreen. An elaborate diversion created so that men like you could be used to serve a purpose. I perpetuated it among you fools only because I needed your help. I wanted to rule the world. I wanted men, women and children all to bow to me. And I needed naïve, delusional men like yourself to help me."

Von Studt's mind raced. Could it be true? Could everything Von Studt believed in, everything he based his life on, all be a lie told by a madman?

"But what about Damascus?" Von Studt asked.

"Damascus." Hitler laughed. "I just showed you who Damascus really is."

He stuck the letter back in front of Von Studt's face. "That is Damascus' real name." Von Studt looked at the letter again signed by Joseph Weinstein.

"I don't understand?"

"Damascus' real name is Joseph Weinstein. And this is the best part, the man you called Damascus is actually a German born Jew."

"You're lying."

"Am I?"

Von Studt looked into Hitler's eyes and despite the fact that the man had gone insane, he realized he was telling the truth.

"Weinstein made a fortune selling arms, primarily poison gases, during World War One. He sold his heinous wares to all sides. And, after the war, every country, every paid assassin in the world was after him. There probably has never been a man with a larger bounty placed on his head. I sheltered him, protected him, but at a cost.

"Do you think the Nazi party just had money sitting in some bank, waiting for me to get out of prison and take over Germany? Weinstein and I formed a partnership, one that benefited both of us. He bankrolled the Nazi party, and I saved his life. I provided protection and gave him the shelter and security of his island, along with the ability to continue to transact his business without hindrance . . . as long as it didn't interfere with my goals."

Hitler laughed. "It is quite astonishing, isn't it?"

"But what about Damascus' books, the language they were written in. Isn't that proof?"

"You just won't face reality, will you? Weinstein was a fanatic, a mindless zealot just like you. Part of our deal was, when I set him up in Malta, I had to guarantee safe passage for his precious books. He told me some crazy story that the books were written in the first language of humans.

"Weinstein believed in some biblical story that before the tower of Babel, all humans spoke the same language. He claimed the books were written in ancient Hebrew. The first language, supposedly. Complete nonsense, of course.

But Weinstein was just as delusional, just as foolish as you."

Von Studt thought about his mother. Had she been lying to him all along as well? He now only wanted death, a death that was final, without rebirth or a new life.

He felt a hand on his shoulder. Von Studt didn't bother to put up a struggle. He knew what would happen next. He welcomed it.

"Good luck, Brutus," Hitler replied.

He felt the end of the gun press up against the back of his head. Von Studt took a deep breath—his last.

A massive explosion rocked the center of Von Studt's brain, ending his existence—for now.

Chapter 8

Hitler stared at the coin. His only solace was that his fate was soon to be the same as Caesar's, and two thousand years later, Caesar was still known for the empire he had built.

"Do you think that will be my legacy as well, Eva?" he asked.

His new wife was slumped over the couch. It had only taken a few minutes for the cyanide to perform its magic.

Hitler stood from the chair and sat down on the couch next to his wife's lifeless body. "I'm sorry the honeymoon was so quick, but there was nothing I could do about it. It's better this way, my love. If the Russians captured us alive—"

Hitler set the Double Dagger coin on the table next to the couch and loaded the Luger.

"I will see you shortly, my love." He kissed her cold lips.

Even deep inside his bunker Hitler could hear the shelling and gunfire from above. They were close now.

He put the gun to his head—

BOOK IV

Greed is Good
Gordon Gekko, Wall Street

Chapter 1

Spring, New York City

"The Trader" incessantly tapped at the computer keyboard. "C'mon. C'mon," he muttered under his breath. Only a few more ticks in the price and he would be out. It didn't matter that he already had a huge profit in the position. He was holding out for every last dollar.

"Almost there, c'mon baby. Don't let me down now."

The Trader was locked in that magical place known to all professional traders as the "Money Zone," and it meant that no matter what he bought or sold, he was making money doing it. The mass of noise and confusion surrounding him on the trading floor went completely unnoticed. The only thing he saw, the only thing he felt, was the constantly changing prices that flashed across his computer screen.

"One more tick," he whispered to the numbers in an almost intimate fashion.

"There!" It was time to get out. He picked up a black phone and punched a single button. The direct line rang only once.

"Jane," answered his trader from just outside the bond pit on the floor of the Chicago Board of Trade. Even with the chaos in the background, her slightly husky yet completely feminine voice aroused him.

"Sell the entire position," he calmly instructed.

"You got it," she replied.

The line went dead and Jack Weston, aka The Trader, grinned. He watched the computer monitor as the volume of the bond futures suddenly spiked indicating that Jane had liquidated the position.

He grabbed his calculator and every time he hit the equal button he got the same figure. His position had just netted him thirty-nine million dollars, give or take a few pennies, depending on the execution prices Jane received for the entire position.

His black phone rang. "Tell me the good news," he answered cheerfully. Even over the phone the roar of the bond traders in the background was deafening.

"You just did very well for yourself, Jacky-Boy," the smoky voice purred into his ear. "You're completely out at an average price of 110.15."

"All right baby!" Jack pumped his fist. The price was even higher than he expected, but it didn't surprise him. Jane was the best bond trader on the floor. That's why he paid her so well. Of course, her sexy voice, raven-thick hair and sultry, "I don't give a damn," good looks didn't hurt either. Jack leaned back in the chair and propped his feet up on the desk.

"Hey Jane," he said in a swaggering tone. "How 'bout I jump on the next flight to Chicago and we go out for happy hour to celebrate the trade with a few cocktails?"

She laughed in a teasing way that only served to instigate him even more.

"Then after that," he continued, encouraged by her initial response, "we'll head over to the restaurant of your choice, I'll book us the presidential suite over at the Ritz Carlton, order up a few bottles of Dom Perignon, some of that Ossetra Russian Caviar you always talk about, and maybe . . . we'll discuss some trading strategies I have been thinking about."

Jack knew Jane was engaged to some humorless though wealthy corporate attorney, but that didn't stop him from playing the game. Anyway, he knew she loved it.

"Hmmm. That sounds great, Jack," she said in her typically seductive voice, "but, I don't think your high society lady friend—what's her name? Susan?—would think too kindly about it. Now would she, Jacky-Boy?"

"I won't tell if you don't," he answered slyly.

She laughed again. "Oh Jack, it's a tempting offer, but you couldn't possibly get here in time for happy hour. So, I guess I'll have to take a rain check."

Jack groaned. She was so damn practical. They had played this game many times, and even though he was half-kidding, if she ever said yes, he would be on the next flight out of LaGuardia.

He couldn't let her off that easy, however, and continued the banter, "But I could still get there for the best part—the Ritz, the champagne. I'm thinking of going long in a certain position, and I'd really like to see what you think about it." Jack put his hand over the phone and laughed.

"I bet you would like that, Jacky-Boy," she cooed. "Tell Susan I said hi. Bye darling."

The line went dead and Jack set the phone down. He took his feet off the desk and sat back in his chair. "Not too bad of a day, ol' Jacky-Boy." He smiled. "Not too bad."

Jack Weston stood up and surveyed the trading floor. He was tall, almost six-feet-two, and there wasn't an ounce of fat on his sturdy, forty-two-year-old frame. He wore a fabulously expensive, custom-tailored suit with all the appropriate trappings of someone in his position: a white designer dress shirt, blue silk tie, solid gold cufflinks and black dress shoes. The shoes alone had cost him two thousand dollars.

In recent years, "The Street" had gone to a more casual attire, but not him. He wouldn't dream of not wearing a suit and tie to work. It was a simple but undeniable fact—men of power and accomplishment wore suits, not cheesy khakis and open collar shirts.

He ran a hand through his thick black hair. He wore it combed straight back, and every morning he added just a touch of hair gel to keep it exactly in place. A pair of black-as-coal eyes offset his chiseled facial features and light olive skin. He was a good-looking man, and he knew it.

As he surveyed the trading floor, his trading floor, a feeling of pride and accomplishment swept over him. He had come a long way from the rough streets of west Philadelphia. Unlike most of his peers on Wall Street, he didn't have a privileged, wealthy upbringing.

When he was twelve, his mother had run off to California with a carpet salesman leaving him and his dad to fend for themselves. The last he had heard, the carpet salesman had left his mother for some younger bimbo, and she had gone to work as a secretary at a used car lot. But that had been over ten years ago and for all he knew, she might be dead. Either way, he really didn't care.

Jack's father had been a freelance plumber and handyman. That was when he could pull himself away from the horse track. His father hadn't been a bad man and Jack even had had some affection for him. At least his father hadn't deserted him like his mother had. It was just that his father loved certain things in life a little bit more than his son—those things being cards, horses and booze.

But his father's passions eventually caught up with him and at the ripe old age of forty-four, he died of a massive heart attack. Jack had just graduated from high school and he was saddened by his father's death, but not surprised.

He still remembered the day after the funeral. A friend of his father's, a seedy attorney named Fishbourne, had come over to inform Jack that his father had left a life insurance policy for him. The policy paid thirty-five thousand dollars, and Fishbourne had tried his best to convince Jack to allow him to invest it.

Jack had grown up in a tough environment, a survival of the fittest atmosphere. He wasn't a fool, so despite the attorney's insistent pleas, he adamantly refused. Jack knew the crooked lawyer would either have stolen the money outright or lost it on some get-rich-quick scheme.

There was no doubt that any one of his neighborhood acquaintances would have blown through the money in no time, wasting it on booze, drugs, horses or women; but not Jack. Every single night when he went to bed, he dreamed of only one thing—getting the hell out of Philly and making something of his life. More specifically, he wanted money, and the prestige and power it brought. The day the check for the life insurance money arrived in the mail, he left Philly for good and enrolled at City University in New York.

He rented an insect infested, one-room studio apartment where he studied finance at night, and worked full-time at Stanley McCallister Investment Bank during the day. He made almost no money working for the brokerage, but that wasn't why he took the job. In his view of the world, to be somebody meant working on Wall Street, and this was the only way for him to get a foot in the door.

Despite working during the day, Jack managed to graduate with honors with a business degree in finance. The day he graduated, he skipped the ceremony and went to the house of a trader who had taken a liking to him. Jack begged the man to take him on as a full-time employee and only after Jack refused to leave his house did the trader finally relent and hire him as a trading assistant.

Now, twenty years later, Jack was the head trader for Stanley McCallister—the most profitable, most prestigious investment bank on Wall Street.

However, the road he had taken to the top had not always been a smooth one. There had been a lot of spilt blood along the way, but that's the way The Street worked. Only the strong survived and Jack had a remarkable penchant for self-preservation.

He stared up at a series of circular clocks lining a section of the wall. On Wall Street, time was money, and the clocks displayed the local times for every major city in the world. And in New York, capital of the business world, it was just before four o'clock on a beautiful spring Friday.

Jack looked across the trading floor studying the faces of the other traders as they talked and sometimes yelled into their phones. He could tell by their facial expressions and mannerisms whether they had made or lost money for the day. It was a type of sixth sense he had developed over the years.

The massive trading floor covered the entire twenty-second floor of a thirty-two story building owned by the investment bank. The building was located on Fifth Avenue, and was the Rolls-Royce of office buildings with no expense spared. Jack had personally rebuilt the trading floor five years ago when he took over as head trader. The floor was about as large as a football field and there was not a single private office.

Sixty-seven traders sat side-by-side in the center of the floor, all connected by a tangled mass of desks, computers and telephones.

Outside of the trading floor were the "sidelines" where an enormous support staff handled all of the traders' administrative and technical issues. Jack looked up to see where the stock market was trading. Stretching along the top of all four walls, huge black and green tickers displayed every bit of financial, market and economic information possible.

Years ago, large windows ran along the far wall overlooking Fifth Avenue; but, much to the dismay, even anger, of his traders, Jack had contractors close them in. He wanted his traders concentrating on the markets, not daydreaming about their upcoming weekend in the Hamptons.

And with regards to the support staff's protests, he had none. All he cared about was making sure they did their jobs so his traders could to do theirs—make money.

Jack's desk on the floor was situated where the twenty-yard line would be on a football field: the "red zone." It was so-named because it was the most critical part of the field, where football games were won or lost; and likewise, Jack's "red zone" was where money was made or lost by the investment bank.

He looked across the room and his gaze settled on a relatively new trader. Jack liked to position all of the less seasoned traders near him so he could keep a close eye on them. The man drew Jack's attention because he was losing money hand over fist, and because of it, Jack was going to get him fired.

Jack shook his head. The miserable bastard couldn't even dress half-way respectably. His cheap off-gray dress shirt was rolled up at the sleeves and he wore a fat paisley tie that looked like a dog had vomited on it. He watched as the soon-to-be-fired trader stared blankly at his computer screen with his mouth gaping open. It was obvious the man had another losing day.

"God damn Ivy League MBA's," he muttered.

Given his choice, Jack would almost always rather hire a street wise, hungry, middle class jerk. As a matter of fact, his ideal candidate was someone who gambled on football during the weekends, spent Thursdays at Belmont, and traveled to Atlantic City to play craps on Sundays.

Forget the overeducated, pencil-necked losers. They could tell you who wrote the *Iliad* or *Moby Dick,* but not a single one could hustle a dollar bill on their own nut, even if their life depended on it.

"Analysis paralysis" he liked to call it. You can't learn how to make money from a book, or from a professor; and that was the problem with most of these Harvard and Yale boys.

Jack sighed. What did he care. Everything he touched turned to gold. In fact, even though he pretended he didn't like it, he was nicknamed "Midas" among some of his Wall Street peers. He also knew he had a few more not-so-kind nicknames, but that was all part of the game.

Sure, he had his share of losing trades in the past. All traders do. Sometimes he even had huge losses, but his gains far exceeded any occasional losing streak. Last year, his total compensation was the highest among traders on all of Wall Street—at least that's what the *Wall Street Journal* reported in its Money and Investing section.

When the article first hit the stands, Jack went out and bought a hundred copies. Being the highest paid trader was a fact he didn't mind sharing.

He took home more than seventy million dollars last year, a bargain in his view considering how much money his trading department made; and that was also a fact he didn't mind sharing, especially with the upper management of Stanley McCallister.

"Hey Jones," Jack yelled over to the hapless trader with the pasty white skin and ugly tie. "How'd you do today?" Jack already knew the answer but he was in the mood to antagonize and humiliate the man some.

Jones exhaled deeply and shrugged his shoulders. "I was doing fine," he answered dejectedly, "until the Department of Agriculture decided to ruin my day by releasing the soybean harvest projections for South America."

"Soybeans!" Jack yelled in a disgusted tone. "You're trading soybeans?"

The soon to be ex-trader nodded his head wearily.

"You should know better, you dumb ass," Jack called out. "Bunch of Harvard Hasty Pudding nitwits. Jones, do me a favor." The man reluctantly looked over at Jack. "Leave the goddamn beans to the goddamn pig farmers. You're not working for Zza Zza Gabor on Green Acres. Are you?"

Jones didn't answer and turned back around. Jack watched in disgust as Jones clicked off his computer, grabbed his jacket and left without even looking back at him. Jack shook his head. He was going to have to tell Johnstone to fire the guy before he caused any more damage.

Sam Johnstone. Talk about a royal loser. He was the President and Chief Executive Officer of Stanley McCallister. It astounded Jack how management types like Sam Johnstone made it to the levels they did. In Jack's humble opinion, Johnstone did not have one bit of talent nor any common sense, and he completely lacked any degree of street smarts or intuition.

Johnstone was probably the most overpaid person in the entire United States. He took home fifty-five million dollars in salary and bonuses last year thanks to Jack and his crew of traders, who, along with the investment bankers, earned all the money for the firm.

All Johnstone did was sit behind a huge mahogany desk for twenty-one, maybe twenty-two hours a week, counting the trading profits and doing asinine interviews for *CNBC* and the *Wall Street Journal*. The rest of Johnstone's time was spent between his men's club on Fifth Avenue, his country club in Greenwich or at his beach mansion in the Hamptons. The man contributed absolutely nothing to the firm's bottom line.

Jack looked down at his black, limited edition Rolex watch. It had cost him twenty-five thousand dollars. It was now after four and the U.S. markets had closed for the weekend. He decided he better go talk with Johnstone before the man left for afternoon martinis at his club.

Jack walked down the sidelines as a slew of sloppy, cheaply dressed clerks busily reconciled the day's trades. No one in the support staff so much as looked up as he passed by. Jack knew the bean counters didn't care for him, but he didn't care. He walked to a series of elevators, jumped in and pushed the button to take him to up the thirty-second floor—home of his illustrious boss.

Chapter 2

The elevator's bell rang announcing that he had reached the thirty-second floor. Jack entered the exceedingly plush, almost vulgar floor for the upper management of Stanley McCallister. The entire floor contained only five offices along with a pair of warehouse-sized conference rooms.

He walked over to Johnstone's secretary with a big smile while she pretended not to notice him. She was a squirrelly looking woman who hated his guts.

"Hey, Deloris. How you doing?" he asked in an overly exuberant fashion.

She looked up from a mass of paperwork with a grimace. Jack loved the fact that just his presence put her in such a foul mood.

"I am well. Thank you," she replied in a cold mortician's manner. Jack guessed Deloris was around sixty and he also surmised that she hadn't been laid in the last forty of those miserable years.

"Whatcha doing this weekend?" Jack continued to goad her. "Any big dates or crazy plans?"

Her attempt to smile was so forced that Jack thought it must have physically hurt her to produce such a faked response upon her iron-clad face.

"I am going to have a quiet weekend. How about you?" she responded caustically.

"Well, Deloris." He sat down on the corner of her desk and picked up her marble name piece. "I'm going to get drunk, then I am going to figure out how I can get the board of directors to fire Johnstone so I can finally run this place like it should be."

Deloris stared at him with a look of utter contempt. Jack knew once he left she would tell Johnstone what he had said, but he didn't care.

"Is Sam in?" he finally asked, deciding he had had enough fun with old Deloris.

"One moment."

She picked up the phone. "Mr. Johnstone. Sorry to disturb you. Jack is standing here and would like a moment of your time."

She paused, which caused Jack to laugh. He knew Sam Johnstone wanted to see him even less than his secretary did.

He leaned over the desk. "Tell him I just made thirty-nine million dollars on the bond trade," he said loud enough for Sam to hear.

"Yes sir," she replied and hung up the phone. "Mr. Johnstone will see you now."

Jack knew the mention of the bond profit would instantly gain him access. His boss might be an idiot but he wasn't a fool—Jack was his bread and butter.

"Have a good weekend." Jack smiled to Deloris. She nodded curtly but didn't wish him likewise.

Jack walked down the oak paneled hallway humming a few lines from his favorite song—the Rolling Stones, "You Can't Always Get What You Want". But Jack could. Johnstone's door was open and he waltzed in.

The large corner office was the size of a small house. The two corner walls were floor-to-ceiling windows overlooking Central Park. The lucky bastard had probably one of the best views in the entire city. A large mahogany desk sat catty-cornered so Johnstone could turn and look out of either window with ease.

He stood behind his desk looking out the window. He turned slowly as Jack walked in. Like Deloris, his smile was an exercise in force.

"Jack," he replied. "Congratulations on the bond trade."

Jack stared at his boss. At sixty-six, he was getting a little plump around the middle and a little light in the hair, but Jack supposed he was still in relatively good shape for a man his age, especially considering his penchant for drinking.

"Well, thank you Sam," Jack said. "Someone has to make sure you get your bonus this year."

Johnstone grunted. "Have a seat." He pointed Jack towards a leather chair in front of his desk.

Besides getting Jones fired, the other reason Jack came up to Johnstone's office was to start campaigning for a bigger bonus. He knew more money would be hard to get in light of his astronomical bonus last year, but he deserved it. It was extremely important to him that he maintain his position as the highest paid trader on Wall Street.

"So," Johnstone said, "to what do I owe the pleasure of your visit?"

"Fire Jones. He's the worst trader I've ever seen. He's a liability, and it's only a matter of time until he does something really stupid."

Johnstone sighed deeply. It brought Jack great pleasure to watch his boss squirm. Jack knew that Johnstone was in a tough position regarding Jones because he was the nephew of one of the most powerful men on the board, a man who had backed Johnstone from his rise through management all the way to chief executive of the firm.

Jack waved his finger. "I told you not to put him on the trading floor in the first place."

"He's young," Johnstone said, shifting uncomfortably in his seat. "Maybe if you took him under your wings a little . . . How much money has he lost?"

"Year-to-date: four million, six hundred and ninety-seven thousand dollars."

Not including the soybean trade he closed out today."

Johnstone frowned. "Cut back his trading limits."

Jack laughed. "C'mon Sam. I'm not a damn babysitter. I've already done that. Just face it. Some people aren't cut out to be traders."

Johnstone turned and looked back out the window. Jack knew he had no choice. Despite the board relationship with Jones' father, money was money, the absolute bottom line on Wall Street.

"I'll take care of it," he replied coldly without looking at Jack. "I'll move him to another area, out of trading."

"I don't care where you put him as long as you get him off my damn floor."

Jack could see that Johnstone was irritated, but even his dimwitted boss understood that the man was hurting both of their pocketbooks.

"I'll take care of it!" he repeated, this time with a hint of anger in his voice. "I have a meeting outside the office. Anything more, Jack?"

"Yes, before you take off to knock back a few scotches at the club. I'd like to talk about this year's bonus."

"Listen, Jack," Johnstone cut him off. "It was hard enough explaining the size of your bonus last year to the board. I can't ask for more."

Jack interrupted him, "I deserve a bigger bonus than last year."

Jack knew it drove Johnstone crazy that he made so much more money than he did, and he loved throwing into Johnstone's face so he added, "With the money I've made this company. To be honest with you, last year's bonus was low."

Johnstone stammered a bit before blurting out, "Low! We paid you more than some entire departments make. Good God! What is this world coming too!"

"I'll tell you what this world is coming to," Jack said. "I make more money for the firm than those departments combined."

Even though Johnstone was his boss, both men knew Johnstone couldn't reprimand or fire Jack, at least, as long as he kept making money for the company.

Jack stood up and before leaving grabbed one of Johnstone's prized Cuban cigars out of a humidor on his desk. "See you Monday," he said as he stuck the cigar in his mouth.

Jack returned to his trading floor and sat on top of his desk. He lit up the Cuban, not giving a thought to the building-wide, non-smoking regulation. He liked to think of his trading floor as his own sovereign nation, like Vatican City. On his trading floor, Jack was king; and like all kings, he had ultimate authority over his territory and subjects.

He blew out a long trail of white smoke and watched it rise slowly into the air. "Thirty-nine million dollars. Unbelievable," he said between puffs.

Now, maybe the compliance geeks will get off his ass. For days the bureaucratic sissies had been crying about the size of the bond position he had taken. It wasn't the first time he had run into problems with compliance, nor would it be the last.

After five minutes of puffing on the cigar, Jack snuffed the half-smoked Cuban in his wastebasket. Typically, Jack stayed late to monitor the after-hour markets, but it was Friday and he had promised his girlfriend, Susan, that he would accompany her to one of her godforsaken auctions.

He stared at a picture of her on his desk. Susan Mitchell was thirty-four-years-old and stunningly beautiful. Her long brownish-blond hair fell half way down her back, and she had the most radiant green eyes he had ever seen. Five days a week at the gym kept her small frame exquisitely tight.

Not only was she a beautiful woman, she was exceptionally bright and well-versed on a whole host of matters, a fact that bothered Jack some.

Even though he hated to admit it, he felt intellectually overmatched in her presence. His only real expertise was in the trading and financial markets. His knowledge of the things that interested Susan, such as art, literature and history, was woefully insignificant. And, despite the fact that he had managed to fake his sophistication, it seemed that Susan was starting to realize that just because someone made a bunch of money, didn't necessarily mean they were worldly.

Their backgrounds were also much different, another sore subject for Jack. He came from the wrong side of the tracks, whereas Susan came from wealth and position. Her father was one of the richest real estate developers in Manhattan and her family had been part of the upper echelon of New York high society for generations.

But, Jack greatly admired Susan because most women he knew in her position would have spent their days shopping at Saks and doing lunch with their friends. Not Susan. She had gone to Yale and graduated summa cum laude with a degree in history and antiquities—a degree that was useful in her position at Sotheby's auction house.

He grimaced as he recalled the first time they had met. It was at a cocktail party given by a mutual friend. When they were introduced, Jack asked her what her degree was in and she told him, "history and antiquities." Then he had stuck his foot in his mouth by foolishly replying, "Oh, I didn't know Ivy League schools offered degrees in antiques."

Jack remembered she had looked at him for a second then burst out laughing. At the time he didn't know what she found so funny until he asked a friend who had explained to him that "antiquities" and "antiques" were two entirely different things.

Despite his faux pas, he got Susan's number and pursued her relentlessly. It took awhile but eventually he convinced her to go out with him. That was over a year ago, and they have been dating ever since.

He had no doubt that she was the perfect woman for him, but he was beginning to wonder if she felt he was the perfect man for her. Jack had brought up marriage two weeks ago and Susan had outright dismissed it. He was still pissed about it. Didn't she know how many women in this city would beg to get that offer.

Much to his growing consternation, Jack felt she was drifting away. She mentioned, quite frequently, that he didn't have interest in anything that she liked, which was basically true. And that was the whole reason he agreed to attend the stupid auction. Maybe if he got more involved in her interests it would demonstrate that he had other interests besides the Japanese Yen or the spot price of gold.

So now, as he rode the elevator down to the lobby, he cursed himself that he was going to have to spend three hours of his valuable time with a bunch of priggish highbrows. Susan had told him the auction was being billed as the greatest collection of ancient coins ever assembled. Jack considered coin collecting a waste of money.

He walked out of the lobby and over to his parked limo. His driver tipped his hat and opened the door for him. "Mr. Weston."

Jack nodded and began to say hello but it didn't quite come out. The driver closed the door and proceeded over to Jack's penthouse eight blocks away on Madison Avenue. The limo pulled over to the curb in front of his building and Jack watched Hector, the Hispanic doorman, hurry over to open his door.

"Good afternoon, Mr. Weston," Hector said with the enthusiasm of a Labrador puppy.

"Pick me up at seven," Jack replied to the driver while stepping out of the car.

Jack quickly walked into his building to escape the way-too-friendly doorman. He liked Hector, and he did a reasonably good job as a doorman, but Jack just didn't want to have a conversation with the guy every single day.

Jack took the elevator up to his luxury penthouse suite. It was the largest, most expensive apartment in the entire building and it came with a steep price.

Jack let himself in and went over to the bar. He made a stiff scotch and soda and took the drink out to the veranda. He had a magnificent view of Central Park. It felt good outside. The cold winter was finally over and spring had blossomed fully.

He took a sip of the 1958 Macallen Scotch, savoring the taste. He toasted himself, "Life is good, Jacky-Boy."

Everything he bought, everything he owned was only the best. He sat down on a Braxton Culler wicker couch, and drank three more scotches before forcing himself to get up and get ready for Susan's damn coin auction.

Chapter 3

After a quick shower and a change of suits, Jack prepared himself to waste the next three or four hours of his life. He poured a much needed to-go Scotch for the trip over to Sotheby's.

When his limo arrived at the auction house, he was in surprisingly good spirits considering what a bore he figured the night would be. His exhilaration probably had something to do with the fortification of the scotch combined with the exhilaration of his earlier bond trade.

However, it was an important night for Susan and he needed to at least try to act interested. Susan had told him she was expecting the auction to set a record for bid amounts. There was some famous coin she kept mentioning, but he had forgotten the details.

He squeezed through the doorway. Inside of Sotheby's, there was quite a crowd milling about. The men were dressed in expensive suits and tuxedos while the women, mostly old hags, wore their finest evening dresses with obscene amounts of expensive jewelry and bad makeup.

He saw Susan talking to an older gentleman. He walked over and kissed her on the cheek. "Good evening, my darling."

She motioned to the man standing next to her. "Jack, I would like to introduce you to Hans Roenert."

"Jack Weston," he said as the two men shook hands.

Hans appeared to be in his late seventies. He wore a classic black tuxedo, and what remained of his silver hair was slicked back across his expansive head.

Susan continued, "Hans is from Bulgaria. He runs the Glockenheimer Group." She looked at the old geezer with what appeared to be immense admiration. "The Glockenheimer Group is one of the oldest numismatic companies in the world."

Jack faked his interest. "Really. How fascinating."

Susan added, "They have amassed the single finest collection of early Roman coins in the entire world."

"So, you flew all the way from Bulgaria for the auction?" Jack asked.

"It is a very special auction," Hans answered in a heavy East European accent.

"Is there any coin, in particular, you are interested in?" Jack asked, trying to sound like he cared.

Hans took a sip of his champagne. "In this auction, there are quite a few we have interest in. I represent a concern that has been in the numismatic business for centuries. We have representatives at all the major auctions. Sometimes we buy pieces, but mostly we attend just to keep track of certain historical coins."

Here we go, Jack thought, as he grabbed a glass of champagne off a passing waiter's tray. He took a big swallow realizing he was going to need the alcohol to get through the night. These guys must have a lot of spare time on their hands, he thought as he listened to Hans drone on.

Finally, Jack interrupted the dissertation. "So Hans, let me get this straight. You attend these auctions just to see who purchases a certain coin. Seems like a waste of time and money."

Susan shot him her "I'm not pleased" look. Jack grimaced. He'd had better be careful. If he screwed up tonight, it would take a long time and a lot of expensive gifts to repair the damage.

Luckily, Hans laughed and seemed to take the question in stride. "Why yes, we do spend a lot of money in that aspect, but that is what we do. Our profession has been passed down for generations. We are historians as much as anything else."

Trying to sound more interested but more importantly, get back in Susan's good graces, Jack asked, "any major historical pieces you have an interest in tonight?"

Hans' eyes lit up and there was an edge of excitement in his voice. "Why yes, as a matter of fact there is. I'm surprised Susan hasn't mentioned it to you. It is why all of us are here."

Susan jumped in, "Jack wouldn't know a Byzantine Aureus from a Republic Aas."

Hans and Susan laughed at their obvious "inside" coin joke. Jack felt a bit of anger rising but he held his tongue even though he knew their laughter was at his expense.

Hans clasped him on the shoulder. "My dear boy, tonight is your lucky night. You will have the privilege of seeing the most famous coin in all of antiquity."

"Really. And what coin is that?"

"The Brutus Double Dagger Denarius, or, as some call it, the Eids of March coin."

Jack knew this conversation was starting to get over his head. He nodded and luckily the Bulgarian continued, "The Double Dagger coin was minted by Brutus after the assassination of Caesar."

"Interesting," Jack said, quickly downing the rest of his champagne. He looked back over his shoulder. Where the hell was that waiter?

Susan grabbed Hans by the arms. "I should say more than interesting. There are less than fifty Eid of March coins left in the world. And this particular one is the most special."

"Why is that?"

Susan looked at Hans and he took the hint to continue, "Because, of the fifty coins known to exist, this one is in the best condition. Actually it is in mint condition, which after over two thousand years is . . ." Hans paused then added almost in a whisper, "a near impossibility. But even more astounding, this coin was specially minted for Brutus by Rome's mintmaster, and Brutus carried it with him until he committed suicide, after losing the battle of Philippi to Marc Antony."

"But how would you know it was the very first one minted, and that Brutus carried it with him?" Jack inquired, looking over at Susan to make sure he hadn't said anything wrong.

"Aah, good question," Hans responded. "First, the coin is marked with the Roman numeral I. The significance of the marking was recorded in historical documents by the Roman historian Titus Livius. But it wasn't until the discovery of the Mettivus parchments."

"Marcus Mettivus," Jack pronounced the name wondering where he had heard it before.

"Hey, how did you know his first name was Marcus?" Susan asked with a somewhat perplexed look on her face.

"What?" Jack said.

"Hans said 'Mettivus parchment' and you said, 'Marcus Mettivus.' How did you know his first name was Marcus?"

Jack was a bit perplexed. "I don't know," he said figuring it must have been just a coincidence. "I'm sure I heard you mention his name before."

Hans laughed. "Well, anyway, Marcus Mettivus was the mintmaster in Rome at the time. Two years ago, a series of scrolls were discovered in a catacomb under Rome, and from them we can finally authenticate that this coin was the first minted. The coin was personally given to Brutus by Mettivus, probably as some type of a souvenir."

"Hmmm," Jack actually found the explanation interesting. "Is your group going to try and buy the coin?"

Hans gave him a rather strange look, then an almost wicked grin came to his face. "Oh no, certainly not."

Susan let go of Hans' arm and said, "The Glockenhemier Group has tracked the ownership of the coin all the way back to Brutus. It has had quite a remarkable existence. One could even say the coin is cursed."

Hans interrupted her with a casual wave of his hand. "Rather, some would say the owners of the coin are cursed."

"Wait a second, are you saying you know of every person who has owned the coin over its entire existence?" asked Jack.

"No, of course not. We can account for its ownership or whereabouts for roughly twelve hundred years. The rest is unknown."

Thankfully, a waiter passed by and Jack grabbed another glass of champagne. "Hans, what do you mean cursed? You actually believe the coin is cursed?"

"Well Jack, it seems a good many of the coin's owners over the years have suffered untimely tragedies."

Jack laughed. "Surely Hans, you don't believe in superstitions and old wives tales?"

The Bulgarian looked dead serious. "Let's just say, I don't like to tempt fate. Remember—beware the Ides of March."

Susan looked at her watch. "Gentlemen, excuse me. It's time to start the auction."

She kissed Jack then Hans on the cheek and Jack watched her leave with a bit of rising lust. Man, she was a good-looking woman.

Hans turned toward him and stuck out his hand. "Nice meeting you, Jack."

"Yes, good to meet you."

The men shook hands then parted ways to find their seats and watch the bidding. Jack's seat was in the back of the auction room, which, for once, he was happy about because he could sneak out without Susan knowing it if he had to.

"Cursed," he mumbled under his breath. If anyone was cursed it was him for having to sit here over the next two hours and watch this nonsense. He looked around and wondered how much money had exchanged hands in this room over the years, probably a mind-staggering sum.

His lovely Susan strode to the podium and the crowd grew quiet. She announced into the microphone, "Ladies and Gentlemen, welcome to tonight's featured Numismatic Auction. We will begin with a series of gold Augustus Imperial coins. The coins are listed on page six of your program."

Jack watched two armed security guards bring out the lot and place the coins on a viewing table next to the podium. Behind Susan, two large screens lit up displaying enlarged pictures of the gold coins.

Susan began: "Bidding will start at forty thousand dollars for the lot."

After five minutes of quiet but steady bidding, an Asian man a few rows in front of him won the lot with a bid of seventy-two thousand dollars.

Jack whistled softly. Seventy-two thousand dollars for three coins. What a waste of money. He needed another drink if he was going to get through this. By the third lot of coins, he had completely lost interest. The auction was progressing at an excruciatingly slow pace. He yawned deeply, settled deeper into his chair and felt himself begin to doze.

Jack woke with a start. "Damn!" he moaned under his breath after realizing he was still at the auction.

He sat up in his chair. The atmosphere in the room had changed drastically since he fell asleep. There was a buzz in the air and the crowd stirred restlessly with excitement.

Susan motioned for the audience to quiet down then said, "Ladies and Gentlemen. I am honored to present the piece we have all been waiting for," she paused and gracefully swung her arm out with palm open, "the legendary, Brutus, Eids of March—Double Dagger Denarius."

Jack breathed a sigh of relief. Thank God, the auction was almost over. The giant monitors behind the stage suddenly lit up behind Susan and gasps rose from the audience.

Jack stared at the enlarged display of the Brutus coin. He felt oddly transfixed by it. And as he continued staring at the coin, it stirred something inside of him, some feeling he couldn't explain. For the first time in the night, he no longer thought about having another drink or leaving.

He couldn't take his eyes off the double daggers portrayed on the coin. His eyes shifted to the inscription—Eid Mar—underneath the daggers. Hans was right. It was astonishing that something that small could remain in such good condition for over two thousand years.

Susan cleared her throat and announced, "As you can see from the monitor, on the reverse is the numeral I. Recently discovered documents from Marcus Mettivus confirm the writings of the ancient Roman Historian Titus Livius. We now have proof that the coin was the first Double Dagger Coin minted and that it was given to Brutus who carried with him until his death. Bidding for this once-in-a-lifetime treasure will begin at seven-hundred and fifty-thousand dollars."

"Goddamn!" Jack said aloud.

A lady in the row in front of him turned and gave him a dirty look. Jack smiled back at her.

Immediately after the starting bid was announced, a frenzy broke out among the once prim and proper high society crowd. Bids and counter bids were shouted out driving the price higher and higher. Jack watched in stunned disbelief as the price went through the roof. When it hit one-point-five million dollars, the number of bidders dwindled rapidly until there were just three men left to fight it out.

All three bidders appeared equally determined. Jack stared at the front row as one of the remaining bidders motioned to Susan that he would accept one-point-six million. He was an enormously fat man wearing a white tuxedo. He was accompanied by a busty young blond who obviously loved the disgustingly rotund man for his money, and not his youthful good looks.

The second bidder was a Middle Eastern man and the last bidder sat in the row across from Jack, although it appeared that he was not the actual bidder because he stayed on a cell phone, obviously taking instructions from someone on the other end.

Susan called out, "the bid is one-point-six. Do I hear one-point-seven for the Eid of March coin?"

Jack watched as the Middle Eastern man shook his head then threw his program down and stormed out of the room like a child having a temper tantrum.

"What a baby," Jack said loudly, causing the old lady in front of him to give him another nasty look.

That left the fat man and the mystery phone bidder.

Susan's face became slightly flushed as she announced, "The gentleman in the back bids two million dollars."

Jack stared at the fat man in the white tuxedo. He looked like a giant albino penguin, and at a cool two million, it appeared as if he was through bidding. He leaned over to his blond escort and whispered something in her ear. The blond shrugged and Jack watched the man shake his head.

Susan raised her gavel. "The bid is set at two million dollars. Do I hear two-point-one for the Brutus Double Dagger Denarius?"

An eerie silence fell over the room. "Very well, two million going once …"

A disturbing thought raced through Jack's head, a thought he was trying to suppress. For reasons unknown, he was considering bidding on the coin. Before he knew what he was doing he raised his hand and yelled, "Two-point-two million."

He wanted the coin, no matter what the cost.

A loud gasp rose from the audience as heads turned to see who the un-expected late bidder was. Jack looked straight ahead, watching Susan squint from the glare of the overhead lights. Surely she recognized my voice, he thought.

"The bid is two-point-two million," she said hesitantly. "Do I hear two-point three?"

Jack looked over at the other bidder who tightly clutched the cell phone. He spoke something into it as he glared at Jack. He didn't look too happy.

The man again rapidly spoke into the cell phone and raised his phone. "Two-point-three," he called out.

More gasps erupted from the audience. Jack knew they loved watching two determined men fight it out. Jack's trading instincts began to take over, and like any other trade, he hated to lose. He had to show this guy he wasn't playing around.

"Two-point-six!" Jack yelled out recklessly without any consideration for the amount of money he was spending.

The excitement in the room reached a fever pitch as all eyes returned back to the cell phone bidder. Once again, he talked quickly into the phone but this time, there appeared to be hesitation from whoever was on the other end. After about sixty tense seconds, the man clicked off the phone and stared over at Jack with a look of pure hatred. He then smiled in such a sinister way that it sent a chill down Jack's spine. The cell phone man abruptly got up and walked out of the auction room.

Susan looked somewhat stunned. She raised her gavel. "The current bid is two-point-six million dollars. Do I hear two-point-seven?"

The room remained silent. "Fair warning," she announced. "Last call. The Brutus Eid of March Denarius bid is two-point-six."

She hesitated for a second then slammed the gavel down on the podium. The sound of the hammer striking the wood reverberated through the room. "Sold for two-point-six million. The auction has concluded. Thank you for bidding."

Susan abruptly left the stage and Jack leaned back in his chair and smiled. He had won the coin. But he still didn't understand why he had wanted it so badly; probably because he now possessed what every person in this room wanted, and it felt good to see the envy in their eyes.

Jack relaxed in his chair, enjoying the moment, as the patrons slowly left with more than a few glancing his way. Finally, he got up and walked out into the reception area to look for Susan and have a celebratory drink.

Jack swiped a glass of Dom Perignon off a passing waiter's tray and spotted Hans. He strode over to him. "So Hans," he boasted, "what do you think of my new purchase?"

Hans' face no longer possessed the pleasant appearance it did when they first met a few hours ago. Jack had to suppress a laugh as he realized the old bugger probably wanted the coin for himself.

"Jack," Hans said in his clipped European accent. "You seem like a nice fellow so I am going to give you some very important advice."

Hans paused while looking around as if he didn't want anyone to overhear. He leaned close to Jack. "Get rid of that bloody coin immediately, even if you take a big loss."

"What!" Jack scoffed. "What the hell are you talking about?"

"The coin. You have no idea of its history. You do not want to own it. Trust me."

Jack burst out laughing. "C'mon Hans. You haven't been drinking too much champagne, have you?"

Jack looked around for Susan then smiled back at Hans. "Okay, are you and Susan trying to play a little joke on me or what?"

Hans waved a hand. "I know it must sound absolutely absurd but we have extensive records of ownership going back two thousands years. Let me tell you, my friend, there is undeniable proof. You have to trust me."

Jack was getting a kick out of this. He was about to give Hans some more grief when he saw Susan approaching. The minute he saw her, he knew something was wrong. She looked furious.

She stormed over to them. "What in hell do you think you are doing?"

Jack looked around, wondering who she was talking to. It took a second for his brain to register that her anger was directed at him.

"What? What's the matter?"

"What's the matter! You just don't get it, do you?"

Jack shrugged his shoulders. He was bewildered. Was she mad because he had fallen asleep during the auction?

"The coin," she said. "How could you have done this to me?"

Jack still had no idea what she was talking about. "Done what? I don't—"

She cut him off. "You asshole! I'm going to be a joke when everyone finds out that my boyfriend purchased the most valuable ancient coin in the world and he doesn't know a damn thing about it. About its relevance. Its importance. Its history. Nothing!"

Jack tried to explain but she was not through. "I have spent six months inviting serious collectors from around the world to attend this auction—people who have spent their entire lives studying and learning about the history and significance of these artifacts. And you, you walk in and have the audacity to buy the coin only because it's some type of a game to you. You don't deserve to own it!"

Jack didn't know what to say. He was aware that others were watching his dressing down, and he didn't like it.

"Susan," he replied in a hushed voice. "I didn't mean to insult you. I mean, I purchased it for three hundred thousand dollars more than the last bid. The seller has got to be happy with that, right? Sotheby's gets a bigger commission, doesn't it?"

"It's all about money to you, isn't it? All one big goddamn game."

"I'll give it back if you want," he replied in exasperation.

"It's too late, Jack. It's too late." She began to leave but stopped and turned back to face him. "Oh, and Jack, it's too late for us as well. Don't call me. We're through."

Jack stood frozen with his mouth open as he watched Susan storm off leaving him alone with Hans. He looked over at the old man in disbelief. "See Jack." Hans smiled. "I told you that coin was cursed!"

Chapter 4

Jack awoke from a restless night's sleep. He looked at his bedside clock. It was six in the morning. He sighed heavily. Goddamn dreams. Ever since his breakup with Susan, he had been plagued with vivid nightmares about a forest, and torments of men and places—he didn't understand. He sat up, soaked in a cold sweat. He couldn't shake an immense feeling of doom. Why was he having these dreams? They were really starting to bother him.

He got up and went out to the veranda. The sun had yet to rise and he felt fatigued, even depressed. Five months had passed since their breakup, and much to his consternation, he found that he missed Susan greatly.

He had not seen, or talked to her since that night at the coin auction. He knew the moment she stormed off that their relationship was over. As a master trader he prided himself on understanding human emotions and behavior, and after dating Susan for over a year, he knew when she had made up her mind about something.

Even though it was still early, it was already sticky outside. The beautiful spring had turned into a scorching hot summer. Jack went back inside, showered and changed into his golf clothes. He took the elevator down to the lobby and had the valet retrieve his car from the garage.

The valet brought his car around and he jumped in. Jack began driving towards Westchester Country Club to play a round of golf, a game he didn't even like. He was good at it, but it just took too much time and he despised the people he always played with.

The traffic was light as he navigated his car out of the city and onto the expressway. He loved driving his new possession, a solid black, custom built Ferrari he had bought right after his break-up with Susan. It had been a rash purchase, but what the hell, he deserved it. It set him back over two hundred thousand dollars but it was money well spent in Jack's mind. He loved seeing other people's envy.

Thirty-five minutes later he pulled into Westchester Country Club and a swarm of valets descended on him, all vying for the privilege of parking his car.

The senior valet won out, and Jack watched in amusement as the man admonished his younger peers. Jack watched other valets drift off in disappointment, once again relegated to parking cheap-ass Mercedes or BMWs.

The head valet, an Asian with a pockmarked face, opened the car door. "Mr. Weston, good morning, sir. How are you?"

"Fine," he answered briskly.

Jack handed him the keys and walked down into the men's locker room. After changing into his golf shoes, he left the locker room and headed over to the golf course. He spotted his playing companions standing around the golf carts.

"Gentleman," he announced, walking over to them.

The group stopped their conversation and turned towards him. "Looky boys, it's our favorite club member," Mitchell James said.

James was a hedge fund manager who Jack hated. Unfortunately, he had to tolerate the son-of-a-bitch because he had a huge amount of money at the firm. James managed about two billion dollars for his clients, and the assets were held in a pooled account at Stanley McCallister. James made all the trading decisions and used the firm to act as custodian and to execute the trades.

The other two men, the Strickland brothers, were generally considered to be the best white-collar criminal defense lawyers in Manhattan; but in Jack's opinion they were degenerate alcoholics whose undeserved reputation for outstanding legal advice was based solely on the enormous fees they charged. Jack never called them by their names and instead referred to them as the "Younger" and "Older".

After the usual set of handshakes and fake smiles, the group headed to the first tee. Jack got out of the cart and pulled out his new Calloway Titanium Driver. The club had cost him more than two-thousand bucks, but the club pro swore it would add ten yards to his distance.

Despite his nonchalance about the game, over the years Jack had spent a tremendous amount of money and devoted countless hours getting his handicap down to a respectable five.

His desire for excellence came, not from his passion or love for the game, but rather from the hatred of losing to anyone, even in a friendly game. Jack watched as his three partners teed off. They were playing for their usual bets which meant the loser could end up shelling out tens of thousands of dollars.

Jack smiled. The Strickland brothers were already drinking, which was a good sign because their games tended to suffer on the back nine when they started consuming alcohol this early.

All three of his playing partners hit decent but unspectacular drives, then it was Jack's turn. He confidently walked over to the tee box, knelt down and stuck his solid gold tee into the ground while placing his fifteen dollar Titleist Double XX pro ball on top of it.

"Hey look," he heard James snicker to the two lawyer brothers as Jack took a few practice swings. "Mister big shot is using those gold tees again."

"What a fagot," said the younger Strickland brother.

Jack ignored them. They were trying to distract him. It was all part of the game. Last week he had won thirty-two thousand dollars from James by making a left to right, eighteen-foot putt on the seventeenth hole.

Jack knew James had been pissed about it because usually he talked to the bastard a couple of times during the week but James hadn't called him once. Instead, he had placed all his orders through another trader on the floor. He knew James was going to try and do everything he could to win back at least some of his money. Jack looked over at James with a causal smile. "Well, the tees sure worked last week. Didn't they?"

The Strickland brothers began laughing like hyenas. As with so many successful attorneys, they never picked sides; they only hoped everyone suffered for their own general amusement and profit.

Jack finished his practice swings and approached the ball. He heard James whistling in the background. Jack chuckled, like that was going to distract him. He stared out over the first hole. It was a long par four, measuring four hundred and twenty yards from the back tees.

With a graceful, powerful swing, Jack drove the ball down the left center of the fairway about two hundred and eighty-five yards out. He heard James mumble something derogatory as he picked up his gold tee. The pro was right. Jack loved the feel and distance of the new driver.

"Almost got a hold of it," he said sarcastically to James with a big grin.

After paring the first hole Jack had a feeling that a good round was in progress, and boy was he ever right. By the sixth hole, his playing companions were all bitching and moaning, especially James. Jack was on fire and stood at only one stroke over par.

After the turn on the ninth hole, the Strickland brothers decided that drinking was more fun and less expensive than gambling, and they refused to bet anymore. Again, as successful attorneys, they realized that their case was hopeless and the brothers cut themselves the best deal possible to minimize the damages. They had wisely conceded their bets after the turn, and each owed Jack five thousand dollars, a considerably smaller sum than if they had decided to continue betting on the backside.

Their bets didn't matter that much anyway because, much to Jack's sheer delight, James had not been as smart as the drunken lawyer brothers. After going double or nothing on both the sixteenth and seventeenth holes James was now down fifty thousand dollars.

The group approached the par-five eighteenth, and Jack surveyed the hole—a dogleg left—measuring five hundred and twenty-six yards. It was a three-shot hole for the group, and the multi-tiered green put a premium on an accurate third shot.

It was still Jack's honor. He teed up the ball on his lucky gold tee. He noticed the breeze had picked up making the stifling heat a little more bearable.

"Hey Jack," one of the Strickland brothers yelled out. "You want a beer?"

Jack turned. Each brother had a fresh beer in his hand. "You two are a pair of drunks." He wasn't keeping exact count but he figured the two brothers must have already consumed a case of beer with numerous shots of whiskey thrown in for good measure.

"If I ever require legal advice," Jack said in all seriousness, "I assure you I won't hire either of you losers."

"You'll need it one day," the Older jeered. "It's just a matter of time before your greed catches up with you. All you Wall Street bastards are criminals."

Jack ignored them and turned back to his ball.

"Hold on, Jack," James replied.

Jack stepped away from the ball and looked at James. "How about letting me double down on the bet?" he asked, causing the Older to spit beer out of his mouth and nose.

"James, you dumb bastard," said the Younger. "You'll owe a hundred grand if you lose this hole!"

"Thank you, I can do the math," James answered back.

Jack grinned. The fool must have lost his mind.

"All right, I'll let you double down. If I win the hole, you owe me a hundred thousand. If you win, we're even."

James nodded. The Strickland brothers were grinning from ear to ear. Jack knew they lived for this kind of action because, as successful attorneys, they loved seeing people in dire straits.

Both men hit decent drives, about two hundred and fifty yards out. The Strickland Brothers didn't even bother to tee off. They were spectators now. They were having too much fun drinking and watching the grudge match. Jack wondered who they were rooting for.

Both men hit lay-up second shots to within a hundred and ten yards from the green. No advantage to either one. It was the third shot that was the important one and Jack took his best club out of his bag—a graphite-shaft pitching wedge.

James' ball was slightly behind Jack's, and he hit first. James' shot was decent, but not great, leaving him a twenty-five foot putt. Jack smiled because under the circumstances, James couldn't have been too happy with it.

Jack breathed deeply and tightened his grip on the pitching wedge. The pin was in the front of the green and there was a slight breeze into his face. He lined up the flag and swung. It was a high shot that started slightly left of the flag and slowly faded back in. Jack knew it was a great shot the moment he hit it. The ball hit the green softly and rolled to within five feet of the hole.

"Shit! You're screwed James," one of the brothers yelled out. Jack smiled and looked over at James whose face seemed to take on an almost pale-greenish color. Jack loved watching the man's obvious agony.

The foursome rode to the eighteenth green in complete silence. Jack strode over to his ball and marked it with his lucky ball marker—the Brutus Double Dagger Denarius. James followed then stopped abruptly and glared down at Jack's ball mark.

"What the hell is that?" James asked, bending over for a closer look.

"A Roman coin," Jack answered.

"A Roman coin?" James looked even closer. "That's not that Caesar coin you bought for two-point-six million dollars. Is it?"

Jack grinned. "Why, yes it is. And just for the record, the coin was minted for Marcus Brutus right after he assassinated Julius Caesar. You should spend a little time learning some history."

James looked over at him with an expression of incredulity on his face. "You mean to tell me you have been using a coin that you paid two-point-six million dollars for as a ball mark?"

"What the hell else is it good for?" said Jack.

"Hey James," the Younger called out, "you're about to get slaughtered just like Caesar." The two drunken brothers were laughing hysterically.

The Older chimed in for good measure, "Hey, we should start calling Jack 'Brutus' and James 'Caesar'."

James shook his head in disgust and walked back to his ball. "You know what?" he replied to Jack.

"What?"

"You're an asshole."

"Shut the hell up you sore loser and go putt your ball," Jack said angrily. Things were getting personal.

James lined up his putt. Then hit it. Jack cringed. The damn ball looked good the whole way.

"Caesar made it! Caesar made it!" the Strickland brothers screamed in unison as the ball rolled towards the hole.

Luckily, the brothers' prediction was the kiss of death. As the ball neared the hole, it turned slightly to the left and lipped out of the cup.

"Shit!" James yelled, as he fell to his knees on the green.

He stood back up, walked over to his ball and dejectedly tapped it in for a five.

Jack couldn't help but laugh. All he had to do was make a five-foot, slightly downhill putt and he would win a hundred thousand dollars. He never missed putts of this distance. Hell, even if by he missed it by some strange fluke, he would tie the hole and still win fifty grand. Those were the types of bets he liked—guaranteed wins.

Jack walked around the hole taking an extra long time studying the putt just to prolong James' agony.

"Jesus, Jack! Putt the goddamn thing and get it over with," James said to him.

"All right," Jack said. He had had enough fun for one day. He lined up over the ball and putted it. He watched as it rolled straight towards the hole. There was no doubt the putt was going in. It was a perfect putt, dead center, but unbelievably, the ball went right over the cup.

Jack couldn't believe it! It was like there was a sheet of glass over the hole. The ball had gone right over it.

"Goddamn it!" Jack yelled. He still couldn't believe the ball had not gone in.

"Looks like you dodged a fifty thousand dollar bullet there Caesar," the Older said to James.

"Ya," James replied. "But I still lost fifty grand."

Jack was numb. He walked over to his ball. It had rolled two-and-a-half feet past the hole, a gimmee any other time, but when playing for money, he had to putt it out. As he re-marked the ball with the Brutus coin the silver from the coin reflected a ray of sunlight into his eye. He stepped back a little. A strange feeling had overcome him.

"You know what boys?" James called over to the Strickland brothers. "I think "our boy" is going to choke. Hey Jack, I'll bet you twenty-five thousand dollars you miss that putt."

"Jesus H Christ! Have you lost your mind," called out the Younger. "The putt is practically in the leather. You're pissing away another twenty-five grand, you dumb ass."

Jack didn't want the bet. Something didn't feel right. A sense of self-doubt, even dread spread over him. If he made the putt, a putt he could make a hundred times in a row, he would win seventy-five thousand. If he missed it and carded a bogey, he would end up owing James twenty-five. He couldn't understand why James would make such a foolhardy bet.

"Well," James said. "Are you going to take the bet Mister Big Shot? It's a lousy two foot putt."

"C'mon Brutus. Give Caesar a chance," Young Strickland yelled out.

Jack smiled weakly. "Fine." He grudgingly accepted the new bet.

"Well I'll be," the Older replied. "James, I think you have the boy rattled some there. Hey Brutus, we'll take twenty-five thousand on that putt as well, okay?"

Have these people lost their minds, Jack thought. The game had gone well beyond the bounds of civility at this point.

He nodded, accepting their bets. Jack stood over the putt and noticed a slight tremble in his hands.

"I think he's going to choke," he heard James say to the Strickland brothers.

Jack felt his face burning.

"C'mon, putt the damn ball," James called out.

Jack's heart pounded like a jackhammer. He pulled the putter back and struck the ball. The moment he hit it, he knew. The ball raced by the left edge. He had completely yanked the putt. It wasn't even close. He had just missed a two and a half foot putt. In a matter of minutes he had gone from winning a hundred thousand to losing fifty.

But it wasn't so much the money that devastated him, it was the way it had happened. He had been played. He had shown vulnerability and others had sensed it and capitalized on it.

His playing partners were howling in delight. Jack knew the three men loved every second of his failure. Pure rage boiled over him. He had to get out of there before he blew up.

He stormed off the green. "Where you going Brutus?" the Older yelled while pulling beers out of the cooler.

Jack grabbed his clubs off of the cart. "I'll settle up with you on Monday," he yelled back to the men. All the way to the clubhouse he could hear them laughing at him.

The ride back down to Manhattan did nothing to calm his nerves. He got stuck in traffic near the Whitestone Bridge and had to sit there and stew. He knew he shouldn't make such a big deal out of the missed putt but he couldn't help it.

"Damn it!" He punched the dashboard with his fist. Traffic was moving at a snails pace. He slammed on his horn again, as if the shrill noise was going to get the traffic moving any faster. He sat in his car in pure agony, and thought, and thought—

Chapter 5

Jack slowly rubbed his temples. His head felt like an overripe watermelon about to burst. He swallowed four aspirin and chased them down with his water bottle that he had spiked with vodka. He had just gotten off the phone with James. It was hard to believe that six months had passed since their golf episode, and although they maintained a professional business relationship, that was the extent of it. Needless to say, they would never play golf again.

He stared at the series of clocks on the wall near his desk. It wasn't even nine o'clock Monday morning and he had already lost ten million dollars on the Japanese yen. He had placed the trade on Friday believing that the yen was due for a rebound over the weekend. Obviously, he was wrong, again.

He pounded the table with his fist and looked around the trading floor with a growing degree of frustration. The floor was only half full.

"Where in the hell is everyone?" he shouted.

He got up and walked over to the desk of a short, stocky trader. "Hey Joe."

The trader looked up from the *Wall Street Journal* he was reading. "Jack. How's it going?" he said in a way-too-cheerful voice.

"All right."

Jack sat down next to him. Joe was a veteran trader and one of the few people in the firm that Jack would occasionally seek council with.

"What do you think about the yen here?" he asked.

Joe punched up the yen quote and a series of graphs displaying the price movement of the currency. He studied the graphs and data for a few moments. He scrunched his face slightly. "I haven't traded it in a while. It's been too damn volatile."

"Tell me about it."

"I don't know, Jack, it looks awfully weak."

"I'm long in a big way," Jack said, trying not to sound too dejected about the losing trade.

"Oh." Joe shrugged while giving him that look that Jack had seen a million times. The look was, "I feel for ya man but better your ass than mine".

Joe hit his keyboard and more graphs of the currency came up. "Technically, it looks oversold, but you know how that crazy currency is. I know the Europeans have been selling the hell out of it for some reason."

Jack shook his head. Joe's non-answer told him what the trader really thought—it was a shitty trade and it was going lower.

"Where the hell is everyone?" Jack asked, changing the subject away from his losing trade.

The stocky trader looked around the floor and grunted, "I don't know, probably still hung-over from the weekend."

Jack looked over the half-empty floor. "Well, I hope nobody is expecting a bonus this year with this kind of piss-ass effort." He left in a huff and skulked back to his desk.

He punched up the yen quote. It had fallen even further. He did a quick mental calculation. He was now down almost twelve and a half million dollars. He had gotten greedy and taken way too big of a position. "This is not the way to start Monday," he said to himself.

He took a sip of cold coffee and chased it with the vodka water. He sat there staring at the flashing numbers. For the first time in his career, Jack felt paralyzed. He didn't know whether to buy, sell, or hold.

He couldn't believe his dilemma. He knew he was suffering from a condition that he had repeatedly warned all new traders about. It was called "analysis paralysis," and the feeling disturbed him greatly.

Jack had had plenty of losing positions before, but he always knew exactly what to do, even if it meant taking a loss and selling out the position. Losses were just part of trading; but now, he didn't know what to do.

He could have dismissed the feeling of uncertainty if this was the first time it had happened, but it wasn't. Over the last six months, Jack's trading losses were starting to pile up. Nothing devastating, but he had been consistently losing on every trade he placed. He actually felt that his trading was slipping out of his control. He pulled up the yearly trade blotter for the Book.

The Book was actually a ledger that recorded the profits and losses of each trader, and of the floor as a whole. Ultimately, the only thing that mattered was where the Book stood.

He stared at the figure. God damn it! Since August, the Book had gone from positive, to down over forty-two million dollars.

"Not good, Jacky boy," he mumbled.

Jack knew it was only a matter of time before Sam Johnstone would call him up to his office to explain the string of losses. Jack started flipping through the morning charts trying to spot a trading opportunity. He needed a big winner and quick, as much for his own psyche as for the profit.

In searching for a quick win, Jack knew he was ignoring another one of his cardinal rules—when in a losing streak, step back and trade very lightly, or not at all. And whatever you do, never, ever place big bets trying to get it all back at one time.

"Corn looks good," he said as he picked up the phone. A thought ran through his head—didn't he chastise and later fire a trader for buying soybeans?

Chapter 6

A week later the inevitable happened. His phone rang. "Jack," he answered briskly.

"Jack." He cringed at the sound of her voice. It was Deloris. "Sam would like to see you," she said enthusiastically.

"God damn it," he muttered under his breath. "Just a second." He hit the hold button and did the math on his last trade.

Corn was trading at $5.26 a bushel. Each contract represented five thousand bushels of grain. He had bought a thousand contracts—five million bushels—and corn was down fifty cents a bushel.

"Jesus H Christ!" he cursed. He was down two-and-a-half million dollars on corn! What the hell was he doing trading agricultures! He never traded those types of contracts.

His phone line kept flashing and he released the hold button. "Sorry for keeping you on hold. I'm in the middle of some trades . . . aah, tell Sam I'll come up after the market closes."

Deloris sighed loudly. "Hold on."

She placed him on hold then almost immediately came back on. "No, he needs to see you right now."

Jack could feel his blood pressure rising. "Fine. I'll be up in a minute."

He slammed the phone down so hard it caught the attention of some of the traders huddled around his area. They quickly looked away. No one liked to be around someone during a losing streak. Jack had noticed a definite change in attitude among his traders over the last few months.

He chewed a couple of breath mints to hide the vodka smell on his breath and took the elevator up to Sam's floor. He walked passed Deloris' desk without even looking at her.

"Hi, Jack. Did you have a good weekend?" he heard her call out a bit too gleefully.

He gave her the finger.

"That's mature," she said.

Jack knew Deloris was aware of the trading losses, and the bitch was taking great pleasure in his failure.

Reluctantly, he walked into Johnstone's office. Johnstone was seated behind his desk reviewing the trading logs for the Book. He didn't look happy. He nodded as Jack entered and motioned for him to take a seat. Jack watched as his boss flipped through the logs, occasionally shaking his head and muttering under his breath. Jack was forced to sit in silence for another couple of minutes before Johnstone finally looked up.

"The Book is down forty-seven million dollars," he said sternly, "thirty-eight of that is yours."

Jack shrugged. "Markets have been tough this year. You know I'll turn it around."

Johnstone didn't seem convinced. "In six months the Book has gone from a profit to a substantial loss. The yen position is killing us. It's a mistake. Sell it. And while you're at it, sell that damn corn. We don't trade those types of contracts here. What the hell were you thinking?"

"Sell the yen," Jack protested. "It's due for a bounce. We'll be leaving millions on the table."

"We can't take the risk or exposure anymore. Sell the damn position," Johnstone repeated.

Jack was stunned by Johnstone's directness. He had never heard him so adamant. He began to protest more but Johnstone cut him off, "Obviously, your research is flawed on this trade and we feel the yen could fall further. We want the risk off the Book."

"We?" Jack snapped. "Since when is this about 'we'? And who exactly is 'we'?"

Johnstone pounded his fist on his desk. "God damn it, Jack! When you're down almost fifty million of the bank's money, then it's a problem."

"It wasn't a problem when the Book made hundreds of millions of dollars last year," Jack shot back.

Johnstone waved his finger at him. "Listen to me, you smart ass. If it was up to me I would have fired your ass years ago. But 'we' felt that you could make some money for the bank if you were kept under control. 'We' now feel that you are losing control and have taken some unacceptable risks for the firm."

"What are you talking about, Sam?" Jack said defensively. "Even with the losses this year, you know how much money I have made the firm over the years."

"I don't want to hear about last year," Johnstone cut him off. "How many of your own traders did you fire after a bad year, or for that matter, a bad quarter?"

Jack didn't have to answer. Being a trader for Jack was a very profitable, but very insecure job. He had fired dozens and dozens of traders, sometimes after only one large loss.

Jack stood up. "Are we finished?"

Sam nodded. "For now. Sell the positions, immediately."

Jack turned to leave.

"Oh, and one other thing. Consider yourself warned. We'll be monitoring the Book very closely."

Luckily, Deloris had left her desk and he didn't have to see her smug look after his dressing down. Jack returned to the trading floor madder than hell. Per Johnstone's orders, he liquidated both the yen and corn positions, and swore he wouldn't let that happen again.

Two weeks passed, and the Book suffered even more dramatic losses. Jack arrived at work and began pouring over the latest economic data desperately searching for a winning trade. It was a bitterly cold, dreary winter day, which mirrored his sour mood. It was a week before Christmas and there was no question that the Book was going to suffer a major loss for the year. The Book was down seventy-two million dollars and Johnstone was absolutely livid. For the first time in his career, Jack was actually concerned about his job.

The only good news was that the year was almost over, and he could at least use the mindset that he was starting fresh on January 1. But he knew Johnstone and the board would not look at it that way. They kept a running total on the losses.

Jack punched up a short-term graph of the United States stock market. For a month he had felt that the market was bottoming from a recent correction and was due for a big rally. Inflation was low and he believed next year's corporate profits were going to be higher than presently expected. The economy seemed ready to take off after spending eighteen months in a mild recession.

Jack had a gut instinct about the trade in a way that he hadn't felt in a while. This trade would bring him back. He was sure of it. But in order to take a large enough position, he was going to have to work a little magic—a little accounting magic.

Jack pulled the new account documents out of his desk and got to work. The paperwork he filled out was for a numbered account registered in the firm's name. Stanley McCallister was custodian to hundreds of billions of dollars in assets, and due to the nature of their trading business, they kept a number of house accounts with assets invested only in United States Government Treasury bonds.

These accounts served not only as collateral for the trading operations, but also as surety bonds to meet the stringent capital requirements that were necessary to operate as an investment bank.

Jack finished the paperwork and faxed the forms over to New Account Operations.

He waited twenty minutes before calling over. "Hey, it's Jack in trading.

You open that new account for me?"

"Ya, we got it," the accounts manager answered. "The new account number is 031544."

"Thanks." Jack hung up with a sigh of relief. Phase one was complete. He faxed the next form over to margin and then called them.

"Hi, Ted. It's Jack."

"Hey, Jack. How ya' doing?"

"Fine, thanks. I faxed over a journal to transfer a 'hundred and fifty mill' from one of the house treasury accounts over to a house numbered account. It's for accounting and margin purposes," he added nonchalantly.

"I just got it. Give me five minutes and we'll handle it."

"Thanks."

The journaling of funds between same name accounts occurred on a daily basis and it only required the approval of a supervisor. The supervisor, in this case, was Jack. This activity was a totally legal and necessary daily procedure at trading firms; except in this instance, the investment bank didn't know Jack was taking guaranteed treasury funds to use as collateral to place huge bets on the direction of the US stock market.

Jack's plan was simple. Buy index futures on the stock market to make enough money to get the Book somewhere close to even, then journal the treasuries back into the house account.

Of course, there was huge risk with the plan. For it to work, he had to make money and he had to make it fast. As he looked at the pre-market quotes, he knew he had crossed a line that just a few short months ago he would have thought was inconceivable.

Chapter 7

Christmas and the New Year came and went, and there was absolutely no joy in it for Jack. He spent the entire holiday at work, alone in his apartment or at a series of bars, all located in places where he wouldn't run into anyone from work or any of his acquaintances from the Street.

And that was where he was now, sitting in a dank tavern, rubbing his finger over the double daggers on the coin, drinking scotch. He stared intently at the portrait of Brutus and laughed. Maybe Hans was right. Maybe the damn coin was cursed.

Shit, ever since he bought the cursed thing, his life had gone to hell. Susan left him. He was fast becoming a full-blown alcoholic. He had lost the bulk of his personal money trading futures, and if the firm ever found out how much they were really down, not to mention his diverting of the treasury bonds. Jack laughed. Hell, he could end up in jail, a thought that sent a cold chill down his back.

Three weeks had passed since he "borrowed" the hundred and fifty million in treasuries to put in the numbered account, and now that account was down over forty million. He was in deep, deep trouble and he wasn't handling it well. He was drinking every single night, and with the stress, he was hardly getting any sleep.

He took out his little sheet and stared at it. The Book was now down over a hundred million with the numbered house account down another forty million. If the market didn't go in his favor and fast, he was in a lot of trouble, and getting fired might be the least of his worries.

The bartender brought him another scotch and soda. It was nine o'clock on a Tuesday night and he was getting loaded in some seedy Irish Pub down in Soho. He had lost count of how many drinks he had, but he knew it was a lot. He was going to feel terrible the next morning, but he didn't care. He felt terrible all the time.

He caught his reflection in a mirror behind the bar. "Here's to self-destruction," he toasted to himself.

He thought it was ironic that of the hoards of people he had known who had self-destructed—whether from drugs, alcohol, marital affairs or financial collapses. They all seem to have the same excuse—that they got caught up in the moment and didn't realize what they were doing or what the consequences could be.

Jack now knew that that was all a pile of bullshit because he was self-destructing, he knew it, and he was fully aware of what the consequences would be.

"Hi." He heard a voice behind him.

Jack turned to find an attractive lady sitting on a barstool next to him. "Hi," he said back.

"What's that?" She pointed to the coin he was playing with.

A little diversion from his trouble might not be so bad, he thought. He held the coin up in front of her. "It's called the Brutus Double Dagger Denarius or Eids of March coin. Believe it or not, it is the single most famous coin in all of antiquity."

"Wow," she said as Jack handed her the coin.

"Brutus minted it to celebrate the assassination of Julius Caesar. See the date." He pointed at the bottom of the coin. "You've heard that expression, beware the Ides of March?"

She nodded. "Ya, I think."

"That was the date Caesar was assassinated—March 15."

"Is it real? I mean, how old is it?"

"Over two thousand years. It was minted in 44 BC to be exact."

"Really?" she replied a bit skeptically. "It doesn't look that old."

"I assure you of its authenticity. I bought it at an auction at Sotheby's."

She seemed impressed by the mention of Sotheby's and turned the coin over. "Who is that?" She pointed to the portrait on the front.

"Aah, that's the culprit. That's Brutus, the chief conspirator in the assassination. Legend has it that he was actually Caesar's son." It occurred to Jack that Susan would have been proud that he remembered so much about the coin.

The girl stared at the coin with a quizzical look on her face. She glanced up at Jack, then back down to the coin.

"What?" he asked.

"That's funny."

"What?"

"Has anyone ever told you that you look like this Brutus guy?"

Jack almost spit out his scotch. He laughed. "No, I don't believe so."

"Well, you do. Except I don't think Mister Brutus had as pretty a pair of black eyes as you do." She smiled at him.

The broad must be crazy. Jack didn't see any resemblance. He took the coin back from her. "The damn thing cost me two-point-six million dollars."

Her face lit up at the mention of the coin's value. "I'm Stacy." She extended her hand.

"Stacy," he repeated while taking her hand. "I'm Jack. What would you like to drink?"

She giggled. "A glass of chardonnay would be great."

He motioned to the bartender who poured her a glass of wine.

"So, what do you do Jack?" she asked while taking a sip of her wine.

"I'm head trader for Stanley McCallister."

Her eyes really lit up. "Really," she replied excitedly. "I work for Smith Barney up on Midtown."

"Oh, what do you do over there?" Jack asked, even though he really couldn't have cared less. He had come here to try and forget Wall Street and trading for a few minutes, though considering the position he was in, forgetting was nearly impossible.

She casually flipped her wavy brown hair. "I'm just an assistant for some stockbrokers right now, but I am studying for my Series Seven. I take the test next month."

The Series Seven was the initial registration test required to sell securities. Jack took a dim view of stockbrokers, believing they were really nothing more than glorified used car salesmen.

"Good luck."

"Thanks. So, any trading tips you can share with me?" she asked, scooting her chair a little closer.

He laughed. "Well, here's one. My Book is currently down almost a hundred-and-fifty million dollars. I don't think you want any tips from me. What do you like?"

She giggled loudly. "Oh, that's funny. Really, what do you like?"

Jack couldn't help himself and burst out laughing. He found it ironic that even when he resorted to telling the truth, he couldn't be believed. The night passed by as they sat at the bar conversing and drinking.

Amazingly, as the night grew later, something wonderful, almost magical, began to happen. It was as if someone had, all of a sudden, turned on a light switch in his mind. The paralysis that had plagued him for the last six months seemed to evaporate, like a revelation from God. It hit him all at once—the trade on the stock market was right. He had just been a little early.

Jack knew what he had to do, now. He actually saw the trade in his mind like he used to. The stock market would move significantly higher, enough to get him out of the hole he had dug for himself.

Stacy asked him something but his mind had been on the trade. "I'm sorry, what did you say?"

She took his hand in hers and turned his palm up. "You seem like a very old soul to me."

He smirked. "Ya, I feel old."

"No, I know these things."

"Stacy," he interrupted her. The only thing he could concentrate on now was the trade. He saw it so clearly. It had to be a sign. He looked into her face. God, she looked so innocent, so young and trusting.

She began to rub his arm. "Do you want to go back to my place?"

He looked over at her. She was a nice person, much too nice to take up with the likes of him. He threw a hundred on the bar and stood up. She smiled up at him and began to get up.

"I've got to go," Jack said briskly. "I'm sorry, Stacy, but believe me when I tell you this—you are much too good for the likes of me."

She looked hurt, but there was nothing he could do about it. She was better off anyways. He hurried out of the bar, hailed a cab and went home. His mind was set. Tomorrow, he would "borrow" more treasuries from one of the house accounts and significantly add to his position in the stock market.

Chapter 8

The month of March roared in like the proverbial lion. Jack lay in bed staring out of his bedroom window. His head ached and his tongue felt like it had been rubbed raw with a piece of sandpaper. Memories of the previous night slowly started coming back to him.

He had always been something of a heavy drinker on the weekends, but somewhere over the last six months, the weekends had turned into all week, which led to early afternoon, which eventually turned into having to have a drink in the morning to get control of the anxiety raging inside of him.

He told himself that it was just temporary. After he straightened out the Book, he would cut back. But the weeks had stretched into months and he knew he was straddling the line of a serious alcohol problem.

He couldn't remember the last time he actually felt good. He rolled over and grabbed the TV remote off of the nightstand and flipped on the business channel. He sighed deeply. The early morning indicators projected another down market. The pressure was mounting and it was consuming him. The Book was now down almost four-hundred million dollars.

"Four-hundred goddamn million dollars!" he screamed as he buried his face into a pillow. Most of that money the investment bank didn't even know about, yet. How could he have let this happen? He was receiving margin calls to deposit more funds to cover the losses and he was running out of ways to come up with it.

He knew all too well that the house of cards he had built could implode at any moment. As a matter of fact, he was surprised it hadn't already happened. It was way too late. He was in so deep that it didn't matter anymore. He had to find a way to get some more money to give himself a little more time for the market to turn. The futures report came on and he sat up.

The numbers flashed across the screen. The stock index futures were down another five points. Not a big loss, unless you happened to have twenty thousand contracts. Each point represented $250 multiplied by twenty thousand contracts, which meant he had lost another twenty-five million dollars.

Jack shook his head in disgust. He literally wanted to cry. He painfully got out of bed. His head felt like someone had taken a sledgehammer to it.

He arrived at the office at seven-thirty and sat there for hours watching the market go up and down in a very tight trading range.

His phone rang and he wearily picked it up, every time fearing that the "borrowed" treasury bonds had been discovered,

"Hey Jack," a clipped British accent yelled. "How's my favorite Yankee bastard doing?"

It was Nils Linquist, a currency trader with the Bank of England. Nils was one of the few people in the industry who had remained friendly with Jack over the years, probably because they never really had any direct business dealing. They just shared information and trading ideas.

"Not bad, Nils." Jack lied.

"Listen, Jack. I've got something big for you, and I mean big."

Jack sat up. Nils didn't give him a lot of tips but when he did, they usually worked out. "Okay, what is it?"

"I've got it on good information," he paused briefly. "Are you ready for this ol' boy? Your Federal Reserve is going to lower interest rates after their open market meeting next Tuesday."

Jack was stunned. At the last meeting of the Federal Reserve, the Fed indicated that interest rate policy would remain neutral and that there was actually a slight bias of a rate increase in the future depending on inflation concerns.

If the Fed unexpectedly lowered rates, the stock market would soar. Jack gripped the phone tightly. Maybe, just maybe, this was the break he was waiting for.

"You sure?" Jack asked hesitantly.

"Jack. I got this information from you know who."

Jack bristled with excitement. Nil's uncle was the Minister of Finance for England, and it was no secret that he shared a close relationship with the Chairman of the Federal Reserve.

"Listen," Nils continued, "I've heard you were having a tough year. I thought you could use the info."

Jack cringed. Traders were a tight-knit community and if Nils had heard rumblings about him, the sharks must be circling. But this was it. If Nils was right, the market would soar after the Federal Reserve meeting next Tuesday.

"Nils, if you're right, I am personally going to fly over to London on Wednesday and take you out to dinner."

"If I'm right! Listen buddy, you just better bring a lot of cash with you."

"Thanks," he replied, and they both hung up.

Jack dialed his index trader and instructed him to double the position in the stock market. He was literally staking his life on this single trade. He anxiously watched the market the rest of the day and it closed higher, cutting into his losses by about four million dollars.

He turned off his computer and got up to leave. His phone rang and he stood there staring at it. He didn't want to answer, but what if it was Nils.

He picked it up. "Jack."

When he heard the voice on the other end, a spark of terror surged through him. "Jack, its Sam. Please come up to my office before you leave. There is something I need to discuss with you."

Jack's heart began to race. Johnstone was the last person he wanted to see. A dreadful thought passed through his mind, did he find out about the treasury bonds?

"Do you mind if I come in Monday. I was just on my way out?" Jack was praying for a reprieve.

"Yes, I do," Johnstone replied curtly, "come up now."

Jack heard the phone slam down. He had to physically fight the urge to run out of the building. God, he needed a drink.

He had no choice but to take the elevator up to Johnstone's office. He walked to the elevator feeling as if he was going to his own execution. He had heard the expression "dead man walking" in some movie before, and now, he felt as if he had the starring role.

He forced himself to walk into Johnstone's office. "Hi Sam. I hope this is going to be quick because I have a big meeting with an institutional client."

Johnstone didn't respond to his obvious lie. "Sit down," he ordered. Johnstone stared down at a sheet of paper. "As of close of yesterday, the Book is down one hundred and sixteen million dollars. What the hell do you intend to do about it?"

Johnstone's face was turning a purplish color and for the first time in months, Jack felt the urge to laugh out loud. He wondered what Sam would say if he knew about the other three-hundred million that the investment bank was actually down.

"The market is going to come back. We'll be all right."

"I've been hearing that bullshit for six months now. I am getting a lot of pressure from the board. These losses have to be rectified or else. . . ." Johnstone didn't finish the sentence. He didn't have to.

"I understand," Jack said, greatly relieved. He had just been directly threatened with losing his job yet he felt as if his death sentenced had been commuted at the last minute. Johnstone didn't know about the treasury bonds, which meant, in all likelihood, he could make it until Tuesday and the announcement by the Federal Reserve. He stood up.

"Oh, and one more thing Jack. We are instituting a whole new risk management system. The board feels that the trading department is taking too many unsupervised trading risks. A risk management review team is coming in next Thursday to audit and evaluate every aspect of trading operations." The son of a bitch smiled broadly at Jack. "I expect you will be cooperative and provide them with anything they might request."

Jack returned the smile as he thought, "Too late, sucker." By Thursday, everything will be square or—he couldn't let himself think of the alternative.

Jack didn't bother to go to his desk. He took the elevator down to the first floor. He had to get a drink. His heart felt as if it could literally explode at any moment. He left the building and found a dark seedy bar called Johnny Macs. The stench of urine, smoke and despair overcame him, but not enough to make him leave. A few losers sat at the bar drinking beers and arguing over some horse race on the TV.

The man behind the bar gave him a double take. Jack knew he didn't see too many "Wall Streeters" in this joint. "I'll have a double scotch with a splash."

The beefy bartender poured the drink and set it down in front of him. Jack threw down his American Express gold card. "Keep it open."

He reached for the drink and noticed his hands were shaking. He proceeded to down the whole drink in two gulps.

"Another," he called out to the bartender.

By the fourth drink, he had regained control over his breathing and his hands had stopped shaking. He stayed in the dingy dark bar for the next three hours and the drunker he got, the better he felt.

At some point, he stumbled out of the bar and hailed a cab to take him home where he spent the entire weekend drinking scotch and pacing his apartment.

Monday finally came and he bought even more contracts on the stock market. The day went by quickly and the market was up sharply, bolstering Nils' claim of an interest rate cut. If Nils knew, other people did as well, and they must be getting their bets in early.

Jack left the office right before closing to make sure he didn't get called up to Johnstone's office. His fate was now up to one trading day. He went home and for the first time in months, he didn't drink or watch the business channels. He went to straight bed.

Chapter 9

Tuesday morning 6:15 A.M.

Jack slept peacefully the entire night and awoke early in the morning feeling refreshed. He took the remote off the bedside table and clicked on the television. The business channel came on. He rubbed the fog out of his eyes and stared at the TV to see what the early futures were up to.

Instantly, he knew something was wrong. Breaking news flashed across the bottom of the screen. A million possibilities raced through his head, most of which would not be good for the market.

He watched in shock as a very flustered anchorwoman was handed a piece of paper. She began reading nervously, "The Associated Press is reporting that a massive earthquake has struck the San Francisco area at 2:29 Pacific time, 5:29 A.M. Eastern Standard. Details are just coming in, but all reports indicate that it was a catastrophic earthquake measuring 9.3 on the Richter scale."

She paused, listening to someone talking in her earpiece. "We caution viewers that these reports are of yet unsubstantiated, but it appears that San Francisco and an immense area surrounding the city have suffered . . ." she paused to collect herself, "suffered catastrophic damage."

The newswoman was visibly shaken and the camera shifted to her co-anchor. Her male counterpart was only slightly more calm. "Ladies and Gentlemen, this has been a horrific day for the United States, on a magnitude that has never been seen before. The President of the United States has just issued a state of emergency for, not only California, but due to California's importance to the country he has declared a state of emergency for the entire United States. At 6:09 this morning, the President signed executive orders sending an initial contingent of three-hundred thousand military personal to California."

The anchorman's voice dropped to a somber whisper, "The loss of life is expected to be in the hundreds of thousands. Damages will most certainly be in the hundreds of billions."

Jack grabbed the remote control off the night table and turned the television off. He went into the kitchen and made a strong scotch and soda. He took the drink out onto the balcony and watched as the sky began to lighten on the horizon.

He knew it didn't matter what the Fed did. All was lost. California was the sixth largest economy in the world and it was devastated. The economic ramifications would be enormous.

There was no question the stock market would collapse at the opening of trading, if they even let it open. He laughed and drank the scotch. He had just learned that history does repeat itself. In 1998, a trader named Nick Leeson had made an enormous bet on the Japanese stock market and an earthquake had hit a key industrial city causing the Japanese market to plunge.

Leeson's trade actually destroyed Barings Bank, a bank that had been in business for over five hundred years. Jack laughed and yelled out over the balcony, "I beat you Nick!"

Stanley McCallister had only been in business for sixty-seven years, but there was no doubt that the bank would suffer the same fate as Barings. Like Nick Leeson, Jack's name would forever be linked to the collapse of an institution. Leeson has spent six years in jail. Jack wondered how long a sentence he would receive?

As the sun began to rise, it occurred to him that he hadn't even felt the least bit of pity or sorrow for the hundreds of thousands of people who had their lives destroyed. His only concern was for himself and his own survival. But as much as he tried to figure a way out, he knew there was none. He knew he was going to jail for a long time, and the thought shook him to the core of his soul. He could think of only one way to make it right.

He went back inside and went to bed. He would have probably slept until the next day if it hadn't been for the constant ringing of the phone. He looked at his watch. It was eight-thirty in the morning. "Hello," he answered.

"Jack, where the hell are you!" It was Johnstone.

"I'm in bed."

"What the . . . Jack, there was an earthquake in—"

"I know," Jack cut him off.

"You know!" Johnstone yelled. "Then what the hell are you doing? Why aren't you here? We have a disaster on our hands. The futures are indicating a stock market collapse that will make eighty-seven look like a bump in the road."

Jack started laughing as his boss let out a string of expletives.

"Jack, listen to me," he pleaded. "Get down here. We have to get some kind of plan together to protect ourselves, somehow."

"It doesn't matter now," Jack calmly replied.

"What do you mean it doesn't matter?"

"There are other accounts you don't know about."

He could hear Johnstone's heavy breathing over the phone. "What do you mean, other accounts?"

"I took money out of the house treasury accounts and placed them into numbered accounts. If the market opens down 15-20 percent, which it will, the position will be down tens of billions of dollars."

"What the hell are you talking about!"

"I leveraged the treasury accounts to the hilt. We are long so many S&P contracts that even an act from God couldn't save us now."

"How many?"

"Does Barings give you an idea?" Johnstone didn't answer but Jack could hear his breathing coming in short ragged gasps. "Punch up account 031544."

He heard a few clicks on a keyboard then complete silence. Then Johnstone gasped, "Oh my God, the bank's . . . I'm ruined!"

They were the last words Jack heard before the line went dead. He wondered if Johnstone had finally suffered that long overdue heart attack.

Actually he felt rather relieved to have finally gotten the truth out. It was almost refreshing to confess his sins. Jack got out of bed, made a cup of coffee and walked out onto the veranda. It was a dreary, blustery day with a freezing rain falling from the sky.

After another cup of coffee, he showered and put on his favorite suit. He dressed while studying himself in the mirror. He looked older than he had remembered. He slowly tied his tie and had to redo it twice to get a perfect knot. It struck him as somewhat funny. He had worn a tie for almost his entire life, yet it always took at least two tries before he got the exact right knot or the perfect length.

He pulled a pair of black dress shoes out of his closet rack and slipped them on. There was a tiny smudge on the toe of the left shoe. He bent down and carefully wiped it off with a wet handkerchief.

He slipped on his suit jacket and took one last look in the mirror. The phone rang but he didn't answer it. He left his building and flagged down a taxi.

"Take me to the park on the East River but first take me through Central Park," he instructed the Indian cab driver.

Jack looked out of the cab's window and observed the people as they rode through the park. It amazed him to think that hundreds of thousands of people had just died in California, while other people just went on with their own lives, as if nothing had happened.

The cab left the park and got onto FDR Drive heading towards the East River. Jack pulled the Brutus coin out of his pocket.

"A terrible thing in California," he heard the Indian cabdriver say.

"Ya, terrible."

The cab driver said something else but Jack didn't quite hear it. "What did you say?" he asked.

The Indian looked at him in the rear view mirror. "The Ides. Beware the Ides of March."

"What?" Jack asked again.

"Today is the Ides of March. The earthquake. It happened on the Ides of March. It is indeed a cursed day."

Jack looked at his watch. It was March 15—the date of Julius Caesar's assassination.

The cab exited the FDR and pulled over to the curb to let Jack out. He pulled out a stack of one hundred dollar bills and handed it to the cab driver who looked at him in dismay.

"Sir, I can't possibly."

"Keep it." He smiled at the cabdriver. "Don't worry, I won the lottery."

The Indian bowed his head. "Thank you, sir . . . thank you."

Jack nodded and watched as the cab pulled away. He walked over to the sidewalk along the river. He walked until he found an empty bench. He sat down and looked out across the East River, watching as its muddy brown waters rushed by.

Jack stared at the coin. He should have known. He got up and walked over to the rail. "God damn coin is cursed!" he yelled.

Without a moment of hesitation, he threw the two-point-six million dollar coin into the churning waters of the East River.

Jack reached inside his suit jacket and pulled out the shiny Gloch nine-millimeter.

He put the gun to his head and pulled the trigger—

Epilogue

The soul returns to earth in a body similar to it's last one
and has similar talents and inclinations.

-Plato

He stood alone on a barren plain. His only thought was that he must be dreaming again. Only this time, something was different. Much different. He didn't feel whole. Part of him was missing.

He slowly turned, and a familiar feeling of doom spread through him. A dark forest stood in front of him. Without commanding himself to do so, he began walking towards the trees. He knew, unlike the other times, he would enter the forest and discover the secret it had been hiding from him for so long.

He reached the edge and without hesitation, passed through the first set of trees. An unfathomable coldness gripped him. Not a physical cold, but a chill that went to the very center of his existence.

He saw or heard no animals—only the trees. He continued walking. The forest grew thicker, darker and a distinct feeling that he wasn't alone came over him. He closed his eyes and visions played in his mind. He didn't know if they were from his past, present or future, but then he understood that time didn't exist where he was.

He saw himself murdering a man in a toga. It was an unforgivable act, a sin punishable forever because he knew the man was his father. The vision ended and he was on top of a horse commanding an army into battle. He could feel the pain as he plunged the dagger into his heart. The visions in his mind were coming faster—he was falling from a wall towards a rocky shoreline far below. Then he was bound to a chair deep in a bunker complex, a gun held to his head by a homicidal maniac. His mind raced as he saw himself on a sidewalk next to a river in New York City. He watched in horrid fascination as he put a gun to his head and pulled the trigger.

Everything stopped. The visions ended. He knew the secret of the forest. He opened his eyes and in front of him stood Marcus Brutus, Michael Claudien, Maxwell Von Studt, and Jack Weston. They stood silently, waiting. He, or whatever he was now, took a step closer as the figures of the men began merging together.

The truth filled him. He was Brutus, Michael Claudien, Maxwell Von Studt and Jack Weston. They had always been one and the same. The cycle of birth, life, death and rebirth had occurred many times, and still he had not learned from the mistakes and sins of the past.

They all merged together and vanished back into the darkness of the forest. He would now have to wait again for his chance at redemption.